DEAD COOL

EVA MACLEAN

BOOKS

By Eva Maclean

The Detective Miranda Murphy Series

Dead Matters
Dead Cool
Sudden Death
Dead Drop

Vinci Books

vinci-books.com

Published by Vinci Books Ltd in 2025

1

Copyright © Eva Maclean 2023

The author has asserted their moral right to be identified as the author of this work in accordance with the Copyright, Designs and Patents Act 1988. This work is a work of fiction. Names, characters, places and incidents are the product of the author's imagination or are used fictitiously. Any resemblance to actual persons, living or dead, places and incidents is entirely coincidental.
All rights reserved. No part of this publication may be copied, reproduced, distributed, stored in any retrieval system, or transmitted in any form or by any means, including photocopying, recording, or other electronic or mechanical methods, nor used as a source for any form of machine learning including AI datasets, without the prior written permission of the publisher.
The publisher and the author have made every effort to obtain permissions for any third party material used in this book and to comply with copyright law. Any queries in this respect should be brought to the attention of the publisher and any omissions will be corrected in future editions.
A CIP catalogue record for this book is available from the British Library.
Paperback ISBN: 9781036700713

Printed and bound in Great Britain by Clays Ltd, Elcograf S.p.A.

Chapter One

2022

MOORGATE TUBE STATION, central London, Monday evening 7pm. The last part of the rush hour. Lots of tired people, the ones who couldn't be seen sloping out at 5.30, or who had stopped for a drink on the way home, were still making their way home, shouldering their rucksacks and cases. They gathered on the platform and stared at their phones. Two northbound trains had been cancelled. Precursor to chaos.

The crowd on the platform was building up and some people were edging beyond the yellow line. There was a bit of shoving and jostling for position when the next train eventually arrived. It was completely full as it pulled in, and the people already travelling on it looked in alarm at the crowd on the platform. They were already welded together and, if too many of this lot got on, they would be suffocating. The most desperate people forced their way into the crowded carriages and the driver shut the doors. As the train moved off, two of the carriages had articles of clothing trailing along, clamped into the doors, as if there just wasn't room for them. One of them was pale blue. Definitely wouldn't be pale blue by the time it got to the next station.

The remaining passengers repositioned themselves. They were definitely getting on the next one, whatever it took. Another train was due in two minutes. During those two minutes the crowd on the platform doubled. Every person in pole position now had at least six people backed up behind them. The people right at the back were relaxed, they knew they definitely wouldn't be getting on this one, not unless it was empty. Some people were giving up and making their way out, having calculated the odds and decided to chance the buses. They edged their way along, past the unending stream of people coming in.

At last, the overhead board showed 'train approaching'. They could all feel the rush of air coming through the tunnel and the lights of the train suddenly emerged. At that moment there seemed to be a scuffle halfway along the platform and a body suddenly tumbled onto the track. A woman started screaming and immediately more people joined in. It's any tube driver's worst nightmare, but it happens so fast that there is rarely time to do anything about it. The tube came to a hard stop with a screech of brakes, throwing all the passengers inside around like skittles. The people on the platform were staring in shock, some had started weeping. Suddenly everybody was shouting at once, the intercom was buzzing, more station staff had arrived and were telling everybody to leave. People in fluorescent jackets positioned themselves in front of the track with their arms out, keeping people away. Others were shepherding the public out, towards the escalators. Some of the people glanced at the tracks as they left, but most didn't want to. It could have been any one of them. The train doors were then opened and the passengers were guided out, away from the front of the train.

This is a regular, if not frequent, occurrence; the station staff know the procedure. They might refer to it as a 'one under'. Sometimes the person is lucky enough to fall into the 'pits' under the tracks and therefore survive. This was not one of those times.

Chapter Two

2012

FLORENCE AND BETH lay side-by-side on inflatable floats in the pool. It was 11am, the sun was already high and the sky was an unmarked clear blue. From the villa next door came the sound of somebody busy with a leaf blower, and a pair of birds were arguing in the tree above them, but there were no other sounds. Florence was wearing her new yellow bikini with spaghetti straps and a bottom half cut so high that, as her dad had grunted, she might as well not be wearing it. But what her dad thought was not important. Getting a smooth tan over as much of her bum as possible – that was important. Beth was wearing a blue one piece. It looked like the same costume she wore for school swimming sessions. Florence had pointed out that she'd end up with a white stomach, but Beth had just shrugged. Well, whatever, that was her choice.

Florence's mum was sitting cross-legged on a lounger reading a book and her dad was scribbling on a newspaper, probably doing the sudoku. Jake was playing some game on a laptop, same as he'd be doing at home, really. Bringing

Jake on holiday was a waste of time. Yesterday he had spent quite a lot of time trying to chat up Beth, but she had made it clear that she wasn't interested, so now he had retreated back to World of Warlocks, or whatever it was called. Florence couldn't blame Beth. Jake was younger than them, apart from anything else – anything else being his weird hair and prominent Adam's apple. For her part, Florence was hoping to snag a gorgeous Italian. This required persuading Beth to walk down to the village with her. She couldn't go sauntering down on her own – she'd look like a saddo and she didn't speak Italian. Beth did at least have a few words. But Beth was proving a bit reluctant to go wandering off. She seemed happy enough to swim, read and talk to Florence's mum and dad (especially her dad, for some unfathomable reason). She just didn't seem to appreciate that she was only here because Florence had invited her.

Over lunch there was a discussion about whether or not Jake was allowed to hire a scooter. He obviously wanted to look like a cool Italian guy (as if...). Florence would also have liked to be going round on a Vespa, but she would want to be doing it with her arms around the waist of the driver (who would definitely not be Jake). Her mum was against it, but her dad, probably thinking of himself at that age, persuaded her that they should let him. He was legally old enough, he wasn't completely stupid (wasn't he?) and there wasn't much traffic, it wasn't like going round the North Circular. Eventually her mum gave in, as they all knew she would, and Jake abandoned World of Woodcraft (and the rest of his lunch) and shot off down to the village.

Once Jake had gone, lunch carried on more peacefully, and eventually wound down completely. Florence then went off to lie in the sun, her mother began slowly taking dishes indoors and her dad and Beth embarked on some discussion about the merits of different universities. Why would anybody be talking about that when they're, like, on holiday? Florence rolled over to expose the backs of her legs (why were they always the hardest bit to tan?) The sun was at its height now and everybody was getting drowsy. Florence's mum had retreated to her lounger and seemed to be asleep over her book. A faint breeze stirred the leaves on the fig tree and an occasional bird called across the valley, but the rest was silence. Her dad and Beth now had their heads down over the crossword. Florence felt just a bit hurt. Her dad had never asked her to join him doing the crossword, not that it was her sort of thing, of course. Maybe he thought Beth was smarter than her.

The silence was suddenly split by a horn, a screech of brakes and a crash. They all looked up, puzzled. Florence's mum was the first to move. She ran through to the front of the villa and out onto the road and they followed as fast as possible behind her. The lorry driver had climbed down from his cab and was bending over something. The Vespa was lying in the middle of the road, without its rider. Florence noted idly, in the few seconds during which her brain seemed to be freewheeling, that it was in that very classy old-school pale blue.

Chapter Three

2022

THE REQUEST for assistance from the British Transport Police came into Islington Green police station just as Detective Inspector Miranda Murphy was about to leave for home. It had been a long day, she had nothing to show for it and her feet hurt.

'Here's one for you,' announced DCI Bellweather with satisfaction, dropping a note on her desk as he swept past. 'Body under a tube at Moorgate. Probably a suicide. Just make sure the paperwork's done properly.'

Murphy gritted her teeth and nodded. She had been on duty for twelve hours, but of course he knew that, the bastard. It was just the latest salvo in the war of attrition being played out between them. He didn't like women that he thought had been promoted above their station, she didn't like arrogant men that, as far as she could see, never did anything anyway. He really wanted her to put in for a transfer, and kept pointedly notifying her of upcoming opportunities, but there was no way she was going to do that – she wouldn't give him the satisfaction. She really prayed for him to put in for a transfer, but hadn't yet dared point him to any vacancies. At the moment neither of them was winning. Deuce.

Having, as far as he was concerned, scored a point, Bellweather shrugged himself into his coat, picked up his case, which probably only contained the remains of his lunch, smiled at his remaining juniors with a startling flash of his teeth and headed for the car park. The CID room let out its collective breath. People grabbed their phones, put their feet on the desks, some of them started pulling on coats.

Murphy took a deep breath, stood up, put on her jacket and grabbed her bag. Kevin Wilcox looked up from where he was typing a report.

'You want to come? It won't be pretty.'

'Sure.' He logged off and stood up. 'As it's an emergency we can take a patrol car and use the siren.'

She nodded. 'Yes. Maybe that will make us feel better.'

MOORGATE STATION WAS SHUTTERED when they arrived and people were standing around outside, piling up forlornly at the bus stops and frantically tapping on their phones. Murphy waved her badge at one of the station staff, the shutters were raised and they were allowed through.

'Nightmare,' said a man in a fluorescent jacket as he pointed them towards the escalators. 'Second this month.'

Down on the platform two women were sitting on a bench looking shaken. The power had been switched off and all trains diverted. 'That means the Bank line is effectively down until this is sorted. All the trains have to go via Charing Cross' said one of the tube staff. 'But this is the Northern line after all – people are used to disruption.'

'It's the family of this poor bugger that are going to

experience real disruption,' said Murphy, as they walked slowly towards the front of the train. The train had been backed into the tunnel and the body could be clearly seen. Wilcox was already pale and she could see him determinedly swallowing. The slight burning smell was reminiscent of barbecues and made her glad that she didn't eat meat.

Having seen enough of the body, Murphy walked back towards two women sitting on the bench. They were witnesses who had agreed to stay behind and talk to the police and were now shifting around and looking in all directions as if they regretted their outburst of good citizenship.

'We really appreciate that you were willing to do this,' Murphy told them. 'It's a very upsetting event. I hope you won't mind us taking your names and details.'

They both looked taken aback at this, but then nodded and gave their details to Wilcox. In the event, although they had no connection to each other, both women told pretty much the same story. There had been a slight scuffle prior to the man falling on the tracks. The person behind him had stooped down as if retying a shoelace.

'But did you see an actual push?' Murphy asked.

'No,' said Winona Francis. 'I wouldn't have thought you could push somebody over from that position. It was probably a coincidence.'

Amy Horsfall agreed with her. 'It looked to me like he fainted,' she said.

'Can you describe the person who bent down?' asked Wilcox.

They both shook their heads.

'He had his hood up,' said Amy. 'It was a dark colour – black or navy blue.'

'That's right,' said Winona. 'I never saw his face.'

'Well thank you both very much for your time,' said Murphy. 'We may contact you again if we need to.' One of the tube staff guided them out.

'Not much to go on,' said Wilcox, keeping his gaze averted from the track. 'Looking like suicide or accident so far. Notwithstanding the person bending down behind him.'

'Probably,' Murphy agreed. 'Unless the pathologist says something different. And this sounds like her now.'

'Jesus Christ. Do I really have to get down there?' Linda Fleming dropped her bag onto the platform with a slam and peered at the body on the tracks.

'Well he's dead!' she shouted to Murphy. 'I can tell you that now. And you know time of death. Do you really need me to put my back out climbing down there?'

'Fraid so,' said Murphy, walking towards her. Linda Fleming was one of the few people she was a bit in awe of, but the rules were the rules.

'Here, give me your arm.' Dr Fleming grabbed hold of the nearest man in a fluorescent jacket and he helped her down onto the tracks. 'Hope you've switched the bloody power off.' He nodded.

She pulled gloves on and bent over the body. 'Electrocution – he hit the live rail. Lot of scorch marks. Pretty hard to avoid it really. And impact injuries – as we would expect. Can't say any more till we do the pm. Now will somebody help me out of here? I'm putting in a dry-cleaning bill for this.'

Linda Fleming climbed heavily back onto the platform, brushed off her skirt, rolled her eyes and picked up her bag. 'Pm tomorrow morning, 10am,' she shouted at Murphy. 'See you then.' And she stomped off.

'Wow.' One of the tube staff was staring after her. 'She's a bit – well – I don't know what to say.'

Murphy smiled. 'She's one of the top pathologists in the country. So, the word you're looking for is probably 'impressive'.'

He nodded slowly. 'Yes, it probably is.'

Chapter Four

2012

THE LORRY DRIVER had already called an ambulance, and thank God for that, Florence decided. She didn't think any of them had enough command of Italian to have done that themselves, or not without a lot of embarrassment.

Jake was unconscious but breathing. Her dad rolled up his jacket and was about to put it under Jake's head, but her mum put a hand on his arm.

'Don't move him' she said. 'There may be spinal damage.'

The ambulance crew arrived a few minutes later and obviously had the same thought. They transferred Jake very carefully onto a rigid board and then onto a stretcher for the journey to the hospital. One of them gently removed his crash helmet and handed it to Florence's dad.

Florence had already decided that she was going to the hospital. She was feeling mean about all the times she had regarded Jake as a nuisance, he was her brother after all, she'd looked out for him all his life, and anyway there might be lots of good-looking doctors – mightn't there? So, when the ambulance crew started to close the doors and said they could take just two people, she leapt in first.

The other person, of course, had to be her mum, so that left her dad and Beth. They'd just have to cope without her. As the ambulance drove off, she looked out of the back window and saw her dad wheeling the Vespa towards the villa, while Beth followed with the helmet.

The hospital was obviously busy as, after a twenty-minute journey, it was another half hour before they were let out of the ambulance. Jake, meanwhile, was stirring and complaining about his arm, so that was a good sign. The waiting room, when they finally got in there, was a wall of noise – whinging children, crying babies, people shouting and gesticulating at each other, the occasional bleep cutting through from somewhere. A few people had presumably been there so long that they no longer cared about the noise and were somehow sleeping through it. Florence was wishing she had run back for her phone and earbuds – but maybe that would have looked bad?

The doctor they eventually saw was female (huh!) and spoke English. After checking Jake over and stitching up a cut over his eye (which she said must have come from flying debris, as he was wearing a helmet) she diagnosed concussion and a broken arm and sent them to another clinic to get it plastered. Then it was another wait until an older man (huh! again) waved them in and did the job. And despite her current determination to be pissed off, Florence found the process fascinating to watch, like a piece of sculpture being made.

They were finally discharged with warnings about keeping an eye on Jake and not letting him fall asleep. Florence's mum had miraculously remembered the name and location of the villa and she found a taxi driver to take them. Jake had now come round and become annoyingly chatty, wearing his sling and plaster like some kind of bravery award.

When they arrived back at the villa Florence's dad was inside on his laptop and Beth was swimming in the pool, although the sun had gone down and it was no longer so warm outside. Beth jumped out of the pool and ran over to Jake like he was some kind of returning hero, while her dad went out to where her mum was paying off the taxi.

That evening they went out to dinner to celebrate Jake not being dead and Beth was unusually quiet. Over the remaining few days of their stay, she stuck close to Florence and on the last day they walked down to the village. It was, Florence decided, a big disappointment. Lots of old women shopping while the old men sat around outside the bars, playing chess or whatever. No sign of cool young men on scooters. Obviously, they hung out somewhere else. It was good to have more of Beth's company, but Florence couldn't help wondering why Beth and her dad no longer did the crosswords together. Had something happened?

Chapter Five

2022

MURPHY SIGNALLED to the mortuary staff that the body could now be retrieved and she watched as it was carefully lifted up off the track. One of the SOCOs handed her a collection of plastic bags containing the victim's phone, wallet and briefcase.

Wilcox got his gloves on and started on the paperwork in the briefcase, while Murphy went through the wallet. The phone would have to be unlocked by one of the technicians. A driving licence and business cards identified the victim as Richard Weaver, age fifty-two, with an address in Camden.

Murphy dispatched the uniformed branch to inform the family and request formal identification. Informing families is the worst job that falls to the uniformed branch – much worse even than traffic duty – and Murphy was not envying whoever would be sent to do it this evening. When it had been confirmed that the body had been identified, she and Wilcox would call on the family and return the victim's effects. It didn't look like there was much else for them to do here, apart from viewing the CCTV. The station master led them into his office and showed them the relevant screen. He rolled it back to 7pm and they saw the departure of the first train without incident. Then they could see the pressure of bodies increasing. The relevant moment was coming up now. They stared intently at the grainy picture from the moment when the lights of the train appeared from the mouth of the tunnel. There was some slight stirring halfway along the track and Wilcox pointed as one of the heads in the picture, just one grey blob among many, suddenly bobbed out of sight. Then there was the (thankfully blurry) sight of the body pitching forward, followed by commotion on the platform and the driver's expression as he tried to brake as fast as possible. They watched it three times, but it didn't get any clearer.

'Well not much chance of identifying anybody from that,' said Wilcox.

Murphy shook her head. Was somebody really retying his shoelace? Why would you do that just as the train is pulling in? Wouldn't you wait until you were on the train? And, in that crush of people, would you even notice that your shoelace was undone? And maybe this had nothing to do with it at all.

Wilcox turned round to look at Murphy as they made their way back up the escalator on the way out. 'The boss will expect us to just sign this off as an accident and get back to the burglaries,' he said.

'I know,' said Murphy. 'He won't want any hit to his budget. And it probably is an accident, or possibly suicide, but I'm going along to the pm tomorrow anyway.'

Chapter Six

2022

FLORENCE WAS PAINTING her toenails when the doorbell rang. Bad timing. Hopefully her mum would get it. If it was left to her, she'd have to go down in bare feet, with cotton wool between her toes. She heard her mother cross the hall and open the door and went back to what she was doing. These miniature palm trees were very time-consuming, she should have gone for something simpler. Still, they should photograph well. The voices at the front door were quite loud, there was more than one of them, then she heard her mum give a loud sob. OK, now something was wrong. Had something happened to Jake? She put the brush back in the bottle carefully and ran down the stairs, cotton wool and all.

The visitors were uniformed police, a man and a woman. By the time she arrived downstairs they were in the kitchen with her mum, who was crying. Her mum and the male officer were sitting at the table. The woman officer seemed to be filling the kettle. Her mum looked up and saw her.

'This is Florence – my daughter.'

Florence and the police nodded to each other. Florence was frightened to ask, but knew she had to. 'What's happened?' she said.

'I'm afraid it's your father,' said the female officer. 'He's been involved in an accident.'

Florence sat down on the bench next to her mum. 'What sort of accident?'

'At the tube station...' the officer began.

'He's been hit by a train,' her mother said. 'He's dead.'

Florence's stomach lurched and dry sobs were all that came up when she tried to speak. When the tears came a few seconds later, it felt like a relief, as if something had unblocked. She felt her voice returning.

'It's not true,' she yelled at them. 'You've made a mistake.'

'I'm very sorry. There's no mistake,' the female officer said quietly, putting a cup of something steaming in front of her mother.

Florence slumped against her mother, who put her arms around her.

The male police officer said 'We'd like you to come and identify your husband – when you feel able to.'

'Let's both go now,' said Florence. There was still some small hope it might not be him.

Chapter Seven

MURPHY AND WILCOX drove back to the station to hand the victim's effects in to the duty sergeant and return the pool car and then set off home. Murphy was trying to forget the sight of the body – God knows, she'd seen plenty of them, but each one was a shock. Wilcox was still pretty silent. He hadn't seen enough bodies yet. Murphy dropped him at his flat and then drove home. She realised that Wilcox had not even clutched his seatbelt and braced his feet against the floor. He must have been well out of it.

Bellweather had intended Kevin Wilcox to be Murphy's nemesis. He was the ambitious, by-the-book, IT-literate junior who would eventually drive her to resign or at least rat her out for any misdemeanours. For a time, it looked as if this would all work out well, but then something had happened which nobody had foreseen. Kevin Wilcox fell in love. He fell in love with one of the civilian call handlers, a bumptious girl called Jade, who always seemed to be on the phone to her mates whenever Murphy passed her desk. But Wilcox was uncharacteristically indifferent to Jade's personal and organisational shortcomings and for the three weeks of their doomed affair he went around in that state where the world seems brighter, and all the rest of it. At the end of three weeks, it became apparent that Jade was a mover, and she moved onto Barry Jackson, who was supposed to be engaged to one of the PCs. The effect on Wilcox was tragic and immediate, suffering bravely borne, but not helped by the fact that Jade was routinely seen laughing with other people. She may not have been laughing at Wilcox, but he evidently thought she was. After a week in which she had been reduced to doing her own paperwork, Murphy decided that this had gone on long enough. She took Jade aside, enumerated her various non-compliances with policy and offered to forget to write the relevant reports if Jade would request an immediate transfer to Wood Green, where a vacancy had just arisen. When Jade hesitated to give such an undertaking, Murphy told her confidentially, woman-to-woman, that Bellweather definitely had his eye on her. Three days later Jade was gone. Murphy and Wilcox never discussed this incident, but there was now a tacit agreement that they had each other's backs.

Murphy swung into her road and began looking for a parking space. There were two others on the same mission as far as she could see, the three of them circling like sharks, waiting to see if anybody was going to leave, although really it was too late at night for that. Murphy had a sizeable advantage as she had the smallest car and the one which had so many knocks and scratches that one more wouldn't make much difference and she duly shoehorned it into the last available space.

She normally tried to be quiet when she came in late, in order to avoid disturbing the lodgers, but tonight it didn't matter because there was noise coming from the sitting room. James and Clive were still up, watching a documentary about whales. She took her shoes off, curled up in an armchair and joined them. Seconds later she was closing her eyes and blocking her ears as a mother seal swam circles around her calf in what was undoubtedly a hopeless effort to fend off a pod of killer whales who were intent on eating it. It felt like tonight was all about death.

Suddenly Clive was shouting to her. 'It's over Murph, it's OK! You can open your eyes now. The seal saw them off! The orcas got fed up with it and pissed off.' When she opened her eyes, she found to her surprise that they were wet.

Chapter Eight

THE NEXT MORNING saw Murphy all kitted up in the hospital morgue, keeping her gaze averted from the instruments. The protective suit kept the clothes clean, but didn't do much to defend the eyes, nose and ears, which were the parts about to be most seriously assaulted. The mask probably kept germs away but the smells always seemed to get through somehow. The mortuary had undergone several upgrades over the years and was now impressively high-tech and germ-free, all gleaming glass and steel, but the reality of what went on there was never going to change. Murphy didn't like post mortems any more than anybody else, but had some time ago accepted that they were always going to feature in her working life. As an exercise in doing something outside of your comfort zone, attending a postmortem can't be beat. What she was expecting this morning was to have her suspicions laid to rest. He was an unfit, middle-aged man, he had underlying health conditions, he had a funny turn and fainted, he had a stroke or his heart just gave out, something like that. Then she can close off the paperwork and Bellweather will get off her back.

One of the attendants wheeled in the body and unzipped the cover. Two of them carefully transferred the body to the table and covered it with a sheet. The clothes had already been removed and the burnt smell was not so noticeable, probably the refrigeration process had helped. Further, much worse, smells were in the offing – Murphy had no doubt about that.

Linda Fleming was in an unnaturally good mood. She announced that she had just become a grandmother and after putting on her gloves she fished out her phone to show Murphy the new arrival. Like all babies, he looked like Winston Churchill, but Linda's judgement was understandably more partisan.

'Isn't he gorgeous?' she said and Murphy expressed agreement.

'It's good to see the beginning of life as well as the end of it' Linda said. 'Now let's see what's happened to this poor chap.'

The attendant drew down the sheet and Murphy winced at the scorch marks caused by contact with the live rail. The face was largely unmarked, which would have been some comfort to whoever had identified him. Some distortion in the trunk suggested a lot of broken bones where he was hit by the wheels.

'Nasty' said Linda, surveying the body. 'At least he's still in one piece.'

Murphy lowered her mask and folded a piece of chewing gum into her mouth. Usually she disapproved of the stuff, especially when she saw it plastered on pavements, but it had its uses in the morgue, if only because the chewing somehow diverted attention from what else was happening.

Linda made the first incision and Murphy kept her gaze well away from what was going on. Counting the ceiling tiles was her usual opening procedure. She heard the top of the head being sawed away and could smell the overheated saw edge cutting through the bone. That was it for the ceiling tiles. Time to start on the floor. Then she heard the squelch as the brain was removed. So at least that bit was over. Linda would now be making the main vertical incision. Stomach contents coming up, any time now. The worst bit, but often the most useful bit evidentially. When Linda declared 'Cancer' she looked over and saw her holding up what looked like the liver.

'They've already cut some of it away' said Linda, pointing to a blunt edge. 'You can do that with the liver and it will regenerate itself. Unfortunately, it seems to have come back, the cancer that is, so further surgery would have been required. Well, he's been spared that.'

'Is that a result of alcohol abuse?'

Linda shook her head. 'Not necessarily. It can happen to people who don't drink at all. It's more a result of bad luck than anything else. With drinkers what you mostly see is cirrhosis. That doesn't look too pleasant either.'

Murphy had often wondered whether Linda had nightmares about bodies and had concluded that, no, she didn't. And the reason she didn't was that her attitude was wholly scientific. A dead body was a puzzle to be solved, not a trigger for emotion. In Murphy's line of work, the case, whether it be murder or anything else, was the puzzle to be solved. The actual dead body she tried not to think too much about.

'So that cancer was terminal' she said.

'Oh yes,' said Linda. 'Can't say when. Depends how fast it was progressing. He would probably be lined up for another op sometime soon and that, together with chemo, could have given him more months or even a year or two. But it would have caught up with him eventually.'

'I guess that makes suicide more likely.' Murphy was thinking aloud at this point.

'Maybe,' said Linda. 'But he may not have been in much pain and people tend to cling to life even when it may not be for long. When we get the bloods done, we'll be able to see whether he was on morphine, but I think it was not quite at that stage.'

The stomach contents held no particular surprises. Mostly beer and an almost completely digested sandwich. 'Cheese and pickle, I think' Linda pronounced. 'That would have been his lunch and then he probably visited the pub on the way home.'

'On the way home' sounded sad to Murphy. On the way home, except he never got there. Or maybe he never intended to get there.

Chapter Nine

MURPHY WAS at her desk the next morning attempting to make some sense of the reports on the door-to-door interviews following the latest burglary. Somebody clearly knew what they were doing. All of the houses targeted were wealthy, all of the burglaries took place in broad daylight while the occupants were out, and none of the neighbours saw a thing. It was a pretty slick operation, you almost had to admire it. Chief Inspector Bellweather didn't admire it, he took it as a personal insult that rich people were being robbed on his watch and was scathing about Murphy's failure so far to apprehend anybody.

He sauntered over now to stand in front of her desk.

'Just a harmless little cat burglar, Detective Inspector Murphy, with a good eye for valuable stuff. Probably not violent or drug-crazed. A gentleman burglar perhaps. More like Raffles maybe? You've had three weeks to finger his collar; what's going on? Shall I call in Special Branch to help you?' This last followed by a mirthless grin that showed off to best advantage the Dulux Brilliant White veneers that had probably cost him half a year's salary.

Murphy was saved from having to reply by her phone ringing. Probably another bloody burglary. But no, it was Linda Fleming, summoning her back to the morgue. She passed the rest of the paperwork over to Kevin Wilcox, who was showing no desire to accompany her, and set off for the tube. That was one advantage of having left Wilcox behind. If he had been with her, she'd have had to walk, and at his pace. Left to her own devices, she could run down the steps into the tube station and then walk briskly down the escalator, instead of just standing there, like some parcel waiting to be delivered.

She found Linda looking almost as animated as when she'd told her about the new grandchild. The body was back on the table, covered by the sheet.

'Rohypnol,' said Linda triumphantly, bouncing on her heels.

'What?'

'Rohypnol, Roofies, whatever you want to call it. We call it Flunitrazepam, but that's by the way.'

Murphy was astounded. 'The date-rape drug?'

'That's right. Administered not long before death, as the concentration in the urine was still quite high.'

'But that's ridiculous.'

'Nothing's ridiculous these days,' declared Linda, whipping off the sheet. 'I've given up being surprised by anything that turns up. Whatever mad thing you can think of, somebody somewhere is doing it.'

Murphy looked at the neat line of stitches going from the sternum to the pubis. She was trying hard to process this. Linda was still talking.

'...so, when I saw the results, I had a closer look and I

found it.' She was pointing at the dead man's left calf on which Murphy could just make out a tiny red dot.

'Is that...?' she began

'Yes.' Linda nodded triumphantly. 'A puncture wound.'

'You mean – he was spiked? With a needle? Through his trousers? Surely not.'

'Surely was. It's not just young girls who get spiked. And trousers are no barrier to a needle, unless perhaps they're leather.'

Murphy could feel her brain struggling to catch up. 'So could that have made him pass out and fall under a tube train?'

Linda took a moment to answer. 'Possibly. It would have induced relaxation, drowsiness, maybe loss of muscle control. And then amnesia, which is of course irrelevant in this case.'

Murphy thought for a moment. 'If you wanted to push somebody under a tube, it would be a lot easier if they were in this condition.'

Linda was covering up the body again. 'Yes, of course. It makes it easier to rape somebody, and easier to kill them too.'

Chapter Ten

BACK IN THE CID room Kevin Wilcox was looking almost as excited as Linda Fleming. 'I think I might have something on these burglaries,' he said.

'Let's leave that for the moment,' said Murphy. 'We may have a murder on our hands. The Moorgate victim had been spiked with Rohypnol. He had terminal cancer but according to the bloods he wasn't yet on morphine, so not in the last stages. Very strange set of circumstances. Let's go and talk to the relatives.'

There was one pool car left; it was the one with the dodgy clutch. Murphy was happy to let Wilcox drive it. This particular bastard had stalled on her once when she was attempting a hill start in pursuit of a suspect and she had never forgiven it. Wilcox had some sort of affinity with machinery – machinery and anything digital – so she was happy to leave it to him. For his part, Wilcox had never troubled to hide the fact that he found her driving alarming – leaving aside the terms of abuse that she flung at other motorists – so, unless she was really feeling up for it, she let him drive the pool cars.

The journey to Camden was slow – such a short journey, but so much traffic. Despite its raffish reputation, the goth vibe and, according to the drug squad, the biggest open-air drugs market in Europe, Camden also had quiet, expensive residential streets lining the route to Regents Park and Richard Weaver lived (or had lived) in one of them.

The door was opened by a slim woman with blonde hair and reddened eyes, flanked by a pretty and much younger woman who looked distinctly alarmed.

'Mrs Weaver?' said Murphy and the older woman nodded. They showed their badges and she stood aside to let them enter.

The two women sat on the sofa and the detectives took the armchairs Murphy was glad of that. The sofa looked like one of those sinkable ones. She might have had trouble extricating herself from that without her joints protesting – probably noisily.

'I'm Alison Weaver,' said the older woman, 'and this is my daughter Florence.' Florence nodded briefly in their direction and fixed them with a glare.

'We're very sorry for your loss,' Murphy began, 'and we're still trying to establish exactly what happened to your husband. We know that he had liver cancer. That must have been difficult.'

Mrs Weaver tightened her lips and nodded. 'Yes, we both knew he only had about another year, but he wasn't in pain and he was still working.'

'How had his illness affected him?'

'What affected him was the chemo, more than the illness. He got tired easily and he was eating less. He hadn't lost his hair, surprisingly.' A tear ran down her cheek at this.

'You don't think it's possible he would have wanted to kill himself?'

Alison Weaver sat up and looked intently at them. 'Of course he wouldn't have wanted to kill himself! We had so many plans. He was going to finish work and then we were going travelling. We were going to start in Australia and then go round south east Asia. We were mapping it all out. He was going to work for a few more months, make as much money as he could, and then we were off. He wouldn't have wanted to lose the last bit of time he had left with us.'

Florence put her arms around her mother and for a few moments they just clung together. The only sound was a distant police siren, another disaster taking place somewhere else. Murphy waited until Alison Weaver turned back to face her.

'We'd like to establish your husband's movements on Monday night,' she said.

Alison grabbed a tissue, blew her nose and sat up straighter. 'He was at work all day. He only works — worked — a short day. Ten till five. Then he was going for a quick drink with Adrian and Arthur, like he usually did on Mondays. I don't know if he did that or not. I guess I should have called them and asked, but it didn't seem to matter once I found out what had happened, and I didn't feel like talking to anybody.'

'Adrian and Arthur?'

'Adrian French and Arthur Wellesley. They're old friends of Richard's from university. The bank has been allowing Richard to finish at 5pm since his diagnosis so, when the others manage to get away early, which is most Mondays, they meet for a drink.'

'Your husband worked for Singapore Commercial

Bank?' said Wilcox, who had gone through the contents of the briefcase.

'That's right. He was in Mergers and Acquisitions.'

'And Mr French and Mr Wellesley. What do they do?'

'Adrian is an estate agent and Arthur is a solicitor. Do you want their contact details?'

'Yes please.' Wilcox passed over his notebook and Alison copied the details from her phone.

'Something surprising was found when the post-mortem was carried out,' said Murphy. 'The pathologist discovered the presence of Rohypnol.'

Alison stared blankly at them and then seemed to find her voice. 'Rohypnol? The date rape drug?'

'That's right.'

'That makes no sense. Why would he have taken that?' She stopped for a moment. 'Could that have made him dizzy?'

Murphy nodded. 'Yes, that's a possibility we're looking into. Did your husband have any enemies? Anybody who might have wished him harm?'

'Of course not. Do you mean that somebody could have administered this drug? Surely not.'

'At the moment we are considering every possibility. The findings were very unexpected and we have to investigate.' Murphy hesitated. 'Are there any other members of the immediate family?'

'My son Jake. He's in his last year at Newcastle university. He's on his way back here.'

'That must have been a horrible shock for him.'

'Yes. We'll be glad when he gets home.'

'I realise,' said Murphy, 'that this is a difficult question, considering the diagnosis that he was living with, but do you think your husband was depressed at all?'

Alison seemed to be thinking for a moment. 'I can understand that somebody might think that, but I think that Richard had made his peace with the diagnosis. He was very resilient and he had plans for how he was going to spend the time left to him. He would never have wanted to die suddenly, without time to say goodbye to us all. So no, despite the diagnosis, he never acted as if he was depressed.'

'Thank you for explaining that,' said Murphy. 'I know it's a really difficult question to answer. Were you aware of any money worries that he might have had?'

Alison shook her head. 'No, he wouldn't have had any money worries. We have enough money. We had no money tied up in anything risky and we both earned good salaries.'

'I imagine he had life insurance.'

'Yes, of course, but you can't possibly think...'

'I'm not thinking anything in particular about it. It's just one of those questions we have to ask.'

Murphy could see that Alison was just holding herself together. It was time to back off.

'OK. I think that's all for the moment' she said. 'We'll probably need to speak to you again and we'll let you know of any developments.'

They all rose together and she and Wilcox made their way out. The daughter had been silent throughout, but stared suspiciously at them as they left. Murphy couldn't blame her; they were hardly the bearers of good news.

'You didn't tell her about the needle spiking' Wilcox observed as he unlocked the car.

'No. I thought I should keep something back. It's always possible that the family could have something to do with it. We need to check the terms of the life insurance.'

Wilcox started the engine and began to pull out. It stalled.

THESE TWO CID people looked like complete losers, Florence thought. The two from the uniformed branch had looked younger and smarter, and that was saying something. The older (much older!) woman really needed to do something about her hair, which looked like she'd had some weird colour job and talk about split ends. Also, she could have done with losing a couple of pounds (no, scrub that, fat-shaming no longer allowed). The young guy with her was a complete dork, looked like he belonged in an IT department. Florence saw him glance in her direction and thought, no way, in your dreams. If this pair were supposed to find out what had happened to her dad, there was no hope, Florence was sure of that. And the idea that her dad had taken roofies, that was just off the wall.

They had all come to terms some time ago with the idea that her dad might not be around too much longer, but new cures were being discovered all the time, new genetic sequencing or whatever, so there was always a chance. That was what her dad said whenever he saw her getting mopey, although she wasn't sure that he believed it any more than she did. However slim it was, that chance had gone now. They had to accept that, having looked at his face on the trolley in the hospital.

In some ways, her dad being gone closed a chapter. There were things that would not now happen, all the pain of the final stages of his illness. But still, she wished he was here now. There were things she should have talked to him about; she should have been prepared to listen. And maybe... no, she wouldn't go there. The future was what counted. And she had plans for that.

Chapter Eleven

ARRIVING HOME THAT EVENING, Murphy opened the door to a barrage of male voices. James and Clive she was expecting to see – they lived here after all. The third man present was her ex-husband. His hair needed cutting, his shirt looked like nobody had ironed it and he glanced up at her with sort of sheepish grin she had long been familiar with and was now impervious to. If this was a bid for sympathy, it wasn't going to get him anywhere. As far as she could make out, the three of them were engaged in drinking beer and tearing lumps out of one of the contestants on Strictly Come Dancing.

'Nul points from me' she said, falling into an armchair. 'Jack, what a nice surprise. Not planning to move back in, I hope?'

He attempted a laugh. 'No, don't worry love. Just thought I'd see how you were.'

'How am I? Much the same, as you can see. Overworked, underpaid, maybe a tad overweight.'

'You don't look overweight.'

James and Clive looked at each other and rose as one. Strictly was drawing to a close.

'Bedtime for us, I think,' said Clive. 'And I still think Sadie and Alphonso were robbed. See you later folks.'

'Goodnight, guys.' Murphy kicked off her shoes and curled up. The third man showed no inclination to move and seemed to be planting himself more firmly in the armchair. 'It's been a long day Jack, and I'm also looking forward to bed, so can you say whatever it is quickly?'

He sighed deeply and looked at his hands. 'I guess I just wanted somebody to talk to.'

Murphy yawned and stretched. She could have done without this. But he was here now.

'About what?'

He looked up at her. 'About Tracey. She's left me.'

Murphy took a deep breath. This was potentially bad. 'To be honest, I'm not sure I'm the right person to help you with that. Do you know why? Did she meet somebody else?'

'No, nothing like that.' He hesitated. 'I think she decided I'm too old. Or rather, I think that's what her friends have decided.'

'That would be right,' said Murphy. 'Peer group opinions are very important for young people. Maybe it got to the point where she could no longer sell you as the sophisticated older man.'

'You're not helping,' he complained.

She sighed. 'OK. In that case is there more you want to tell me about it? When did it start to go wrong? Did you miss the signs? Go ahead, unburden yourself.'

He gave her a sharp look and then sat back. 'It was after Cornwall. We went down for about five days last month.'

Murphy could remember holidays in Cornwall. The beaches, the body boarding, the pasties, the cream. The long drive there and back. Jack was always very keen on the West Country, the kids loved it as long as it didn't rain, and somehow it invariably did. She knew how this would have played out.

'Don't tell me, let me guess. You insisted on staying in a tent because it was cheaper and she had to spend half her beach time in the launderette drying the clothes off and the other half cooking over Calor gas and washing the camping dishes in cold water.'

'No, not at all. Are you going to listen or not? OK. For a start we didn't stay in a tent. We had a very acceptable Airbnb with a washing machine and a dryer – and a dishwasher. It was very civilised. And we ate out, she didn't have to cook at all. Well, to be honest, she doesn't cook much anyway. I think the problem was that she posted a lot of pictures on Facebook and some of the comments we got were ... not very kind.'

'You mean comments about you?' Murphy tried to look shocked but she was fighting hard to keep her face straight.

'Yes – you're laughing!'

'No, I'm not. I'm just yawning 'cos I'm tired.'

'Alright, well some of them pointed out that I looked old – they made the point in various more descriptive ways.' His tone was suddenly tinged with outraged respectability. 'People say stuff – the most disgraceful things - on social media that they would never dare say if they met you in the street.'

Murphy yawned. 'From what I see every day, some people do much worse things than trade insults when they actually meet each other in the street. But carry on. What happened then?'

He sighed. 'I thought we could laugh it off, it was all just ignorant rubbish, and who cares what anybody else thinks?

But Tracey didn't agree. She was really upset about it. These were her friends I suppose, so it was important to her in a way that it wasn't to me. I guess she lay awake thinking about it, and the next day she told me it was over – just like that. I couldn't believe it. I'd thought we were going to spend our lives together. I'd made so many plans. We were going to travel, I was looking at RVs, we'd talked about it, we were going to go to the US, do the national parks, Yellowstone and Yosemite. It was a bit of a shock; I have to admit that. I couldn't talk her round. The upshot was that I had to move out.'

Murphy yawned and stretched again. 'I think that's just how it happens, Jack. Young women today have a social media reputation to keep up and social media is merciless. Appearing in selfies with someone who looks like your dad doesn't generate a lot of likes. Tracey did what she had to do. I think you'd be better off with somebody nearer your own age. There's probably lots of slightly older women who would love to roam around North America in an RV with a mature man. Maybe amend the Tinder profile a bit.'

'I'm not on Tinder' he shot back.

'No, that's right. You found Tracey in real life, didn't you? IRL, they call it. I'm not sure that IRL works these days. Anyway, you had to move out, so where are you living now?' She held her breath waiting for the answer.

He sighed. 'I'm renting a bedsit in Queens Park. It's not up to much. I can't believe the rents you have to pay these days.'

Murphy relaxed and exhaled. 'You've joined Generation Rent – that should make you feel younger. OK, I'll stop joking. Queen's Park. I used to know Queen's Park. I had a flat there once, about a century ago, before I met you. It's a good area – good tube service, nice pubs, decent shops. Do you need any stuff – furniture, dishes, whatever?'

'No, that's fine, it's fully equipped. Well, enough for one person anyway.' He hesitated. 'Perhaps we could have dinner sometime.'

'Dinner? In a decent restaurant? Paid for by you? You bet your ass we could. I'll give you a ring when I get a free evening. No chance at the moment, murder investigation ongoing. And now I really have to get to bed.'

'Yes, of course.' He rose and headed for the front door. 'Thanks Miranda.' He stooped to kiss her cheek.

'For nothing. Take care.' She waved and closed the door. Then she leaned against it. Crisis averted, but maybe not for long.

Chapter Twelve

ADRIAN FRENCH'S office occupied a small corner of the first floor of a glass and steel building in the smart, new high-tech centre of Kings Cross. Even the pigeons looked well-groomed.

'Whole area's unrecognisable,' said Murphy, looking around. 'This used to be one of our regular patrols and there was always stuff going on – fights, muggings, drugs, prostitution, vehicle theft, drunk and disorderly. What I always wonder is – where has it all gone? Our clientele must have moved on – but where to?'

'Don't worry,' said Wilcox. 'It will all surface somewhere else, and we'll be the first to hear about it.'

Adrian French was on the phone when they arrived and introduced themselves to the receptionist. He was a balding man of middle age with fashionable glasses and a body shape, seen from above the desk, which suggested that he didn't often skip lunch. He was engaged in trying to terminate a conversation which was evidently going nowhere.

'...as I've tried to explain, Mrs Foster, I can only send

people to view your house if it is what they are looking for. Otherwise, I'd be wasting your time as well as theirs. The housing market is not buoyant at this time of year and a number of vendors are dropping the asking price … well no, that was just an observation, you are of course free to maintain your asking price … shall we give it a week and see if anything moves? Perfect. I'll be in touch next week.'

He put the phone down, came round from behind the desk and advanced towards them, hand outstretched. Murphy noticed that it was quite a small hand. They introduced themselves and the welcoming smile faded from Adrian French's face. They were not potential buyers of Mrs Foster's house.

He sighed. 'How can I help you?'

'We want to talk to you about Richard Weaver,' said Murphy.

A couple of expressions flitted across his face – shock, fear, resignation – could that be right? He waved them into an inner office, brought in an extra chair and shut the door.

'What is it? Has something happened to Richard?'

Murphy looked carefully at him. 'I'm afraid so, yes. He was killed at Moorgate station on Monday night.'

Whatever he had been expecting, this was clearly not it. The shocked expression took several seconds to clear from his face.

'Killed? You mean he's dead?'

'Yes, he is.'

'Oh my God.' He seemed to sink lower into the chair behind his desk.

'We gather you saw him earlier that evening,' said Wilcox.

Adrian French turned to look at him. He took a moment to reply. When he did his voice sounded hoarse.

'Yes, we had a drink after work – Richard and me and Arthur Wellesley. We've known each other since university. Oh God – poor Alison. What happened?'

'We're still piecing together exactly what happened, but he was hit by a train.'

Adrian French flinched. 'You mean he went under the tube? In Moorgate?'

Murphy nodded. 'Exactly.'

'So, we'd like to hear everything about that evening, Mr French,' Wilcox continued. 'Every detail you can remember.'

He dropped his face into his hands for a few seconds, then took a deep breath and looked up at them.

'It was a pretty unremarkable evening. We met in the Ropemakers Arms in Fore Street. We've been meeting there on and off for years. This last year we've just been meeting on Mondays and only for about an hour. It's convenient for Richard and Arthur as they both work round there and I'm here in Kings Cross so it's easy to get to.'

'Richard worked for an investment bank, I gather,' said Murphy.

Adrian French stared at his hands for a moment.

'Yes, that's right. SCB – Singapore Commercial Bank. Why? Is there something wrong at the bank?'

'Not as far as we know,' said Wilcox. 'Should there be?'

He shook his head. 'Not at all. Just wondered, you know. Anyway, we met at about 5.30, just had one pint and then we left, probably about 6.40. I got on a bus and Arthur went back to the office. Richard made his way to … Moorgate.'

'Why did you all leave so early?'

'Because of Richard, really. He only stays for one pint. I don't know if he's actually allowed to drink, with the drugs he's on, so he doesn't push it. Do you know about the cancer?' Murphy nodded.

Adrian French carried on. 'Because he's not well, he has a special arrangement at work, so he doesn't start until 10 and he finishes early. So, we go for an early drink.'

'So how was he that evening?' said Murphy. 'What did you talk about?'

'He was pretty much the same as usual. He never seems to be in any pain or discomfort – I guess he wasn't at that stage in the progress of the cancer. And he didn't seem upset about anything. What did we talk about? Let me see ... we spent a bit of time slagging off the government. That's pretty standard. Then we got onto Arsenal and what's been going wrong there. Arthur's firm has been retained to defend some high-profile grooming case, which Richard mentioned, but Arthur said he couldn't talk about it, not while it was ongoing. Richard told us a bit about his last hospital visit, but he didn't want to say too much about it. He was being very brave, I thought, but – is that what happened? Did he kill himself?'

'We don't know that yet. Would you have expected him to kill himself?'

He shook his head. 'No, definitely not. For one thing, he hadn't given up hope that the thing might go into remission again. And for another, he wanted to keep working as long as possible to build up funds for Alison and the children. He hadn't given up, not at all.'

'Mr French,' said Wilcox, 'can you tell us what time you arrived home that evening?'

'I didn't take much notice of the time. About 7.15 I think.'

'Was anybody else at home?'

'My wife and son were there. Not sure that my son

would have noticed me arriving though – not if he was playing Fortnite.'

'OK. You have known Richard Weaver a long time, is that right?'

'Yes. Since university.' He smiled briefly. 'I had more hair then.'

'In that time, have you been aware of him having any enemies, anybody who would wish him harm?'

'No, absolutely not. Does this mean you think somebody deliberately pushed him?'

'We're not ruling anything out at the moment. Do you know if he was taking any drugs?'

'Well, he was probably taking all sorts of chemo drugs, but nothing else, I'm sure. He wouldn't have taken anything else in case it interfered with the chemo.'

'And did you notice anything unusual that evening? Anything about Richard, or any altercation with anybody else in the pub, anything like that?'

He shook his head. 'No nothing at all. It was a perfectly normal Monday evening. The pub was pretty crowded, but it always is.'

Murphy stood up. 'Thank you for your help, Mr French. If you think of anything else, please get in touch with us. And if you can just let us have your wife's phone number?'

French scribbled on a piece of paper and passed it over. Wilcox had the number ringing by the time they were down to the ground floor and out the door.

'Seems OK' he said as he disconnected. 'She confirms that he got home sometime after 7, though she can't give an exact time, and I must have got through to her before he did.'

Murphy was staring at the shoes in the shop window next door. 'Yes, I thought his distress was probably genuine' she said. 'But he did look very worried when we first mentioned Richard, before he knew he was dead. Was he hiding something else or does he know something about this incident? Plenty more to find out.'

She dragged her attention away from a pair of suede kitten heels with a hefty price tag and they got in the car.

Chapter Thirteen

WATERFIELDS WAS on the second floor of 20 Gresham Street, a steel and glass structure occupying the corner of what was once a bustling medieval street. The office itself was bustling, people hurrying around with bundles of folders or speaking intently into mobiles.

Arthur Wellesley was a totally different body-type to Adrian French – tall, slim and well-muscled. A man with a gym membership, no doubt. A bike helmet could be seen nestling in his bookshelf. This made sense to Murphy – if you were a lawyer you had to do whatever it took not to look like a lawyer. He waved them into his office and shut the door.

'We want to talk to you about Richard Weaver,' said Wilcox.

'Of course,' he said. 'I've heard what happened. Very shocking.'

'Did Adrian French call you?' asked Murphy.

He nodded. 'Yes. And then I called Alison. She's in bits. I can't really believe it.'

Murphy looked carefully at him. He looked much less stunned about it than Adrian French had, but of course he had had time to get over the shock. Or maybe he was less surprised? It was always annoying not to be able to observe a person's initial reactions.

'Can you tell us your movements that evening?'

'We met in the pub early — about 5.30 — and we had just one pint and left about an hour later. I guess we're pretty slow drinkers. I came back here to finish some work and collect my bike and I then left about 8.30.'

'Was anybody here at the office when you came back?'

'No, everybody else had gone. Bit unusual. A lot of the senior people were at a conference and the junior ones had seized the opportunity to leave at a normal time. The cleaner arrived about 7.30.'

'Can you tell us whatever you remember about that last meeting? What you talked about, stuff like that.'

'OK, well we talked a bit about football. Quite a lot about football actually. Richard described his latest hospital visit — not in detail, but he managed to make it sound amusing, which I'm sure it wasn't. He was very good company like that. I'll miss him a lot.'

'Arthur French also referred to a case you are going to be defending,' said Murphy. 'A grooming case.'

'Yes, that's right, although I can't say much about it. There are a number of victims, so it will be high profile.'

'How would you describe Richard Weaver's state of mind that evening?' said Wilcox.

'Do you mean was he suicidal?'

'Yes, that as well. Do you think it's a possibility?'

'He seemed to be in a good mood, but that was how he always was. If he had been planning to kill himself, we would not have known, he would have acted same as normal. He was a strong character.'

'Are you aware of him ever having any enemies?' asked Murphy.

Arthur Wellesley rubbed the back of his head. 'He'd spent years on the trading floor, where every deal you secure is in competition with other traders, so he would have inspired lots of professional rivalry, but no, nothing personal. He was a very likeable person, he got on with everybody.'

'Do you think he could have had problems at work?'

Arthur Wellesley opened his mouth and then closed it again. He took a deep breath. 'I don't know much about what went on at his office. They were being very decent to him, shorter hours, time off when he needed it, so I can't think there was anything wrong.'

'Adrian French told us he had known Richard since university. Had you known him that long?'

'Yes, we were all in the same year at Durham – Richard, Adrian and me. Richard did economics, Adrian did history of art and I did law. But we were all in the same lodgings during the first year and, somehow, we stayed friends. We had a terrifying landlady, so I guess we bonded in adversity.'

'And you all ended up in London,' said Wilcox.

He nodded. 'Anybody who wanted a career, unless it was a public service career, and maybe even those, tended to drift down to London. It was where all the jobs were. Durham is a lovely, historic city, but it was far away from where everything was happening. I doubt many students stayed there after graduating.'

'And what about Alison?' asked Murphy. 'When did Richard meet Alison?'

Wellesley looked at the floor for a second and blinked a

few times. 'Let me see, it must have been during our second year.' He was silent for a moment. 'Yes, that was it.' He smiled. 'So they were together a long time.'

'Just one more thing,' said Wilcox. 'The pub you were at on Monday – the Ropemakers Arms – was it busy when you were in there?'

'Oh yes, packed. It's pretty well always packed. We managed to hold onto a small patch of the bar, but people were piling in behind us. It's a popular place for people to have a drink before going home.'

'Would you recognise any of the people who were in there that night?'

'Probably not. It was just a crowd. I wouldn't recognise any particular individual.'

'I guess the bar staff there know you,' said Wilcox.

He thought for a moment. 'They might do. We've been going in there once a week for about a year, but the bar staff have probably changed a few times. There's one barman that's a regular – bald head and a gingery beard.'

'Thank you. That's very helpful,' said Murphy. 'We may need to speak to you again. And if you think of anything else, please call us.'

Chapter Fourteen

'THIS WILL BE a good time to check out the pub,' said Murphy, 'before the evening drinkers pile in.'

Wilcox summoned up the directions on his phone and they set off at the sort of measured pace that he favoured and that drove Murphy mad. He was young and fit – shouldn't he be the fast walker? On this occasion he was dictating the pace because he had the directions. Murphy had several times tried following directions on her phone, but the map always seemed to be upside down whichever way she looked at it and she had ended up in weird places.

'You walk as if you're still on the beat' she said. 'Plodding along. Proceeding – that's what it is. If you had to stand up in court and say 'as I was proceeding in a westerly direction', that would be an accurate description of what you were doing.'

'Well, I always think it's important to know where I'm going and how to get there without getting lost' he replied, pointedly.

At that moment they turned the corner and the pub

appeared. 'I guess that must be its original name,' said Murphy. 'They haven't renamed it as the Hedgehog and Cabbage or whatever.'

'Dates back to 1781' said Wilcox, consulting his phone. 'Probably had a few makeovers since then.'

The place was obviously getting ready for the evening rush. A young woman was wiping the tables and the man behind the bar polishing the glasses had a bald head and a ginger beard.

'Bingo' muttered Murphy. 'You can get the drinks as you're so efficient at doing your expenses. I'll have a tonic water.'

When the barman had placed the tonic water and a Coke on the bar, Murphy showed him her badge.

'We'd like a few words' she said.

He held his palms up. 'Sure, no problem.'

'Can I start by asking your name?'

'Stan. Stan Welby.'

'OK Stan. Were you in here on Monday night?'

He shrugged. 'Yes. I'm in here every night.'

'Do you remember three middle-aged blokes coming in about 5.30? From what we have gathered, they stood by the bar and just had one pint each. They come in about once a week.'

Stan smiled. 'Yes, I remember them. A short plump bloke, a tall slim bloke and one somewhere in between. They're Monday regulars. Nice enough guys but we don't make much money from them. Why, has something happened?'

'Have you had any incidents of needle spiking here?' asked Wilcox.

Stan folded his arms and shook his head. 'Absolutely not, and we would call the police immediately if it was ever reported. We do get quite a lot of young people in here but nobody has ever complained about that.'

'Sometimes,' said Wilcox, 'people don't know it's happened until some hours later. It's not necessarily painful. If they're in the middle of a crowd and they've had a few drinks they might not notice.'

He nodded. 'Yes, I've heard that.'

'Was it crowded in here on Monday night? Say about six to six thirty?'

He nodded. 'Pretty crowded. That's our early evening influx. Piling in from work. It thins out about seven.'

'Stan,' said Murphy. 'If you cast your mind back to Monday night, can you recall where those three blokes were standing? I take it they were standing?'

He indicated a section of the bar about two feet from where they were standing. 'They were there' he said. 'I think that's where they usually stand.'

'And you would have been aware of them all that time, on some level?'

Stan nodded. 'That's part of working a bar. You always have to know who's where and who's next to be served. I was hoping they'd leave soon, to be honest, because they were blocking off a bit of the bar and they obviously weren't going to buy any more drinks.'

'So, they were in other people's way?'

'Yes, a bit. But you always get that. People work around each other.'

'Did you see any shoving, altercation, anything like that?'

'No. And I wouldn't stand for anything like that.'

'If you think back, can you picture anybody else in the vicinity of these three people?'

'Anybody specific you mean?'

'Yes. Is there any face that comes to mind?'

'Let me see, there were one or two girls at one point, one of them was quite good-looking. There was one young guy, maybe on his own, maybe not. There was a group that had all piled in from the same office, some of them were a bit noisy. I'm not sure that I could provide descriptions of any of them.'

'Do you know which firm they worked for?'

'No. Probably one of the legal firms.'

'But if we were to come by with photos, you might recognise some of the people who were here?'

'I might, yes. I've got a good memory for faces. But what is this all about? Was somebody spiked?'

We can't be sure at the moment,' said Wilcox. 'So we'd ask you not to discuss this with anybody else.'

He nodded. 'Sure thing.'

'He'll definitely discuss it with everybody else' said Wilcox as they closed the door.

'You bet he will, but there's not much we can do about that. He's an observant chap. I think he might prove to be useful. OK, tomorrow we'll visit SCB.'

Chapter Fifteen

RICHARD WEAVER'S boss was a large man called Andrew Castle, with a confident manner, a firm handshake and a beautifully cut suit. No dress-down Fridays here, Murphy was sure. Nevertheless, she thought she could detect some underlying nervousness. It was there in the almost over-eager welcome, the immediate offer of coffee (In an expensive place like this? She almost bit his hand off).

'This is some view you have' she said, looking down from the tenth floor of the Gherkin at the bodies hurrying below.

'It's quite something isn't it? We were very lucky to get in here.'

Murphy resumed her seat and gave him her best smile. 'You will have heard about what happened to Richard Weaver?'

'Yes. I called his mobile when he didn't appear for work on Tuesday and it was answered by somebody at the police station. It was a terrible shock. I've told the staff here, the ones who knew him are very upset. We don't really know what to think.'

'We're not sure yet exactly how it happened,' said Murphy. 'Tell me what you can about Richard.'

He sighed. 'Richard was here for ten years, most of that time on the trading floor. SCB did well to get him. I think he was headhunted from one of the hedge funds. He was one of the best traders in the business, could spot any movement in the market just before it happened. And he could take it right to the wire. You need good nerves for that. Once or twice, it was touch and go, margin calls were due and, if it had been me, I would have closed out our position, but Richard had the confidence to just hang on. He was very talented. And a lot of young people benefitted from his expertise and went on to do really well. We'll miss him a lot – as a person, of course, not just as a colleague.'

Or as a cash cow Murphy thought uncharitably. 'So he made the bank a lot of money?'

'Yes, he did. And of course, he was well rewarded.'

'Of course. But there must have been some changes when he got his diagnosis.'

'Yes, that was a shock. He told HR about it straightaway. He wanted to carry on working and the bank wanted to keep him. At that point his health was the top priority. He had hospital appointments and he needed rest, so the trading floor was no longer the right place for him to be. Apart from anything else, the traders work till late in the evening to tie in with the US markets, and those sorts of hours were really contraindicated for anybody undergoing chemo. At that point he transferred here to M&A – mergers and acquisitions.' The last added helpfully for lay people.

Wilcox frowned. 'How good are your Chinese Walls between M&A and the traders?'

Castle looked taken aback for a moment, but recovered quickly. 'Our Chinese Walls – although we're not strictly allowed to call them that any more, we say information barriers – are pretty impregnable. We have very strong internal controls and procedures.'

'Transferring staff between trading and M&A puts maximum stress on those controls, doesn't it?' said Wilcox.

Castle was now looking at Wilcox as if seeing him properly for the first time. He was sounding just a bit rattled.

'Yes, it does. And for that reason, we wouldn't normally do it. We certainly wouldn't transfer in the other direction, from M&A to trading, or not without a substantial period of gardening leave. But in this case, we made an exception and...'

His voice trailed off. Murphy realised that he had been about to say 'it worked out well' and then thought better of it.

'How was he doing in his new role?' she asked. 'Wouldn't he have found it a bit dull?'

Castle frowned and she realised he was a bit offended. But he went ahead and answered. 'It's a bit less exciting, if you like. But it's just a different skillset. More client interaction, a lot of meetings and discussions. Richard was doing fine. He was very well respected. And still very well paid, of course. We kept him on the same salary.'

'Did he have any particular friends here?'

'Well, like the rest of us, he had mainly acquaintances. The trading side of the business doesn't leave much time for personal interactions. People work very long hours, to cope with the time differences around the world, and some of them burn out or move on. Not all of them stay with one firm as long as Richard did. And in this department, he hadn't really had time to form any close ties. He had two direct reports in M&A and they were probably the people he was closest to, in the last few months at least.'

'When we've finished here, could we have a chat with them?'

'Of course. I think they're both in today.'

'Can I just ask you' Murphy began, 'when you heard what had happened, what was your immediate thought?'

'I have to admit, my immediate thought was suicide, simply because of his terminal illness. I can understand anybody wanting to get it over with. But it didn't fit with my understanding of Richard – he wasn't somebody who had given up. Then I thought it must have been an accident. He was on powerful drugs, I thought maybe they could have made him black out.'

Murphy nodded. 'Of course. Any of that is possible. We'll know in due course. OK, I think that's all for now. Perhaps we could have a word with his two reports – separately I think.'

'No problem. If you just wait here, I'll send them along.'

Parvez Shah was a slight young man with a smart suit and fashionable spectacles. Murphy introduced them both and asked if they could talk to him about Richard Weaver.

'Of course.' He spread his hands wide. 'Although I don't have any particular information.'

'Can you just tell us a bit about him, what he was like?' said Wilcox.

Parvez hesitated for a moment. 'He was one of the best people' he said. 'He was always helpful, he never got angry. It's a tough environment here and several times I thought of quitting, but not since I've been reporting to Richard. Some of the others, I think they worry about us younger guys coming through and taking their jobs, so they don't really want you to do well, but he was always encouraging.'

'So you'll miss him?'

'Yes. A lot.'

'You're in M&A, is that right?'

'Yes, at the moment.'

'What do you think of the internal controls here?' said Wilcox.

He shrugged. 'The digital controls operate well. I can't really answer for the rest.'

'The information barriers?'

'That's harder to control, but I don't have knowledge of any breaches.'

'Understood.' Wilcox nodded. 'Thank you for your help.'

Parvez made as if to leave then turned back. He hesitated for a moment. 'Can I ask? Did he really jump?'

'We're not sure yet. We're still investigating. Do you think it's likely?'

'I find it hard to believe because ... well this will sound stupid, but he should have been doing my appraisal today. It was an important appraisal and we had discussed it and agreed the date and time. It just seems odd that he made that appointment with me when he knew he was going to kill himself first.'

'That is interesting,' said Murphy. 'Thank you for telling us that.'

'No problem.' He raised a hand and let himself out.

A few minutes later Melanie Thomas entered the room and they introduced themselves. Melanie also wore glasses and had a confident handshake. Murphy thought she was a girl who would have been very attractive with a bit of makeup and slightly less unisex clothing. But she had obviously decided that being taken seriously was more important. Good for her.

'We asked to talk to you because, as one of Richard's direct reports, you probably saw him regularly' she said. 'We haven't definitely established what happened and we're hoping you may be able to help us.'

Melanie nodded. 'Of course. I'm happy to help.'

'So can you give us some idea of what he was like to work for?'

'He was a good senior. He was very fair and he didn't pass blame down the line. If something went wrong, he took responsibility for it. I really respected that. I'm so sorry he's dead.'

'You would have known he had cancer?'

'Yes, but I guess there's always hope. People do go into remission. And there's always research going on.'

'Do you think he was hoping for that?'

'He never spoke about his illness. It was never referred to.'

'Do you think he liked being in M&A?'

'I think he missed the trading operation to begin with, but we were doing good work in M&A.'

'This sort of organisation can be a tough place for a woman, I think,' said Murphy. 'Or maybe that's no longer the case.'

Melanie smiled. 'There's none of the blatant sexism there used to be' she said. 'Or if there is, it's not overt. People are terrified of being hauled up before HR, being suspended, losing their jobs, whatever. It's a very different climate now to what it was a few years back. I'd say there's still some low-level casual sexism, but it's pretty easy to ignore. And Richard was very good like that. He pushed to get at least two women that I know about promoted when he was on the trading floor. And if anybody aimed anything sexist at me, he would call them out on it immediately.'

'Thank you for talking to us, Melanie,' said Murphy.

'You're welcome.' She left the room.

'I guess that's all we can do here,' said Wilcox.

Murphy nodded and they made their way out, passing Andrew Castle who waved them goodbye from an outer office.

Wilcox was thumbing through his phone. 'Do you think we're done for the moment?'

Murphy nodded. 'Yes, that's all we can do for today. I'm due at my sister's in an hour.'

Chapter Sixteen

SUSANNAH HAD CLEARLY MADE an effort in the culinary stakes and Simon was on his best behaviour – pouring the wine, making a fuss of the girls, asking Murphy about the job (as if she'd be telling him anything). Murphy wasn't won over. As far as she was concerned, somebody who'd run off with the nanny, and then returned three months later when it didn't work out, should have been spending a lot longer in the doghouse. But that was just her, mean-spirited old witch that she was. Susannah and the girls were obviously happy to have him back and it was what they felt that counted. For their sake she was keeping a smile plastered to her face. Nevertheless, she amused herself, when he wasn't facing in her direction, by looking him over and planning exactly where she'd hit him (hard) if he did it again.

She dragged herself away from contemplating this in time to hear what Susannah was saying.

'There's a lot of volatility in the market right now, so I'm going to be working late for the next few weeks. Simon's going to be doing a lot of cooking. And it's like buses, they all arrive together – ABS, Credit Deutsch, SCB, Waverings.'

'What do you know about SCB?' she asked, realising too late that she'd suddenly slipped into police officer mode.

Susannah looked surprised at this sudden direct questioning and they both started to laugh. Murphy realised she hadn't seen Susannah laugh in months. So maybe everything was OK.

'Well officer,' Susannah began, 'I don't know anything for a fact. They're not one of our clients or I wouldn't mention them at all. But there has been a bit of speculation about them. Nothing definite, which would of course be ruinous, just idle talk. The shares of some of their clients have been a bit volatile and there was something of an upswing prior to the announcement of the latest merger brokered by them. But, 'she shrugged, 'could all be nothing. We forensic accountants are liable to look for patterns which don't exist.'

'If the pattern did exist' said Murphy, 'what would that mean? Insider dealing?'

'Could be. That's what we'd wonder about. But you didn't hear any of this idle gossip from me.'

'Of course not, and we'll change the subject right now.' She turned to Katy and Emma. 'Time for an update on this school play, I think. And I want to know all about the new nanny.'

'Daddy's going to be in the play,' said Katy. 'He's playing one of the baddies.'

'Is he indeed?' said Murphy, smiling in his direction.

'Yes, but all of the grown-up parts are baddies,' said Emma, 'so there wasn't much choice.'

'The goodies are all children then?'

'A few children, but mostly dogs.'

'Of course,' said Murphy. 'Just like life. I've never had to arrest a dog.'

'And our new nanny is called Ben,' said Katy. 'He takes us to school in the morning and brings us back. Us and Joe and Betsy.'

'He's a professional skateboarder' Emma announced.

'Wow' said Murphy. 'He sounds really glamorous.' She winked at Susannah, who rolled her eyes. 'That's an Olympic sport now, isn't it? When he makes it to the Olympics, you'll be able to say he was your nanny. I take it he doesn't live in?'

'No' said Susannah. 'He lives up near the tube station. With his girlfriend.' Emphasis on the last three words.

'So he's spoken for?' said Murphy. 'That's a shame.'

Susannah laughed. 'I think a lot of the mothers agree with you. The crowd at the school gates have definitely smartened up since he arrived.'

'I think girls,' said Murphy, 'that you should find a part in your play for Ben. He could be the lone goody who whizzes in on his skateboard and saves the dogs, or whatever. It would probably increase attendance. And maybe he could wallop some of the baddies with his skateboard.' She smiled at Simon. 'I think they make quite good weapons.'

Chapter Seventeen

MURPHY HAD JUST PERFORMED A VERY messy three-point turn in order to grab the last space in the car park, thereby depriving the head of the Drug Squad who was driving in behind her in his brand-new Land Rover. She saw him glare in her direction as he went past. Well, he probably wouldn't have fitted in there anyway. In her haste to claim the spot, she failed to notice Wilcox streaking past her on his bike and almost nailed him to the wall.

'Good job you had your helmet on' she said, brushing the back of his jacket down, as they walked in together.

They had been back in the CID room about five minutes when Bellweather homed in on Murphy like a heat-seeking missile.

'I assume you're now wrapping this Moorgate case up.'

'Not yet sir. We still don't know exactly what happened.'

He tutted and rolled his eyes. 'We all know exactly what happened. He fell under a tube. You can't get more exact than that.'

'Yes, but we don't know why he fell. There may have been somebody else involved.'

Bellweather widened his stance and folded his arms. 'I've read your initial report – such as it is. You don't have any witnesses saying somebody else was involved. The guy was terminally ill. He either fell accidentally because the drugs he was on made him woozy or he threw himself in front of the train because he was dying anyway and he wanted to get it over with.'

'I don't think it's as simple as that sir. They found traces of Rohypnol in his urine and a spike mark on his leg.'

Bellweather's jaw dropped momentarily and Murphy fancied she could see the recalculate operation struggle to get going, like a sluggish sat nav. Then he was suddenly back on the route.

'I don't see how that changes anything. He must have been taking the Rohypnol, perhaps as an aid to relaxation. And the mark on his leg could have been caused by anything, not necessarily a needle. I think it's time we wrapped this up.'

'There are a few more avenues to pursue,' she told him. 'I'd like another chat with the family and it's possible there may have been something going on at the bank where he worked. We don't want to close it off and then discover afterwards that there was a crime involved.'

He narrowed his eyes at her and she could see him weighing up the odds.

'OK. Another forty-eight hours on this. Then drop it and do the paperwork.' He marched into his office and slammed the door.

Chapter Eighteen

ALISON WEAVER WAS DRESSED for going out when they arrived, in well-cut trousers and a fitted jacket. She caught Murphy's glance and smiled tightly.

'Yes, proper clothes. I'm actually leaving the house this morning. I decided work was what I need at the moment, so I have a seminar group this afternoon. Was it me you wanted to see?'

'If you have half an hour,' said Murphy. 'We don't have any news for you, it was just a chat. Perhaps we can also have a quick word with Florence and Jake?'

She rolled her eyes. 'Be my guest. Get them off the laptops.'

She held the door open and shouted up the stairs. Thumping noises suggested she had been heard.

Alison took off her jacket. 'Come and sit down. I'll make some coffee.'

She disappeared into the kitchen and a stick-thin young man appeared and regarded them warily.

'You must be Jake,' said Murphy, and made the introductions. 'We're very sorry about your dad.' Jake nodded briefly. 'I gather you've come down from Newcastle' she continued.

'Yes. I'm at the university. Computer science.'

'That's what I did,' said Wilcox.

Jake looked surprised at this. 'So why are you…?'

'In the police? Well, I didn't really want to spend all day staring at screens. And computer science is relevant to so many jobs now. Cool scar, by the way.'

Jake touched his forehead. 'Yes. It was a scooter accident in Italy.' He gestured towards a framed photograph standing on the bookshelf.

Murphy went over to have a look. Five people smiled in the sun, in front of a pool, flanked by a holiday villa. What was not to smile about?

'That's the four of you' she said. 'Who's the other person?'

'That's Beth,' said Jake. 'She was Florence's best friend.'

'No, she wasn't.' Another voice cut in and they were joined by Florence, looking bored and impatient. 'I had lots of friends and she was just one of them.'

'OK.' Jake shrugged. 'I liked her anyway. And she's quite high-profile now, isn't she? Posh job and all.'

Florence rolled her eyes. 'I wouldn't know. I haven't seen her in years.'

Jake frowned. 'But wasn't she at your school reunion?'

Florence opened her mouth to reply but was interrupted by the entrance of Alison, bearing a tray.

'Here we are.' She set it down with a clatter. Jake and Florence started heading for the door. 'Just a minute, you two.' They stopped.

She turned to Murphy. 'Do you want to ask them anything?'

Murphy turned to Florence and Jake. 'I just wanted to tell you both that we are working hard on finding out what happened to your dad. And if anything occurs to you that you think is relevant, please let us know. That's all. Good to have met you both. We'll let you get on.'

Jake gave a brief nod and they both disappeared.

'I'm afraid their social skills are not up to much at the moment,' said Alison.

'That's no problem,' said Murphy. 'They've had an awful shock. I'm sure it will take them some time to get over it.'

Alison sighed. 'That's true enough. I have intermittent periods when I totally forget for a few minutes and then it comes flooding back and I realise I'll never see him again.'

Murphy nodded. 'Of course. It's good that you still have your daughter at home.'

'She was hoping to have moved out this month,' said Alison. 'She was planning to move in with her boyfriend, but she seems to have delayed it. I'm grateful for that. Jake will have to go back to university in a few days. After the funeral. Life stays suspended until after the funeral. After that I'll have to think about the house.'

'You mean selling the house?' asked Murphy.

'Maybe. I'm trying not to make any hasty decisions, but I can't imagine rattling round here on my own. And I think I might need a clean break, there are a lot of memories in this house. But, for the time being, I have Florence, so I can put things off.'

'What does Florence do career-wise? asked Wilcox.

Alison hesitated. 'At the moment she's working in a coffee shop, but I think she and her boyfriend -Cal, his name is – are planning a business venture. She did Media

Studies at university – against my advice, but there you are – so I guess it's something media related.'

'They'll need seed capital for that,' said Murphy.

'I guess so,' said Alison. 'If I sell the house, I'll be able to help them out.'

'We wanted to ask you again,' Murphy began, 'about Richard's job. Whether he had any job worries, problems within the organisation, anything he may have confided in you about. I wondered if you may have thought of something.'

Alison looked surprised. 'No, nothing. To be honest, we didn't discuss his job much. We didn't discuss my job either come to that. We weren't one of those couples that come home and tell each other about their day, I don't know why. And I think he was probably often under stress – it's a very high-pressure environment – but he was good at coping with that. I think when you've had a cancer diagnosis not much else is going to worry you.'

'I'm sure that's right,' said Murphy. 'Are you aware of any problems, disagreements, upsets, people he wasn't getting on with?'

'No, nothing that I was aware of.' She looked intently at them. 'This investigation isn't going anywhere, is it?'

'So far, it's not yielding much' Murphy admitted. 'But we'll get there in the end. Thank you for the coffee and for your time.'

As the front door closed behind them, she looked up to the first floor and spotted Florence. Their eyes met and Florence withdrew hastily.

'Now what is young Florence not telling us?' she pondered out loud.

'I don't know,' said Wilcox. 'I guess she's at that age where you have a lot of stuff going on that you don't want older people to know about. Probably nothing to do with her dad dying. But I'm afraid Mrs Weaver was right. It's not going anywhere.'

'OK' said Murphy grimly. 'Let's head back to the bank. I heard some interesting gossip from my sister last night. Let's go in a bit harder. See if we can shake anything out there.'

Chapter Nineteen

FLORENCE PULLED BACK from the window, but not fast enough. Of course, the stupid woman had to look up at precisely the wrong time. Now they'll be thinking she looks guilty. Something uncomfortable flashed through her brain at that moment. Some thought she didn't want to give house room to. It was crap, not going to go there.

Florence had forgotten how annoying Jake could be. She missed him when he was away, but then he came back and in no time at all she was pissed off with him again. Showing off his scar to the goons, telling them about Italy, as if it was the only holiday they'd ever been on, bigging up bloody Beth, who had a boring job in a law office and wasn't even Florence's BFF any more. And that stupid comment about the school reunion, like she was fourteen or something.

She picked up her phone and flicked through a few sites. Melanie Katz was beating her on followers, but not by much. The reason Mel had pulled in more followers was because she'd taken the plunge and had the cheap lip fillers.

Florence couldn't imagine having a needle stuck in your lips – and then what if it went wrong? That was what half these followers were there for. They wanted to see what she would look like when it went wrong. Her lips looked pretty swollen right now, but Mel was saying that was normal, the swelling would soon go down. Well, maybe.

Charlie and Bill were still smashing it out of the park, of course. Charlotte Evans was pretty, that had to be admitted, and Bill was – well, Florence wouldn't chuck him out of bed, that was for sure. But Charlie and Bill were touring South America, so that gave them access to so many more products – trekking gear, insect repellent, sunscreens, solid shampoos, water purification tablets, money belts, underwear that wicked away your sweat. What did wicking mean? She'd have to look it up. It was obviously important. While she was stuck here promoting self-tan and hair straighteners and putting up with interference from Lindy. The sooner she could separate Cal from his sister, the better.

Chapter Twenty

ANDREW CASTLE WAS SURPRISED to see them back so quickly and probably a bit put out, but he was too professional to let it show.

'Our investigation is still ongoing' Murphy began, 'and we're following up a number of leads. The evidence so far suggests that somebody else could have been involved in Richard Weaver's death, so we are having to investigate all possibilities, however remote.'

The look of surprise and faint annoyance was slowly turning to shock. That was good.

'One of those possibilities is that his position here at the bank has some relevance to his death.'

Castle opened his mouth to argue, but she carried on. 'So, what we would like to see is a list of all share transactions – mergers, acquisitions, disposals and small trades - involving your clients, that took place after Richard Weaver's transfer to M&A.'

'You surely can't think...'

'We don't think anything in advance of the evidence,

but our job is to check everything, and I would like to eliminate this area of enquiry.'

'I'm afraid that's not possible. Those records are confidential.'

'That's no problem,' said Wilcox. 'We'll just pass it on to the Financial Conduct Authority and they'll investigate on our behalf. They'll have much more idea of what to look for than we will anyway.'

Castle held his palms up in the time-honoured gesture of submission.

'Very well. We would not wish to impede a police enquiry. Give me a few minutes to clear it with the trading department. You can use the office next door and Melanie will show you where to access the data.'

THREE HOURS later Murphy was ready to give up. Her eyes felt scratchy, her shoulders were stiff and her mind was wandering.

'Was this my idea? It wasn't one of my better ones. I hope, however much he hates me, that Bellweather never has me transferred to the Serious Fraud Office. I wouldn't last a week. How do people do this all day?'

'I'm finding it quite interesting,' said Wilcox.

'Oh, are you? Well, if he ever threatens me with the SFO I'll offer you up instead. Actually, the SFO wouldn't want me. I think you have to have brilliant maths and computer skills and a tidy mind and a tidy desk and lots of patience. You probably have to be a slow walker as well. You'd be a shoo-in.'

Wilcox wasn't listening. His attention was focussed on the screen as he scrolled up and down.

'I think I've got something.'

Murphy's physical complaints immediately evaporated and she abandoned her laptop to ram herself in front of his.

'Here.' He righted himself and pointed with a pen. 'Both of these major takeovers were preceded by two small - relatively small – purchases through the same broker. When I say small, that's like probably transactions involving individual investors, not pension funds or whatever. These are both companies which didn't have much share movement up to that point, apart from the odd sale, because prior to the takeovers they weren't doing too well, so investors were dumping the shares. That means the prices had dropped considerably. Then suddenly these random purchases, followed by the takeover, and then of course the shares shoot up. So did they then sell them again?' He scrolled a bit more. 'Yes! One of them did anyway. Look, same broker.'

Murphy frowned. 'So, what are we saying here? Insider trading?'

'Looks a possibility. Digital controls are good, like Parvez said, but the information barriers – well it's hard to control the barriers between the firm and the outside world, the leakage to complete third parties. We need to get onto that broker and get the names of his clients. We can threaten him with the FCA too.' He smiled. 'Seems to work well.'

LATER THAT AFTERNOON they sat in Adrian Finch's office while he looked frantically around at the walls, as if in search of escape.

'As you can see, Mr French,' said Murphy, 'we have not asked you to accompany us to the station. That's because we are confident that you will co-operate fully and make such a move unnecessary.'

He nodded rapidly. 'Of course.'

'So just explain how it worked. Richard gave you both the nod – just a quick whisper over a pint?'

'Yes, that's all it was.'

'And how much profit did you make on the transactions?'

He swallowed. 'Ten thousand pounds.'

'That's a reasonable return,' said Wilcox. 'How much did you transfer back to Richard?'

'We agreed on forty percent. So that would be four thousand.'

'And Arthur Wellesley made the same profit – or more?'

'Possibly more. I don't know.'

'What I don't understand,' said Murphy, 'is why Richard Weaver, with a no doubt substantial banking salary, should have undertaken this serious risk for a relatively small return. He surely didn't need the money. Or was it you who needed the money? Housing market a bit sluggish, is it?'

He licked his lips. 'Yes, things are not going that well at the moment. The market has slowed down a bit, it always does at this time of year, and I think a lot of people are cutting out agents and selling online. In some cases, people are digging out their basements rather than moving somewhere bigger. I needed the money more than Richard did. In fact, he didn't need money at all. I think he did it partly because he was bored.'

'Bored how?'

'He missed being on the trading floor. There's not much excitement in M&A. And he knew the big salary would be coming to an end when he finally had to step down. He wanted to leave as much money as possible for Alison and the children.'

Murphy frowned. 'Surely Alison also has a good salary and the children have good careers ahead of them. Are they really going to be short of money?'

He shrugged. 'Alison doesn't like her job much, or not from what she says. I think the atmosphere in universities has changed a lot. Academia has always been cut-throat but it's even worse these days. And students are now regarded as consumers, they're the people paying the money, so they get to review the lecturers. If the students decide they don't like you, you're out. It's not like in our day when the faculty members were respected. Before Richard was diagnosed, she told me she couldn't wait to leave and do something else, maybe start a business. I think now Richard has gone, things will be up in the air a bit, she'll probably have to stay a bit longer in the job. He wanted to make sufficient money so that she would be able to leave if she decided to.'

'What about Florence. What's she planning to do?'

'I think Richard was worried about Florence. She's a clever girl, but she never liked school much, and never worked that hard, according to Richard and Alison. They hoped she might do medicine, but she wasn't good enough at science. So, she ended up doing Media Studies. Media Studies graduates don't tend to get the jobs in traditional media outlets, like the press or the BBC, those jobs go to people with more traditional degrees, so a lot of them try to make a career in social media – that's where the advertising spend goes these days.'

'So, you think Florence is hoping to make it as an influencer?' said Wilcox.

Adrian French nodded. 'That was what Richard was afraid of, anyway. Jake is doing a good degree, but he's got the best part of a year to go. He'll be fine once he graduates, there will be lots of jobs for computer scientists. But Florence doesn't have much of a career plan.'

'It's quite a lot to worry about when you've also got a terminal illness to deal with,' said Murphy.

'That's right,' said Adrian. 'That's why he needed the diversion of work. And of course, if he broke the rules, he had nothing left to lose.'

'Well thank you for your co-operation,' said Murphy. 'You can further co-operate by not telling anybody else about this matter – not Arthur Wellesley or anybody else. We're investigating a death, so financial irregularities are not really part of our brief, but we could be minded to pass the financial aspect onto the National Crime Agency.'

'That won't be necessary,' he replied immediately.

'I thought not. We'll be in touch if we have any further questions.'

'What do you think?' asked Wilcox as they walked back to the car. 'Would that be a motive for murder?'

'I don't know,' said Murphy. 'If it was detected, they would strictly be liable to a fine or a custodial sentence – but it's such a small amount of money, I don't think they would be sent to prison. For Adrian, he might have to pay a fine and could then lose his business, but maybe in estate agency it wouldn't matter so much. He could just start up again. Richard would be regarded as the most culpable – but he was maybe past caring anyway. The person with most to lose would be Arthur Wellesley. If he was convicted of profiting from insider information, he would be thrown out by his professional association and he would presumably never work as a solicitor again.'

'If Richard was going to die soon, then the risk would probably die with him.'

'Yes, to some degree. It's altogether not a very convincing motive – even for Arthur Wellesley. Let's leave him on the back-burner for now.'

THERE WAS something drifting in the atmosphere when Murphy got home that evening. James was on his laptop at the kitchen table and Clive was over by the cooker, chopping onions with murderous intent. They both acknowledged her presence with barely a grunt and went back to what they were doing.

'OK' she said. 'You two have had a row, right?'

Clive put the knife down and then picked it up again and pointed it at James. 'It was him, fawning over the Instagram posts of that complete…'

'Clive, put the knife down right now.' Murphy used her best police-issue voice. Clive complied.

'Do you realise how much of my working life is taken up with knife crime? Let's not elevate this to a domestic. Now', she sat down next to James. 'Let's see this complete whatever he is.'

He folded his arms and stared at her for a few seconds then picked up the mouse and clicked on a site.

'Well the six-pack is good,' said Murphy, regarding the two hundred-odd pounds of self-satisfied brawn, 'and those look like powerful leg muscles. But I think he's got a weak chin.'

Clive wandered over. 'How can you tell?'

'Easy. He's got a beard.'

'But you can't say that about every man with a beard,' said James.

Murphy shrugged. 'I can and I do. I quite like stubble, even long stubble, as long as you can still see the shape of their chin. But a full, biblical-prophet-type beard? No. To me they're hiding something.'

'I have lots of friends with beards,' said Clive.

'Sure you do,' said Murphy. 'And I'm sure they're great people, with strong chins. I was just telling you about my irrational prejudice, not inviting you to share it.'

Clive wandered back to his onions.

'While we're on the subject of what people look like,' said Murphy, pouring herself a glass of water, 'have you ever heard of somebody dumping their partner because they didn't generate any likes on Facebook?'

'Loads of them,' said Clive, sloshing olive oil around. 'You might be happy with somebody who looks like an ogre, but that would be a relationship you couldn't post to Facebook or Instagram, so it wouldn't be sustainable in the long term.'

'So social media is part of a person's long term?'

James looked up. 'Of course. Getting more so all the time. Even young kids are busy curating their image, photoshopping themselves, monitoring their likes and shares. None of that is going to go away. And by the time it gets to their kids, it will have taken over peoples' lives completely.'

'Perhaps in a few years the pendulum will swing back and kids will go back to playing in the streets' said Murphy hopefully.

James shook his head. 'Streets are too dangerous these days.'

'That's true enough' said Murphy, 'I should know.' She thought for a moment. 'So there must be a lot of money being made out of social media – and not just by the social media companies.'

'A lot of money.' Clive's onions had now made it into the pan and he was stirring them vigorously. 'If you want to advertise something that's bought by young people – and quite a lot of older ones, come to that – your audience is not on TV, it's on social media. So you pay your money to influencers and they push your product to their followers. Just like James's muscle-bound oik there.'

'Why? What's he selling?'

'Beard oil' said Clive with satisfaction.

Chapter Twenty-One

ALISON WEAVER OPENED the door the next morning in her dressing gown. It was a nice waffle dressing gown in a pale green colour. Murphy wondered where it was from. Alison was presumably disconcerted to see them on her doorstep, but dealt with the situation with an aplomb that Murphy could only admire.

'Come through to the kitchen,' she said cheerfully. 'I'm just having breakfast. Late, I know.'

Sitting at the kitchen table in front of a cup of coffee and the remains of a piece of toast was a slim, reasonably attractive (Murphy decided) middle-aged man. Thankfully for all concerned, he was fully dressed.

'My old friend Tom.' Alison waved an arm airily.

'Tom Finlay.' He rose and shook hands. 'Time for me to get going Ali,' he said. 'Thanks for breakfast.'

'Don't leave on our account,' said Murphy.

'No, really. I have to get on.' He picked up a coat and briefcase.

'I'll see you out.' Alison followed him into the hall.

Dead Cool

Murphy decided the coffee smelled good and hoped she'd be offered some.

'Disgraceful, isn't it?' said Alison as she returned. 'Entertaining gentlemen callers in my nightwear. Would you like coffee?'

'You can entertain gentlemen callers in anything you want,' said Murphy. 'And I'd love some coffee.'

Alison filled the kettle and switched it on. 'Tom's a friend of mine from university' she said. 'I ran into him a few years ago at the twenty-year reunion for our year. He was the only one of the men that was still recognisable. It was bizarre, looking round at all these men with grey hair and stomachs and realising that they were the skinny, sexy guys with the cool record collections that we'd all fancied. Some of the women didn't seem to have aged at all.'

'Did you meet Richard at university?' asked Murphy.

'Not exactly. I was at Manchester; Richard was at Durham. I'd gone up to Durham to visit Arthur – well of course he was Art in those days – and I met Richard.'

'So you and Arthur were an item?'

'Me and Art.' She smiled. 'Yes, we were, for a while.'

'Is he married now?'

'Divorced. Just like Tom. Seems like a lot of women are kicking out the men these days. The children grow up and the wife takes off. And Tom's not my lover, although maybe he'd like to be. Anyway, at our age, what does it matter?' She sat down abruptly. 'What does any of it matter?' Her voice was wavering.

'You must be missing him,' said Murphy. 'Richard, I mean.'

She looked up. 'I am. So much. You know, it was always sitting there in future time, that we would lose him, and I was dreading the end, the final few months. The pain and grief. The deathbed scene. Then, when he was suddenly dead, there was nothing to dread anymore. It was all over. It was almost a relief. But now I don't feel any relief. I would give anything to have him back, even if it was just for a few months more and I knew we would have the nightmare at the end of it.'

'That's understandable,' said Murphy, while Wilcox, who didn't enjoy displays of emotion, scrolled intently on his phone. 'And I'm sorry we haven't been able to bring you any closure. We are still investigating and there is one aspect I wanted to ask you about.'

Alison tore off a piece of kitchen paper and blew her nose forcefully. 'Of course. Go ahead.'

The kettle had boiled. She refilled the coffee pot and brought it to the table with two more cups.

'We've visited SCB and spoken to some of the people there,' Murphy began, after taking a sip of her coffee. 'That was a high-pressure environment he was working in.'

Alison nodded. 'Certainly was. But I think he was used to coping with it.'

'Do you think he was disappointed to be transferred to M&A?'

Alison was silent for a moment. 'Yes, I think so. He needed time off for appointments and he needed a lot of rest, he couldn't be working till nine or ten o'clock at night, so he couldn't put in the hours needed for trading, and it was good of the bank to find him another role. He appreciated all of that. But yes, I'm sure he missed the adrenaline, the buzz, whatever.'

'And do you think he was worried about money?'

She looked surprised. 'No, he's never really worried about money. He was good at making money.'

'But do you think he was worried about you having enough money after he died?'

Alison was looking confused now. 'I don't think so. I've still got a job. Why? Are you thinking that he was worried so he killed himself? That makes no sense.'

'No, not at all. But do you think he was looking for other sources of income?'

'Not that I knew about, and I'm sure he would have told me.'

'Do you think he was worried about the children?'

'Everybody always worries about their children, but I don't think we worried any more than anybody else. I guess we would have liked Florence to get a proper job, but I'm sure she will eventually.' She was silent for a moment. 'Are you thinking' she said 'that it was suicide after all? That he took Rohypnol in order to make it easier to throw himself in front of the train?'

'We don't have any reason to believe that,' said Murphy. 'Nobody we have spoken to had seen any sign of depression or suicidal tendencies. He seems to have been a strong character.'

'He was.' Alison smiled. 'He was totally reliable, never fazed by anything. Kitchen fires, flooded bathrooms, break-ins, punctures on the motorway. He took everything in his stride. Even when we learned about the cancer, I was the one who broke down. He was having to comfort me. So no, I really don't believe in the suicide idea.'

'Did he make a will?' asked Murphy.

Alison nodded. 'We both did a few years ago. Just the usual provisions. Everything left to the surviving partner and after that equally to the children.'

'There's something else we should tell you,' Murphy said. 'It will come up at the inquest, so you need to know.

The post-mortem found an injection mark on Richard's leg.'

'You mean like from a hypodermic?'

'Yes, exactly that. We think that's how the Rohypnol got into his body.'

'I can't believe that. That's more the sort of thing I would worry could happen to Florence, not Richard. Couldn't it just have been a chemo injection, something like that?'

'No, we checked all that. We don't have any explanation for it at the moment.'

She shook her head. 'That's just bizarre. Why would anybody want to do that to him? Was that why he fell? Because he was drugged?'

'We just don't know at the moment,' said Murphy, 'but it could have been a contributory factor.'

'I'm sorry to have sprung that on you,' she added. 'I was waiting to see if we could get a clearer idea of what happened, but now obviously you need to know. Thank you for answering all these questions.' Murphy drained the last of her coffee and rose. 'I just wanted to get a clearer idea of Richard's state of mind. And thank you for the coffee. We'll be in touch.'

'YOU DIDN'T ASK her about the insider trading' said Wilcox, as they walked to the car.

'I wanted more to skirt around it.' said Murphy. 'She would just have denied all knowledge if we'd asked her outright. And it didn't look to me as if she did know anything about it. She certainly didn't seem to think he needed money.'

'Yes, I thought the same.' He waved an arm around.

'This is an expensive part of town, I couldn't afford to live round here, and she has a better-paying job than me. Their mortgage is probably paid off. I wouldn't have thought money was much of an issue. And she'll be wealthy in her own right now. She'll own the house, plus whatever's in his bank accounts.'

'Perhaps that's it,' said Murphy. 'Richard's only motive was to enable his friends to make some money. Maybe he didn't need any for himself. He just did it for the buzz. I guess all the buzz had gone out of his life. Maybe he wanted to do something that would put him back on the edge.'

Wilcox checked his fitbit and speeded up. They reached the car just ahead of a traffic warden, who was bearing down on it with paperwork at the ready. Wilcox opened the door, slid inside and started the engine. The traffic warden mouthed something and walked off.

'Amazing!' said Murphy, as they joined the traffic. 'You can walk fast when you need to.'

'I make a special effort for traffic wardens.'

'Have we got any access to his bank accounts yet?' Murphy asked.

'Should have it today.'

'We can check whether he received any funds in from French or Wellesley. If he didn't, that confirms that he wasn't doing it for money. It also reduces the likelihood of any charge being brought against any of them. If he didn't receive any of the money, there's it's harder to prove that he passed on the information.'

'Maybe they were supposed to pay him his share, but they hadn't yet. And now he's dead, they won't have to.'

Chapter Twenty-Two

FLORENCE WAS SQUINTING at her buttocks in the mirror. It was difficult to get a proper view, whichever way she turned. Looked at from one angle she could see a darker brown line, but if she looked from the other side it didn't seem to be there. So far, she wasn't impressed with this stuff. Application wasn't a no-brainer like they claimed. Still, a deal was a deal. Perhaps the too-brown bit would have evened itself out by the time she arrived at the flat tonight. If not, she'd just have to keep that side away from the camera. Another fifteen minutes before she could put her clothes back on, just time to touch up the toenails.

People who thought this was an easy job didn't know what they were talking about. The constant pressure to look good, the crappy products you had to pretend you were using, the abuse from trolls – or people who were just jealous. If somebody recognised her in the street on a bad day and took a photo of her looking like shit, that would be on all the channels in no time. No chance then of making big money, appearing on TV, getting invited to openings – it would all not happen. Except maybe if she could confess to her followers that she sometimes looked and felt like shit, and then she could do a whole series on handling that – exercise, diet, colonic cleanse, meditation, hot stone massage, whatever. All bloody hard work when you still had to work in a bloody coffee shop to make ends meet.

It would be so much easier when she had moved in with Cal. She'd be on-site as it were. But it didn't seem right to leave her mum at the moment, especially as Jake was heading back next week. Maybe after the funeral they'd all be able to sort themselves out. She'd have to make sure her mum was OK before they went travelling. Maybe this creepy Tom person would be keeping her company. Would that be a good thing or not? Had he been here all night (gross!) or did he just drop in for breakfast? He was already sitting in the kitchen by the time Florence surfaced, grabbed food and went back to her room, so she couldn't be sure.

And, as if that wasn't enough, they had the fuzz barging in again, the old bag and the nerd. They obviously had no clue what had happened to her dad, so they were hassling her mum – maybe they thought they could pin it on her?

The toenails were now looking good but another glance in the mirror confirmed that, yes, there really was a line down her bum. She'd see what Cal said – maybe they could sandpaper it off. Anyway, no time to mess around, she was due at the café at ten. She waved each foot in the air to dry it off and climbed carefully into her underwear.

Chapter Twenty-Three

'TOM FINLAY,' said Wilcox, looking up from his screen as she came in. 'I've got him here. Management consultant, specialising in the oil and gas industries. Not exactly industries of the future.'

'No' said Murphy. 'But still highly lucrative industries for right now. And they probably have lots of funds to spend on consultants who will find them something to diversify into. Is he on anything other than LinkedIn?'

'Hang on. Yes, he's on Facebook. But we'll need to get access.'

'May as well set that in motion. But it doesn't look likely. Would you murder somebody in order to take over his wife, if the poor bugger was dying anyway?'

'Actually, no,' said Wilcox.

'In fact,' said Murphy, taking off her coat, 'there was a slim chance he might not have been dying that imminently. I spoke to his oncologist earlier this morning. They were planning to enter him for a drug trial. The chances of success are not that high. The drug might not work, or it might not work for all patients, or it might only add a few months to his survival time, or he might have been on the placebo anyway. But it was a chance. I can't see that it would affect anybody's decision to kill him. We haven't found any motive, least of all a time-sensitive one.'

'So do we have anywhere else to go on this?'

She shook her head. 'I don't think so. At the moment it looks like he was spiked by person or persons unknown, either deliberately or not, maybe somebody thought he was somebody else. That caused him to lose his balance and fall under a tube train. Shit, here's Bellweather.' She looked up with a smile as the DCI bore down on them.

But Bellweather's face was not wearing its customary sarcastic grin. In fact, he looked remarkably serious. He stopped in front of Murphy's desk and dropped a note.

'Body just hauled out by the river police — it cross-references to your case. Better get onto them.'

He swept off. Murphy put the call through, frowned and scribbled a name. 'Amy Horsfall' she said as she ended the call. 'Where is that name from?'

Wilcox accessed the case documents and typed the name into the search function. He raised his eyebrows. 'The tube station. She was one of our witnesses.'

AMY HORSFALL HAD PALE SKIN, brown hair and eyes and a noticeable overbite. Murphy was finding it hard to match up the image of the girl she remembered speaking to at Moorgate with the body in front of her. Prolonged immersion in river water had inflated her cells, robbing her face of any contours. And it looked like the fish had also played a part. Murphy felt acute compassion for the weeping parents she had encountered on the way in.

'I hope you're not expecting time of death,' Linda Fleming barked, as she lined up the instruments.

'No' said Murphy. 'Not the exact hour, but maybe the twelve-hour period?'

'As a rough estimate I'd say forty-eight hours immersion. I doubt we'll get much closer than that.'

Murphy counted back. Amy had died within about twenty-four hours of the tube station incident.

'There's nothing that will tell us where she went into the river, is there?'

Linda shrugged and picked up the scalpel. 'Not really. I'm sure we'll find river water in the lungs, but the river's tidal, so no bit of water stays in the same place. It's lucky she was found relatively quickly. I had one last month that had been in the river for weeks. That wasn't fun.'

The next hour wasn't fun from Murphy's viewpoint and she hadn't learned much by the end of it. Amy was well-nourished, slightly overweight, not pregnant, no sign of recent sexual intercourse and no sign of assault. The internal organs were as expected for her age. There was water in the lungs, as predicted. She had died as a result of drowning.

'There would be the initial cold-water shock,' said Linda. 'If she survived that, she would then be swimming for her life. It's possible she wasn't a very good swimmer, and she was fully clothed, which would have made it much more difficult. No sign that she was hit by any river traffic. The only trace we found was a rust mark on her jacket which survived the river water. That could have come from some bit of old chain or a rusty old dredger. But I don't know whether you could ever find the exact source. One bit of rust is the same as another really. She may have brushed up against something as she entered the water, but there's no sign of any injury that could have been caused by an actual impact.'

'So she could have jumped or been pushed?' said Murphy.

Linda nodded. 'Basically yes. We can't tell one way or the other. A push may not have needed to be that hard to overbalance her, and we'd be unlikely to see any sign of it. When the samples come back, we can see if any drugs or alcohol were involved.' She looked across at Murphy. 'This is the second this week that you've had of people falling into things. Is there some connection?'

Murphy shook her head. 'Possibly, but whatever it is, we haven't found it.'

'No,' said Linda. 'They're certainly not the same demographic. Hopefully it's not some nutcase roaming around pushing people off bits of infrastructure.'

'I don't even want to entertain that thought,' said Murphy.

'No, I'd keep that to one side' said Linda, now engaged in sewing up her handiwork. 'I'll let you know what else we find.'

Murphy thanked her and made her way gratefully out into the open air.

SERGEANT BILL WEBSTER had been ten years with the Marine Policing Unit and told Murphy he had seen dozens of bodies pulled from the river.

'It's never a nice sight' he said, looking across at the granite piers holding up Battersea Bridge. 'We all hate it when it happens. Just a few hours in the water bloats the features and if the body's been in for some time and the fish or the crabs have been to work on it, well, it becomes hard to recognise people. I always feel sorry for whoever has to identify them.'

'I had no idea it happened so often,' said Murphy.

He nodded. 'More often than you'd think. And of course it's been happening for thousands of years, and probably most of those bodies are never recovered, just end up out at sea or buried in the riverbed. Sometimes people jump in for a lark, or a dare, especially when the weather's hot. They think it's just the Thames, it's not the sea, nothing will go wrong. They can just swim across to the other side and then wave at their mates, good photo to post on their Instagram or whatever. And they always overestimate their own swimming abilities. It's not something to do for a lark. What these people don't realise is that the river flows faster than an Olympic swimmer can swim. That means nobody can outrun it. And the currents as you go deeper are very powerful. Not to mention your chances of being hit by a dredger or a patrol boat if they don't spot you.'

Murphy looked up from the murky water. 'Somehow I don't think this girl went in for a lark.'

'No,' he said. 'She was fully dressed for a start. People going in of their own accord would strip off a layer, at least take off their shoes. She's one of the other cases. Suicide, murder or a bid to dispose of a body.'

'I suppose that's right,' said Murphy. 'If you were committing suicide you wouldn't care about your shoes. Where do you think she went into the water?'

He shook his head. 'Almost impossible to tell. If she'd gone in off one of the bridges, that would have made a loud splash, so there's a good chance somebody would have heard it. If there was nobody around, she could have gone in somewhere along the Embankment without making too much noise. There were reeds tangled around her legs, so they could have held her in position for a while. The first thing the guys on the patrol boat saw was her handbag.'

'Her handbag?'

'Yes. It was one of those cross-body bags, so it stayed attached to her and the officers in the boat saw it floating just below the surface. And that's how we were able to identify her so quickly.'

'Yes, that's been a great help,' said Murphy. 'Finding out what happened to her is going to be another matter altogether.'

Chapter Twenty-Four

'WINONA FRANCIS WILL SEE us about six o'clock, when she gets home from work' said Wilcox, when Murphy arrived outside the house in Hammersmith where Amy Horsfall lived. 'She didn't sound too thrilled. Probably wishing now she hadn't been so public-spirited.'

'Naturally' said Murphy. 'No good deed unpunished. Anything else useful in the handbag?'

'Not really. Wallet, travel card, makeup, couple of condoms. Enough to establish a name and address. But no phone. And the keys.' He held them up and they headed for the front door.

'She's on the top floor,' said Wilcox. 'Or she was at least. Her parents agreed to stay away until we've checked the place. Can't imagine they're looking forward to coming in here.'

'No. I wouldn't be looking forward to it either, if I was in their position. OK, let's go.'

The stairs got progressively narrower as they made their

way from the ground floor up to the first and then second floors.

'The flat at the top is always the cheap one,' said Wilcox. 'I should know.'

The top floor gave access to two front doors. 'These places must be pretty small,' said Murphy.

Wilcox unlocked the door. 'Just bedsits really,' he said. 'But I think they call them studios these days. OK for one person, or two people who like each other. Landlords cram as many in as possible. Lots of money in rental properties.'

Amy Horsfall's studio had plenty of signs of occupation. Clothes were draped across the bed and the sofa, dirty dishes were piled in the sink and a towel covered most of the floor in the tiny bathroom. SOCO had been and left powder marks everywhere.

'Evidence of a life interrupted,' said Murphy. 'She would never have intended anybody else to see it like this. If she'd known we were coming she'd have tidied up.'

'If she was in any condition to know we were coming, we wouldn't be here' said Wilcox, with faultless logic.

They pulled on gloves and began a search.

'I don't see that we'll find any more than SOCO did,' said Wilcox. 'What will be most useful will be when we get into her laptop. Pity about the phone.'

Murphy started going through the wardrobe. Amy obviously spent a lot of time in Primark.

'That's another reason why I think somebody else was involved' she said, picking up stuff that had fallen off the hangers. 'Her handbag was zipped shut. It's possible the phone was in her pocket and floated away, but the pockets on her jacket were deep.'

'She could have fallen off the wall taking a selfie,' said Wilcox. 'There have been a few people doing that this year.'

'True,' said Murphy, who was now in the kitchen area and restraining her urge to start washing the dishes. 'But think about it. She's at the tube station when a man falls under a train and is killed. Admittedly, hundreds of other people were also there, but she came forward as a witness. And then a day later she falls in the river and is killed. We know that's unlikely to be a coincidence.'

She stepped back from the sink. 'Looking at this dirty crockery, it all seems to be for one person. One wineglass, one water glass, one plate, one bowl, one saucepan, various bits of cutlery. Doesn't look as if she was entertaining anybody.'

A door banged close by. 'The next-door neighbour,' said Wilcox. 'Somebody's come home.

He went out to the hall and knocked on the other door. After a short interval it was opened by a young woman still wearing her coat, who looked at him blearily. He introduced them both and she gave her name as Belinda Roberts. She spent several seconds trying to focus on his warrant card.

'I've just come off nights,' she said by way of explanation.

'Hammersmith Hospital?' said Murphy and the young woman nodded.

'I can see you're very tired,' said Murphy, 'but could we come in and talk to you for a few minutes? It's important.'

Belinda Roberts nodded wordlessly and held the door open. The studio looked very similar to the one next door, but marginally tidier. She sat down and motioned them to do the same.

'Do you live here alone?' asked Murphy and she nodded again.

'We want to ask you about the other person on this floor,' said Wilcox.

'You mean Amy?'

'That's right. Can you tell us when you last saw her?'

She hesitated for a moment. 'Sunday. It would have to be Sunday, because I've been on nights all this week. Why?' She frowned. 'Is she missing?'

'I'm afraid she's dead,' said Wilcox.

Belinda put her hands over her mouth and then removed them. 'How?' she said. 'What happened to her?'

'She was found in the river yesterday,' said Wilcox. 'Drowned.'

'Oh my God, that's awful. Poor Amy.'

'Did you know her well?'

'Not really. We didn't do anything socially. My friends are mostly at the hospital and I have different shifts each week. But we got on fine. I can't believe this.'

'When you saw her on Sunday' said Wilcox, 'how did she seem?'

Belinda dragged her fingers across her eyes, as if to keep them open. 'Fine. She was just fine. She was taking her stuff to the launderette. There was nothing wrong. Are you thinking she committed suicide? I can't believe that.'

'Have you ever seen anybody else visiting her flat?'

'No. Not that I'm around that often. Her parents once, but nobody else. I don't think she had much of a social life. Well, nor do I, come to that.'

'Do you have any idea how her life was going?' said Murphy. 'Did she like her job? Did she want to do something else?'

'She definitely didn't like her job, she told me that. So I'm sure she was looking for something else. She worked at the Jobcentre. That was probably pretty boring. Also, we get abusive people in the hospital, but I think it's worse at the Jobcentre.'

'Which Jobcentre?' asked Wilcox.

'I'm not sure. Somewhere in the City'

'And no boyfriends that you know of?' said Murphy.

Belinda was removing her coat now. She shook her head. 'No. We did talk about men once, a couple of weeks ago, just casually, and she said she'd been to one of these speed dating events. She didn't think much of it.'

'So she didn't like her job and didn't have a boyfriend,' said Murphy. 'Did she have any plans to change any of that?'

Belinda shrugged. 'I really don't know. She said she wanted to work in the fashion business. I think she'd applied for a few jobs but she didn't get anywhere.'

She was really yawning now. 'I'm sorry, but I have to go to bed now.'

'Of course you do,' said Murphy. 'Thank you for your help.'

They went back into Amy's flat and Murphy had another look in the wardrobe.

'Looks like she bought a lot of clothes' she said. 'But I'm not seeing much fashion sense here. I think she probably had more time to serve at the DWP.'

'I think 'fashion sense' is an old-fashioned concept now,' said Wilcox. 'Fashion is whatever you can get away with.'

THE GROUND FLOOR of the house was occupied by an elderly couple who explained that they were the owners.

'Our children left home' explained Sally Burton, 'and so we felt we really should downsize, it didn't seem right just two of us in this house, but Ray had put half his life into that garden – hadn't you love? – so we decided to stay and we had the two upper floors converted.'

Ray, who had hitherto managed the odd grunt, sprang into life at this point. 'Cost a pretty penny too' he said. 'Bloody cowboy builders.'

'So how long has Amy Horsfall been living here?' asked Murphy.

Sally and Ray looked at each other. 'About six months' said Sally. 'We were fairly choosy about who we had in. Amy is a civil servant and the other tenants are all in the NHS. Why? Has something happened?'

'I'm afraid Amy is dead,' said Murphy. 'Her body was found in the river yesterday.'

Sally lowered herself onto the sofa. 'Oh no. The poor girl. I can't believe it. How did that happen?'

'We're still investigating,' said Wilcox. 'Perhaps you can tell us when you last saw her.'

'We don't see that much of any of them,' said Sally. 'They all come and go and we wouldn't know. But I did see her a few days ago. Tuesday, I think, in the evening. I went out to put some rubbish in the bin and she was just leaving. Looked dressed-up, like she was heading for an evening out.'

'What time do you think that was?' asked Wilcox.

Sally hesitated for a moment. 'Let me just think... Yes. It was just before seven, because I went back in and the news was just coming on.'

'That's very helpful,' said Murphy. 'I suppose she didn't tell you where she was going?'

'No, and I didn't ask,' said Sally. 'I make a point of not prying.'

'Did you ever see any visitors coming to her flat?'

They both shook their heads.

'Is there anything else you can tell us about her?'

'I'm afraid not,' said Sally. 'She was a nice, quiet young woman. I never thought there was anything wrong.'

'Who lives on the first floor?' asked Wilcox.

'Steven and Isobel,' said Sally. 'Steven Frost and Isobel Hardman. They're both doctors but they're on holiday at the moment – walking in the Brecon Beacons, I think. They went at the weekend.'

'We'll have a word with them when they get back,' said Wilcox. 'Thank you for your help.'

'SOMETIMES' said Murphy, 'I wish people did make a point of prying. But not often.'

'We're seeing her parents this afternoon,' said Wilcox. 'They'll probably know less about her life than anybody else.'

'That's for sure,' said Murphy.

But they were both wrong. Mrs Horsfall claimed to be in constant communication with her daughter, over email, Skype and Facebook.

'I know she would never have killed herself,' she sobbed. 'We spoke every day. She told me everything.'

'Everything?' Murphy wasn't convinced. Maybe young people these days were different. Her generation never told their parents anything.

'Of course.' Sandra Horsfall wiped the mascara streaks from her face. 'She told me all about the people at work, what she was doing, where she went, how she was feeling, what her stars said for that day – everything.'

'And how was she feeling?' Wilcox asked.

'She was fed up with her job, but I told her to hang in there, something better would come along. She didn't really have any friends at work, but I told her she should make an effort, go for drinks with them. And she did. She bought some new outfits – quite nice they were. She tried them on and showed me. And I think she had a party coming up – that would have been this weekend.' She started crying again, then dried her eyes. 'So I told her that was the best place to meet people – better than those speed dating things. She hadn't really gotten into online dating yet. And then she told me something exciting was going to happen, but she wasn't going to tell me about it just yet. I thought perhaps she'd met a nice chap.'

'Does Amy have any siblings?' asked Wilcox

Sandra shook her head. 'No, she was our only one. That's probably why she and I were so close. We were like sisters. I wish she'd stayed at home. She was never really happy down in London.'

At this she broke down again and her husband squeezed her shoulder.

'We still don't know exactly what happened,' said Murphy. 'But we'll continue investigating until we do. We'll let you know of any developments, and if you think of anything which might be relevant, please let us know.'

'Something exciting was going to happen,' said Wilcox resignedly as the door shut behind them. 'More like something bad. She'd met a chap alright.'

Chapter Twenty-Five

WINONA FRANCIS LIVED in Kentish Town, in one of the Victorian terraces leading off from the high street. Half the houses in the street were run-down with three bells outside, the rest were expensively restored. Winona's house could have done with a coat of paint, but there were no signs of multiple occupancy. The hall was almost completely blocked by two motorbikes.

'Jesus. It's a Bonneville,' breathed Wilcox reverently, as they squeezed past.

Winona smiled. 'Yes. My son Josh is rebuilding it. The other one's not worth so much, but you can't leave them outside, no matter what sort of locks you have. Thieves roam around with oxy-acetylene equipment these days.'

'Thank you very much for seeing us,' said Murphy, when they had successfully negotiated past the bikes and seated themselves around the kitchen table. 'We just wanted to ask you a bit more about Monday night. Obviously, at the time everything was a bit frantic, but we wondered if you have thought of anything else since that we should know.'

Winona crossed her arms. 'To be honest I've tried not to think about it. I hope to never see anything like that again.'

'That's understandable,' said Murphy. 'The other person who came forward as a witness – a girl called Amy – did you exchange any words with her?'

Winona frowned. 'As I remember it, one of the station staff asked if anybody saw what happened. So I said yes, I saw him fall. Lots of other people did too, but they were all running for the exits. Then this girl appears and says she saw it as well. That made me feel better, like I wasn't the only one. She seemed quite – well, excited is not really the right word – but I guess shocked and a bit awestruck – like the horror of it hadn't really sunk in.'

'If you think back to where you were standing when it happened' said Murphy, 'you will have been aware of some of the people around you, even if you weren't looking directly at any of them. Did you notice Amy at that point?'

'No, I didn't see her at all until she popped up at the end. Maybe she was behind me. Why? Has something happened?'

'Amy Horsfall has been found dead,' said Wilcox. 'She died the next day. She was found in the river.'

Winona stared at him. 'Oh my God. The poor girl. And you think...?'

'We don't have any reason yet to think that the two incidents are related,' said Murphy. 'But obviously we have to consider everything.'

'Of course.' Her expression changed. 'Is that why you're here? Should I be worrying?'

'We have no reason to think you're in any danger,' said Wilcox. 'But it does no harm to be careful.'

'Try not to let it worry you,' said Murphy. 'But just be

aware of your personal safety. We'll let you know of any developments. If anything worries you, give us a call.'

They rose and picked their way back out. Winona waved them off and shut the door firmly.

'It feels bad frightening her like that,' said Wilcox.

'I know what you mean,' said Murphy. 'But it would have felt negligent not to have done so. I'm going to ask for this address to be added to the patrol route. I'm glad she has a son who lives at home and rebuilds motorbikes.'

Chapter Twenty-Six

'AND IF YOU enjoyed this video, please subscribe to our channel for lots more interesting stuff. Just hit the red button below.'

Florence switched off the microphone and logged off Camtasia. Cal switched off the webcam.

'That wasn't bad' he said. 'Should bring in some new subscribers.'

'The problem,' said Florence, 'is that this is not the best tanning product I've used. And if people buy it and come to the same conclusion, then they might stop following me.'

'With a bit of luck' said Lindy, 'not too many of them will buy it. Remember it doesn't matter to us, we'll be paid anyway. We just need to move on quickly to a better product.'

'We need to get our number of followers up' said Florence 'or we won't be able to bid for better contracts.'

Cal put his arm around Florence. 'Loosen up. We're young. Time is on our side. In a few months we'll have the vehicle and the dog and then we'll be travelling the world and making money. City guides, bar and restaurant reviews, camp sites, hiking, beaches, equipment, cool clothes. It will all be good.'

'I think we need a lot more UK business before we have the funds for that,' said Lindy. Florence stared at her. Who asked her?

'You have anything in mind?' asked Cal.

Lindy frowned as if she was concentrating hard on something. 'I'm thinking shapewear' she said finally.

'Shapewear?' Florence was appalled. 'I'm not promoting bloody shapewear. I don't need it.'

'Shapewear is massive right now,' said Lindy. 'It's not just for overweight – I mean curvy – women. You can use it to pull in your waist and that will make your hips look bigger. Big bums and big hips are very fashionable right now and you don't have either.'

'Nor do you' said Florence, looking Lindy's slim frame up and down. 'What I have is youth and good looks and personality. I don't need a big bum.'

'I don't think we need to get into a disagreement about this' said Cal hurriedly.

'Of course not,' said Lindy. 'If Florence doesn't want to do shapewear, we may want to work with somebody else on that.'

'Or we may want to work on a different product,' he added pointedly.

Florence narrowed her eyes. She was interested to see how Lindy would handle this minor defection on Cal's part.

Lindy shrugged. 'Of course. I'll look for something else.'

Florence was cheered by her small victory. Time to be magnanimous.

'Yes, I guess we need to make more money before we can take off' she said. 'Anyway, everything's crap right now.

I just don't feel I can leave my mum at the moment. At least, not until the police have decided what happened to my dad and cleared off. And I don't see that happening any time soon. I've met the detectives and they're a right pair of saddos.'

'Maybe they're just pretending to be saddos' said Cal. 'Like whatsisname.'

'Columbo? Yeah, right.'

Chapter Twenty-Seven

MURPHY DIDN'T EXPECT the inquest to reveal any new facts about Richard Weaver's death, but it was usual for the police to attend and she was interested to observe the people involved.

There seemed to be little in the way of press interest, she could only see one reporter, and a junior one at that. He had his attention on his phone throughout the proceedings, probably playing Candy Crush or something similar. It made sense – the probably-accidental death of a terminally-ill middle-aged man wasn't going to sell a lot of papers, or generate a lot of website hits. What they needed to avoid was the suggestion that there was any link between this case and the death of Amy Horsfall. That would definitely generate press interest, none of it helpful.

She recognised some of the tube station staff and first-responders from Moorgate and then Adrian French and Arthur Wellesley walked in together. Adrian French looked apprehensive; Arthur Wellesley completely relaxed. Murphy reflected that, as a solicitor, he probably wasn't fazed by any legal-type proceedings. Alison Weaver arrived in a covetable black bouclé suit with ivory-coloured buttons. Murphy couldn't take her eyes off it, while conceding that she personally wouldn't wear it half so well – and probably not in that size.

Alison looked upset but composed. Not so the young people. Florence was wearing dark glasses and had most of her hair hanging over her face. Maybe her eyes were red from crying? Jake was looking hunted, casting glances around the room, which was thankfully modern, boring and not at all intimidating. Murphy felt sorry for Florence and Jake and wondered if, in Alison's place, she would have left them at home. But probably they wanted to be here to support their mother. Then they were joined by more support in the person of Tom Finlay, giving them the appearance of a nuclear family. Finlay was obviously serious about Alison if he was prepared to put in an appearance at a non-fun event like this. Or maybe he wanted to hear what the evidence was? Murphy looked around the small cast of characters and wondered if the killer was here. Or should she be looking for somebody else entirely?

At that moment the coroner entered from a side door and Linda Fleming from the main entrance. The proceedings were opened, the tube station staff and paramedics gave their evidence concerning what had taken place and it was all as Murphy remembered it. No surprises there. Linda was next to the stand and she ran through the post-mortem findings in a matter-of-fact tone. Alison knew about the spiking, and had presumably told Florence and Jake, but Adrian and Arthur looked shocked when this detail was aired. The coroner was also nonplussed and was unwise enough to mildly question Linda's findings. She gave an answer which caused him to immediately retreat back to his paperwork. The solitary newshound suddenly sat up and looked interested. Candy Crush was abandoned.

Alison then took the stand and explained about her husband's illness and the effect of the diagnosis on him. She agreed that he was probably sometimes a bit depressed but was at pains not to exhibit any signs. She emphasised that he was not suicidal. The tragic, good-looking wife created something of a stir, while her body language made it clear that creating an impression was the last thing she was interested in. The solitary reporter scribbled in his notebook. When she returned to her seat Tom Finlay squeezed her arm and Florence moved closer to her.

Wilcox then delivered a dry-as-dust report on the police investigation so far, which avoided detailing any significant lines of enquiry. The atmosphere subsided, the reporter went back to his phone and a few minutes later it was all over. The coroner returned an open verdict.

'Not much else he could do,' said Wilcox as they left the building. 'It could still be accident, suicide or murder.'

'That's right,' said Murphy, but her attention was on something else. The attendees were standing around outside, shuffling awkwardly as people do when wondering how best to make their escape. Alison was holding onto Tom's arm, Jake was looking upset and, a few feet away, an animated conversation appeared to be taking place between Adrian Finch and Florence. Murphy was too far away to hear anything, but it was interesting, that was for sure.

Chapter Twenty-Eight

BACK IN THE CID ROOM, Wilcox was deep into Richard Weaver's bank statements.

'The only money going into this account is his salary,' he said. 'It's a pretty good salary, but it's all there is.'

Murphy looked up. 'So he's never received any money from the sale of shares?'

'No. That means he never did any trading himself and he never received any money from Adrian French, despite what Adrian French told us. Unless there's another account we don't know about.'

'Arthur Wellesley hasn't sold his shares, has he?'

Wilcox drummed his fingers on the keyboard. 'No. So that means he can't easily be accused of using insider information. The longer the period between the purchase and the sale, the less it looks like a get-rich-quick scheme.'

'I guess he's just smarter than Adrian Finch,' said Murphy. 'Or less in need of money.'

'Probably both. He's a lawyer. He knows how to stay on the right side of the law.'

'How much did Wellesley pay for his shares?'

Wilcox scrabbled through the paperwork. '£60,000. And they are worth, as of today' he paused and fished out a calculator 'just under £93,000.'

'So he has £33,000 profit there ready to cash in. Will he feel that it's safer to sell now that Richard is no longer around?'

'Maybe,' said Wilcox. 'Plus, he won't have to give Richard anything. Adrian French said 40%, so if that's true he would have to hand back £13,200, leaving him with £19,800. Which would be liable to tax.'

'But these are paltry sums of money,' said Murphy. 'Nice to have maybe, but you don't kill somebody for twenty grand. Certainly not if you're on a legal salary.'

'I would guess, in Arthur Wellesley's case, it's more a case of something being found out,' said Wilcox. 'He's a member of a professional body. If he was accused of something shady, he could lose his right to practise.'

'Be far worse if he was accused of murder,' said Murphy. 'I think Adrian French is the weaker link here. We can go and lean a bit more on him, see what else he has to say. In the absence of any other leads.'

She picked up her phone and listened for a moment. 'You don't say? Well, that's another link certainly.' She put the phone down.

'That was Linda. Blood tests are back. Rohypnol was found in Amy's blood, but no spike mark. So it must have been in a drink. There was also a small amount of alcohol. Get her half-unconscious and push her in the river. Our perp is really finding that the date-rape drug suits his purposes.'

Wilcox shook his head. 'But why? Why would anybody

want to kill her? Could it be some deranged person who's just picking off anybody they can find?'

'Don't say that. Don't even think it. This is some clever bastard but we're going to catch him – or her.'

'So we're back to trawling pubs and bars?'

'Yes. Let's start with the ones near the river, say between Hammersmith where she lived and Battersea where she was found. If we don't find any sightings, we'll have to widen it. We can use copies of the picture we got from her parents.'

Chapter Twenty-Nine

FLORENCE WAS FOLLOWING Tom Finlay and, so far, it was going pretty well. She'd hung around outside his office near London Wall, waited for him to emerge, followed him down the street and into Moorgate tube station (wish it wasn't Moorgate, but never mind) and manoeuvred herself into the same carriage. Then she realised that the carriages were really very well lit. How had she never noticed this before? Luckily, she was wearing her hoodie with her hair bundled inside it and she kept her face focused down onto her phone. She could see where he was by watching his feet.

At Bank they switched to the District line, which involved the long walk through to Monument. He was going at a fairly leisurely pace, so Florence had no trouble keeping up. A few times she had to stop to avoid getting too close. At the District line entrance, she swiped a copy of the Metro, just for something else to bury her face in. The platform was crowded so she had to edge a bit closer. If he made it onto the next tube and she didn't, it would all be a waste of time.

Dead Cool

They both made it on, but it was standing room only and more people got on as they headed west. By the time they got to Embankment she was completely hemmed in and she couldn't see any bit of him, not his shoes or anything else. At Westminster and St James's Park it just got a bit worse. Finally, at Victoria, all the people heading for southbound commuter trains got off. Florence was now so crumpled she no longer cared. He'd probably got off and she'd missed him. But no. She did a quick sweep and there he was, still on the train.

Just before Sloane Square he stood up and she got ready to follow him off. She stood six people behind him on the escalator and just hoped he wouldn't look round. At the top she hung back as he went through the barrier and when she had spotted which direction he was taking, she went through the barrier and set off after him. Really, this was no problem.

Florence wasn't familiar with the Kings Road; Chelsea was not where her generation hung out. Dalston, Spitalfields, Hackney – these were the areas where she felt at home. She slowed a few times, letting him get a bit further ahead, and looked into the shop windows. They were full of expensive rubbish as far as she could tell. She was staring in disbelief at the four-figure price on a really quite boring pair of shoes when she suddenly remembered to look up and he had vanished. She put on a spurt and he suddenly reappeared as if doubling back on himself. She hung back as he seemed to check something in a window and then they were off again. She paused as she came up to the window he'd been looking in. Curtains? Was he into soft furnishings? Oh well.

He was now pausing outside a pub and after a few

seconds he went inside. Maybe he was meeting somebody? Please, not her mum. Her mum would spot her straight away. Perhaps she could just wait outside and look through the window. She was just getting up on tiptoe when the door opened and he stuck his head out before she could move.

'Come on in Florence. What are you drinking?'

Chapter Thirty

STEVEN AND ISOBEL were still surrounded by bits of tent, half-unpacked rucksacks and steaming socks when Wilcox arrived.

'Please sit down – anywhere you can find,' said Steven. 'We're both on duty tomorrow, so we have to get all our stuff organised.'

'Looks like you've had active week,' said Wilcox.

'It was lovely,' said Isobel. 'But so was getting home and having a shower.'

Wilcox inserted himself between two pairs of trekking trousers spreadeagled across the sofa and got out his notebook.

'You'll have heard what happened earlier this week,' he said.

'Yes,' said Isobel. 'Sally told us. Poor Amy. I can't really believe it.'

'I guess you were in Wales on Tuesday night.'

'That's right,' said Steven. 'And we were wild camping, so no alibi, I'm afraid.'

'Can you tell me what you know about Amy?'

'Not very much in terms of hard facts' said Steven. 'She moved in about three months ago, as far as I remember. We took her to the pub with us a few times because she seemed to be on her own, but she wasn't much of a drinker and to be honest she wasn't great company. I guess I shouldn't say that now. But she was a decent person and we're very sorry this has happened to her.'

'Amy was somebody who was waiting for something,' said Isobel, moving one of the pairs of trousers and sitting down next to Wilcox. 'She was waiting for her life to start. She wanted some exciting future to just come along and she seemed to think that she just had to be patient and it would all happen.'

'Or maybe some exciting man?' asked Wilcox.

'Yes,' said Isobel. 'Some exciting man, who would take her away from all this. This being, I guess, the poky little flat and the job she didn't much like. It seemed to me that she was lonely.'

'So do you think she would have been likely to fall for the wrong sort of man?'

Isobel nodded. 'I think that's probably very likely. She would have been grateful for the attention. Do you think that's what happened?'

'We don't yet know' said Wilcox, 'but it's something to consider. How about the job? Was she looking for a different job?'

'Yes,' said Steven, 'she told us about it remember? She followed all sorts of people on Instagram and she thought she could have a career in the fashion industry if she could just get a break.'

'Do you think she was depressed at all?' said Wilcox.

'I hope not,' said Isobel. 'I hate to think of her on her

own up there being depressed and nobody to talk to. Belinda's not around much, and we tend to work long hours, but maybe we should have looked out for her a bit more.'

'I can't see her killing herself,' said Steven. 'She had lots of hopes and she told us she believed in fate. She used to read her horoscope and believe it. She wouldn't have thrown away her chances by committing suicide. And drowning yourself is not that easy, not if you can swim.'

A bit easier if you're drugged, was what Wilcox thought as he thanked them and left.

Chapter Thirty-One

'SO TELL me what your sleuthing has uncovered so far.' Tom Finlay stretched and sipped his beer.

'You're laughing at me'. Florence raised the bottle to her lips.

She wanted to be angry but he was kind of disarming, which was in itself annoying. He wasn't bad looking for an older man, not of course that she would be interested. Absolutely not. But at least he wasn't fat or bald.

He was smiling now and shaking his head. 'No, I'm not laughing at you, I swear. I'm interested, that's all. I didn't know your father well, but what happened was terrible and I can understand your feeling that you need to do something. Am I the only person you're investigating?'

'Well, I thought I'd start with you.'

'Because I was the dodgiest person around? I can see why you might think that. After all I've just pitched up out of nowhere. And I seem to have designs on your mum. So I totally don't blame you for thinking that.'

'Do you? Have designs on my mum, I mean.'

'I really don't know. We were friends – well we were an item for a while – at university. Then things moved on, we had relationships with other people, we both married other people, we lost touch. Then my marriage broke down – my fault – and I thought again about your mum, so I got in touch. It's very easy to reconnect with people these days. You'll know all about that. So we got together and had a chat and I learned about your dad's diagnosis. It was very hard for Alison. She loved your dad very much. So I just became someone she could talk to about it. And that's all I am right now. I do value her company and her friendship, I must admit.'

'I do want my mum to have somebody,' Florence began, 'because me and Jake won't always be around.'

'Of course you won't. You'll be off doing exciting things. Alison told me you have a very clever boyfriend, although she hasn't met him yet.'

'No, well, my dad tended to be a bit interfering about my boyfriends. I don't know why that was, he never looked into Jake's private life.'

Tom nodded. 'Men worry a lot more about their daughters. I was the same.'

'Well, that's certainly how he was. So I was in no hurry to introduce Cal. I didn't want my dad frightening him off. Also, I suppose I was waiting to see if it was going to be serious. Bit late now. But I will introduce him to my mum.'

'I think that's a good idea. If you were with somebody nice, that would be one less thing for her to worry about.'

Nice, thought Florence. Such an insipid word. Was Cal nice? Would she even want to go out with somebody nice?

Chapter Thirty-Two

MURPHY HAD TO ADMIT, it was the smartest Jobcentre she had ever visited. Most of the others had been in rough areas of town, and had been decorated with maintenance in mind, lots of hardwearing materials and wipe-clean surfaces, but this establishment in London Wall was very different. In a way, she wondered what it was doing here, in the square mile that paid the highest salaries in the country, but maybe some of these smart offices had ongoing needs for admin assistants and cleaners. If you had to work for the DWP, this must be one of the best places to end up.

Amy Horsfall's manager was a stout woman in a too-tight suit who expressed profound shock at what had happened.

'We kept trying to call her,' she said, 'but there was no answer.'

'We don't actually know what happened to her phone,' said Murphy. 'It wasn't on her when she was found. I'd like to talk to the people Amy worked with, see if she had any problems, anything like that.'

Lona Hedges looked affronted. 'We have very good HR here and a strong anti-bullying policy. I'm sure if there was anything that she was worrying about it would have been properly handled.'

Murphy shook her head. 'We have no particular reason to think that she had problems at work, and we are not even sure yet what happened. We're just trying to build up a picture of what was going on in her life. Are there people who worked closely with her who might be able to help us?'

'There are three other people in Amy's section. You're welcome to talk to them. If you want to wait in here, I'll send them along.'

The first two arrivals had no insight to offer. They claimed to have had no conversations with Amy apart from those related to work, and both advised her to 'talk to Stella'.

Stella had red hair, freckles and a properly robust attitude. 'Amy was kind of waiting for her life to happen' she said. 'I used to tell her that she had to decide what she wanted and do something about it. She didn't like working here, it's not a very fun place, she wanted something more interesting, but she seemed to think something would turn up. And she wasn't very good at fighting her corner.'

'Was she being bullied?'

'No, not at all. Nobody dares bully anybody these days. Or that's how it seems to me. We have to treat everybody with respect – whether or not they've earned it. But Amy tended to end up doing more work than other people simply because she was more interested in pleasing other people than in pleasing herself. I used to tell her there was no future in that, but I don't think she could change – it was just the way she was.'

'What sort of job do you think she was looking for?'

Stella rolled her eyes. 'She was interested in social media and fashion, not that she knew much about either, as far as I'm aware. She seemed to think that, if she could get into the fashion business in any sort of role, she could have a modelling career.'

'Was that realistic?'

Stella seemed to be considering this. 'It might have been. Even ten years ago it would have been impossible, because models had to be skinny and beautiful, the clothes had to hang on them properly, all that. Nowadays models don't have to be either of those things, they can just look ordinary and be overweight. So Amy figured she had a chance as a 'curvy' model. She had posted a few pictures of herself to Instagram, posing in outfits, but I don't think she had many followers.'

'Can you think of anybody who would want to harm her?'

'Nobody at all. She wasn't the sort of person who would have enemies. She didn't make enough of a mark for that.'

'No boyfriends that you know about?'

'No. She would have liked to have a boyfriend, but she didn't have one. I introduced her to a few guys, but it didn't go anywhere. None of them really made a play for her, there was no chemistry. And there are no fanciable blokes here, in case you haven't noticed.'

'How about suicide?'

'I sincerely hope not. I would never have expected it. She was kind of marginally dissatisfied, but not really unhappy. I would hate to think that underneath it all she was actually in despair.'

'There's a lot we have to find out yet,' said Murphy. 'Do you think she would have been attracted to the sort of man who wouldn't be good for her?'

Stella drew a deep breath. 'She would have been attracted to any man who paid her any attention – well obviously not if he was fifty years old with a beer gut, but you know what I mean. I don't want to sound harsh, but really, she was an innocent. I tried to toughen her up but it didn't work.'

Murphy stood up. 'Thank you for your help, Stella. Please get in touch if you think of anything else.'

'Certainly will. This shouldn't have happened to her. She was a good person. Naïve, but good.'

'Naïve, but good' thought Murphy as she made her way out. Classic victim profile.

Chapter Thirty-Three

'TOM FINLAY HAS a serviced office just off Finsbury Square,' said Wilcox. 'Probably can't afford it. His consultancy posted losses for the last two years.'

'But he probably needs it for PR purposes,' said Murphy. 'No point running a business consultancy unless you look like you're making lots of money. Nobody would want your services otherwise.'

'Yes, I'm sure that's it. He has a flat in Tufnell Park. No answer from the office number, so that's probably where he is now. I haven't brought my car in today, though.'

'No problem.' Murphy grabbed her bag. 'We can go in mine.' And she led the way out.

Wilcox climbed cautiously in and moved stuff around to make space on the floor for his feet. He cleaned his car at least once a fortnight, including vacuuming the interior. Did women not do this? His train of thought was interrupted by his head slamming into the headrest as Murphy accelerated at speed out of the parking space and his whole attention was then focussed on unravelling his seat belt which seemed to be knotted around something. Conscious that he could die in the time he took to sort this out, he finally managed to release it and heard the satisfying click as the belt snapped shut. He sat back and drew a deep breath.

Murphy had noticed none of this and seemed to be talking to herself. 'Can't be right. I came down here last year. Something's moved, they've changed the name of the street.'

Wilcox decided to engage. 'What does the sat nav say?'

'The sat nav's saying nothing.'

'That's because the sound isn't enabled.' He switched it on and the smooth tones of the robot immediately began issuing directions.

'That's rubbish,' said Murphy. 'That's not the way.'

Wilcox sighed. 'Maybe just do as she says and see what happens.'

A few minutes later they pulled up with a hard stop outside an Edwardian semi.

'This is it,' said Wilcox, climbing out gratefully. 'I think he's on the first floor.'

MURPHY INTONED 'POLICE' into the entryphone, and the front door was unlocked. Tom Finlay was waiting for them at the top of the stairs.

'Come on in,' he said. 'I had a feeling you'd be looking me up before too long.'

The flat was roomy but sparsely furnished. Finlay saw Murphy looking around. 'I'm not actually some cool minimalist. Wife got most of the furniture,' he said, by way of explanation. 'The idea seemed to be that she'd chosen most of it and I'd only paid for it, so it was hers more than mine. Still, you don't need much for one person.'

Murphy looked sideways at him. 'Who divorced who?'

'She divorced me,' he said. 'Come and sit down and I'll tell you all about it.'

The sofa was a modest two-seater and upright rather than squashy. Murphy decided this would be easy to get out of, so she commandeered it for herself. Wilcox seemed happy to walk around flexing the back of his neck and Finlay took the other available chair.

'I might as well tell you the whole truth about my sorry marital situation, rather than let you drag it out of me.'

Murphy nodded. 'It's quicker that way.'

'OK, well I had an affair, a very ill-advised affair, and she divorced me.'

'An ill-advised affair with a much younger woman?'

'Yes, that's right.' He looked pleased with himself just for a second.

'And this much younger woman suddenly did the math and realised she could end up as your carer?'

He wasn't looking so pleased now. 'Well I'm not sure it was quite as cut and dried as that, but yes, she had second thoughts.'

'And your wife took full and proper advantage of the fact that you were the party at fault?'

'She took me to the cleaners, yes.' It was said without any trace of rancour, just a self-deprecating twinkle. Murphy could suddenly see why Alison Weaver might be attracted to this man.

'How long have you known the Weavers?' she asked.

'I've known Alison for decades, because we were at university together' he said. 'Then we knew them as another couple for a few years, but didn't see that much of them. I saw Alison again at one of those ghastly university reunions. She was the only person I really talked to much. A lot of the people there I couldn't remember who they were. Then that was it for another couple of years.'

'Until you got divorced?'

'Yes. We got divorced and our only son went off travelling. So there I was, alone again. At that point you look around to see what friends you have left. So I looked up Alison on LinkedIn and got in touch.'

'What did you think of Richard?'

He took a moment to answer. 'He was a highly intelligent man, good company. I don't think he suffered fools gladly. I liked him a lot.'

'And do you think theirs was a happy marriage?'

'Whoa now. What would I know about that? Me with my brilliant track record?'

'Well you might have some strange insight that nobody else has picked up on.'

'I might, but unfortunately not. They always seemed happy to me. Until Richard was diagnosed of course. That was a terrible shock.'

Murphy nodded. 'And what about the children? What can you tell me about them?'

He shrugged. 'I think they're typical of their age group. Jake is a bit nerdy. He's a clever chap. Florence is outwardly more sophisticated but I think she's struggling a bit.'

'Struggling in what way?'

'You mustn't place too much store on what I say, it could be all wrong. Anyway, I think Florence is trying to find a niche where she fits in and she hasn't managed it yet. She's finished university, but with no career path mapped out. I think she's always been feisty, but her parents were indulgent in a lot of ways. Even now she's still living at home and paying nothing. She has a boyfriend that her father never met, because he has a bit of a history of frightening off her boyfriends, and now of course it's too late. So I think she's a bit – unmoored.' He smiled. 'She followed me across London yesterday.'

Murphy stared. 'Followed you? Why?'

'I think she fancied herself as a bit of a sleuth. Maybe she thinks if anybody is going to find out what happened to her father it will have to be her. So she picked me as the obvious first suspect. Or maybe she just suspects my intentions towards her mother.'

'What happened?'

'I led her a bit of a dance actually, on and off a couple of tubes and so on. I enjoyed it, to be honest. She kept up manfully – or womanfully.'

'Bet she was well pissed off,' said Murphy.

'When she caught me up? Yes, she wasn't too amused. But we had a drink and talked about it. Maybe you should give her a job.'

'So she picked you as a suspect – why?'

Finlay sat back and folded his arms. 'I guess she wonders whether I offed her dad in order to get off with her mum.'

'And did you?'

He shook his head. 'No. I'm not even sure I want a relationship with Alison. Or not like that. We're good friends and I think she needs support at the moment.'

Murphy raised her eyebrows. She was inclined to disregard all of that. 'Where were you that night?'

'I left the office in the City about 6.15, maybe 6.30, got back here about 7.20.'

'You came back on the Northern line?'

'Yes, and before you ask, I did use Moorgate station, but there was no disturbance, so I must have been on a train before the one that hit Richard.'

'OK. Did anybody see you leave the office?'

'No, there's only me there, it's just a space that I rent, and nobody saw me arrive here either. So I guess I'm not properly alibied.'

'What do you think happened to Richard?'

'I think it must have been an accident. He wouldn't have killed himself, certainly not like that. He wouldn't have done that to his family.'

'Did you know anything about Richard's financial affairs?' said Wilcox, who obviously thought this relationship stuff had gone on long enough.

He shook his head. 'No, nothing at all. I know he had a well-paid job, so I'm sure his affairs were all in order. And I'm sure he will have left a will.'

'In favour of Alison?'

'Yes, I'm sure. Who else would he want to leave his money to?'

'So she will be quite wealthy,' said Wilcox.

'I'm beginning to see where you're going with this,' said Finlay, 'and I don't like it. I'm not looking to snare some merry – or even not so merry – widow. Alison is an old friend and I want her to be OK. That's it.'

'I had a look at the financial statements you posted,' said Wilcox. 'No profit for two years.'

'That's true. Revenue is way down because I parted company with the other director, so now it's just me. And the losses are after paying salaries.'

'So you're not personally in financial trouble? Not even after paying the wife?'

'I wouldn't say so, no. Last year was bad because I had to buy back the shares and I had to pay the settlement but I'm hoping to get back into profit this year.'

'Well I think that's everything.' Murphy levered herself

off the sofa and they made for the door. 'We may need to speak to you again, and if you think of anything else useful, give us a call.'

When they get outside it had started to rain. 'Bugger' said Murphy. 'Hope the wipers don't pack up again.' Wilcox gritted his teeth.

Chapter Thirty-Four

IT WAS LATE when Murphy arrived home, she'd forgotten to have lunch and she was vaguely wondering whether there would be any food around – with a bit of luck Clive and James would have made extra. It was not to be. Sitting at the table with them, having apparently eaten the last of the aubergine parmigiana, which Murphy would have gratefully consumed herself, was Maisie.

'Mum' she murmured, and rose to give Murphy a hug. Very nice, but you couldn't eat it.

'I'm afraid we've eaten it all Murph, we weren't sure what time you'd be back,' said James. 'Let's make you an omelette.'

'No,' declared Maisie. 'It's my fault. I'll make the omelette.'

Murphy sank into a chair and decided to let them sort it out between them. From what she remembered, Maisie would devastate the whole kitchen just making an omelette, but never mind.

'It's lovely to see you darling' she shouted above the crashing noises. 'Was there anything in particular...?'

'No, nothing at all, just thought I hadn't seen you for a while.'

So it definitely was something, and Murphy had a good idea what. But they'd get round to that.

'Have you heard from Ben?' she asked.

'Yes, we had a chat the other night when he came off duty. He sends his love. He's very busy as usual. I don't know how they do these twelve-hour shifts.'

'Me neither,' said Clive. 'I'd be a wreck.'

'You'd be a wreck just from the sight of blood,' said James.

'Funnily enough' said Murphy, 'the sight of blood is something you get used to quite quickly. The sight of death, not so much.'

'Yes, that's what Ben told me once' said Maisie, slamming a frying pan onto the cooker.

'And now' said James, 'we're off to watch some on-screen blood and death. See you girls later.'

'Cheerio' said Murphy. 'This looks good' she told Maisie, a few minutes later when the omelette appeared.

'Actually, my cooking's improved a lot since I left home.'

Murphy wasn't too sure how to take that, so she smiled and nodded and started eating. The omelette was surprisingly edible and she ate it all.

'OK, now down to business' she said, putting the plate to one side. 'Has he sent you here?'

'No, of course not.' Maisie's air of affront was just not convincing. Her daughter seemed not to realise that Murphy had spent years being lied to by the best in the business.

'OK, let's approach it a different way. Has he been in touch with you?'

'Well of course he's in touch with me. He's my dad.'

'And what did he say to you about his personal situation?'

'He told me a bit. Like he's living on his own in a flat in Queens Park.' *While you're still living in the house* was the subtext, but Murphy decided to ignore it.

'OK. That much we know. What did he tell you that sent you haring over here?'

Maisie hesitated. 'I think he's lonely.'

'I'm sure he is,' said Murphy, 'but that's very much part of the human condition. Don't you get lonely sometimes?'

'Not really, because I have Chris.'

'And your dad has nobody. OK, that much I understand. I'm sorry his relationship didn't work out, but there's not much I can do about it.'

Maisie was silent for a moment. 'I guess not.'

'Maisie, listen, who was that guy who dumped you? Rob, wasn't it? Well, if Rob reappeared and you didn't have Chris and I said you should take Rob back because he was now lonely, how would that be?'

'That would be crap, but it's different because I never had a family with Rob.'

'But when you've had a family and that family has now left home, you're back at square one. Your dad and I now, we're like two single people. I'm very glad we were married all those years, because otherwise we wouldn't have you and Ben, but it doesn't mean we have to spend the rest of our lives welded together. Probably in a few months he'll meet somebody else and you'll no longer have to worry about him.'

'I hope so,' said Maisie.

'Well if he doesn't,' said Murphy, 'it will be his problem, not yours. He'll have to find somebody less active on social media.'

'I couldn't believe she dropped him, just like that.'

'Clive and James tell me that's par for the course these days. Everybody's obsessed with their profile.'

'Yes, that's true of young people – even the little kids in my class – but it shouldn't be like that for old people.'

Murphy smiled. 'I think maybe that was the distinction Tracey drew. She decided that she wanted to stick with the young people. And who can blame her?'

Chapter Thirty-Five

FLORENCE WAS SITTING in Starbucks with Cal, sipping a Caramel Frappucino. It was covered in whipped cream and some sort of toffee sauce and the amount which had made it down to her stomach was making her feel a bit queasy. Worse than that was the embarrassment of sitting behind this thing which looked like a child's dessert. Cal was drinking a black coffee, a proper grown-up drink. Why hadn't she ordered that?

They were round the corner from Cal's flat in Shoreditch and Florence was making her case for why she should move in. Cal seemed not to appreciate the desperate urge of anybody trapped in middle-class north London to move to Shoreditch, to be with the tribe.

'The thing is, babe, I can't ask Lindy to move out just yet. She's my big sis after all and she's a big part of the business. You and me – that's something different.'

'But couldn't she find somewhere else?'

'Of course she could, she's really well networked, you know that, but at the moment she wants to stick with me.

She's always looked out for me; I can't just ask her to leave. But just be patient, the time will come. Anyway, don't you want to stay home and support your mum a bit longer?'

'My mum has some sort of boyfriend, so she probably won't need me too much anymore.'

'Has he moved in?'

'No, but he might.' She wrinkled her nose. 'Gross.'

Cal laughed. 'Good for her. Even old people need somebody. This thing with Lindy – it's a business arrangement. That's how you need to view it. We're a threesome. She has the connections in the advertising world, I have the photography skills, you' he kissed her, 'have the fabulous face and body. We're unstoppable. She keeps the contracts coming in, we keep the followers increasing, keep them engaged, and that's it. There could be something exciting coming up with a new acne remedy.'

'And how am I supposed to promote that? I don't have any spots.'

'No, you don't.' He kissed her again, lightly. 'You're beautiful. Maybe we can put them on with makeup, or even photoshopping. Lindy will have an idea.'

'But it will have to look realistic,' said Florence. 'And I don't really want to appear with spots. That's not how my followers are used to seeing me.'

'The thing is' said Cal, 'acne's really big, it's mega. People who have it are desperate to get rid of it. They'll do anything, pay anything. And this spot remedy might be brilliant, people might find it really works. Are we going to deny our followers that chance just because you don't have spots?'

In some distant region of her brain Florence felt that this argument didn't quite work, but he was looking at her with those dark blue eyes that she just wanted to drift into, so she smiled and said 'I guess not.'

He hooked an arm around her shoulders. 'We're going to be such a hot item. And we can make lots of money just by being us – no more having to work for anybody else. All we have to do is keep building our platform and keep giving our followers what they want.'

The making lots of money was taking rather a long time to arrive, Florence thought. If money was being made, she hadn't yet seen any of it.

Chapter Thirty-Six

MURPHY AND WILCOX were sitting on deckchairs in Hyde Park.

'If Bellweather came past now and saw us, we'd both be up on a disciplinary charge' said Wilcox.

Murphy snorted. 'If Bellweather came past here I'd ask him what he was doing in the park when he's supposed to be at work. These things cut both ways. The reason we're sitting here, me enjoying the sunshine, you shifting around like you've got leeches attached to your arse, is because I want to be able to discuss all of this without him grimacing at me with his terrifying dental work.'

'I don't think he likes you' said Wilcox regretfully.

'Oh really? And I thought he was one of my biggest fans. You're quite right – he doesn't like me. I guess he doesn't have much use for mouthy women. And to be honest, the prospect of being liked by him doesn't have that much appeal either. So, for you, the sad fact is that he probably regards you with the same jaundiced eye, so he's not going to assist your progress up the greasy pole. Let's take that as read. But look on the bright side. A boring probable-suicide comes in, he gives it to the most unpopular girls in the school. Then it turns out to be something much more complex. He's now probably wishing he had given it to one of his pets. But he didn't, so we've got it. Now we've got to work out what to do with it. So where are we at?'

Wilcox consulted his notes. 'We have three suspects for Richard Weaver's killing – Adrian French, Arthur Wellesley and Tom Finlay. All had motive and opportunity and the means was provided by London Underground.'

'I don't really like any of those motives' said Murphy. 'They're just too thin. Adrian French doesn't look to me like somebody even capable of carrying out a murder. He's one of those people who probably look guilty when they've done nothing. And just for a sum of money that he could probably borrow from the bank? If it's him, there has to be another reason. Wellesley is more capable, he could carry it off, but again, he wouldn't do it for a stupid sum of money. And Tom Finlay has just pitched up and seems to have designs on Alison, but her husband was dying, so surely any sensible person would just bide their time.'

'Unfortunately, those are our three contenders at the moment,' said Wilcox

'We may have to widen it,' said Murphy. 'How about the wife? Most murders are committed by close family. How about his boss – whatsisname? – Castle – maybe he'd become a liability in the office and they wanted to save the salary but they couldn't fire him because he was ill. And I've been thinking of something else. If Alison Weaver decided to sell her house, now she's the only one living in it, who do you think she'd get to organise the sale?'

'Adrian Finch, I guess. He's a family friend, isn't he?'

'That's right. Now, after your rummaging round in the bowels of Companies House, we know that Adrian French is not doing all that well financially. He's probably just hanging on. How much could he make out of selling Alison's house?'

Wilcox logged onto Rightmove and paged through a succession of screens. 'That's actually a very sought-after property,' he said. 'It's got the location factor and it's Georgian, so it's not replaceable.'

'So what are we looking at?'

'Somewhere around £1.8m.'

'Blimey. What would the estate agent make? 2%?'

'At 2% that would be £36,000.'

Murphy thought for a moment. 'I think we can assume the mortgage is paid off, or Richard's life insurance will pay it off, so the proceeds all come to Alison. And say she gave half to the kids and spent the other half on a flat, which she purchased through Adrian.'

Wilcox nodded. 'That would be £900,000 at 2% - another £18,000.'

'OK' said Murphy. 'Total £54,000. Not a fortune. But if your business was in trouble, it could make a lot of difference.'

'You probably wouldn't kill somebody for that,' said Wilcox.

'No, I wouldn't think so' said Murphy, 'but we do have to consider the financial aspect – and it also applies to Tom Finlay. Alison's not just an attractive woman, she's an attractive woman with assets. And I noticed Adrian having an intense conversation with Florence after the inquest. I just wonder if he was sounding her out about the house, pointing out to her that if the house was sold, some of the proceeds would probably come her way. So that's my take on Adrian. Might be something, might be nothing.'

'I suppose if she sold the house and bought a flat, she could have Arthur Wellesley doing the conveyancing,' said Wilcox. 'I don't know how much he would make out of that. But it's not a motive for murder. You don't murder someone so you can do the legal work on his wife's house sale.'

'No, you don't,' said Murphy. 'But there's another angle in respect of Arthur Wellesley. Alison was his girlfriend and she then transferred her affections to Richard. The point about it is that Richard, Adrian and Arthur were mates. Alison was Arthur's girlfriend. She came to visit him and Richard snaffled her somehow. And these men are still mates.'

'But that would have been a motive for a punch to the jaw twenty years ago,' said Wilcox. 'Not murder now, when they're all old anyway.'

'It might not sound very rational,' said Murphy. 'But murder is not a particularly rational act. And we shouldn't disregard the emotional responses of people over forty. You might write them off, but they're not writing themselves off. I wonder if Arthur – Art – has designs on Alison now that Richard has gone. And if so, he won't be too pleased that Tom Finlay has just drifted in from left field. But maybe I'm getting carried away. The perp could of course be somebody we don't even know about yet.'

'Like a random killer?'

'Could be, but maybe not that random if we need to tie in the death of Amy Horsfall.'

'That's the most perplexing bit of all,' said Wilcox. 'I

haven't been able to find any link between the two victims. Perhaps their deaths are unconnected.'

'The only thing that connects them,' said Murphy, 'is Amy staying behind to talk to the police. If she hadn't done that, we would have never known that she had been at Moorgate that night and no connection would be suspected. Her death would be investigated by a different team.'

'So did somebody kill her because she spoke to the police?' said Wilcox.

'I think the question we have to ask,' said Murphy, 'is why did she speak to the police? She didn't really tell us anything, she had no useful information to impart. Why did she want to hang around?'

'Because she wanted to be seen talking to the police?'

'Something like that. Maybe she saw more than she was telling us. And maybe she told someone else that she was helping the police with their enquiries.'

'But she couldn't have gone after the person in question because she was waiting to speak to us.'

'No, but she might have known how to contact that person – or she might have some idea where they worked. After all, the same set of people must go into that tube station at the same time every weekday night. Granted, that's a couple of thousand people, but it's not impossible. Maybe we should look more closely at her work colleagues. Many of them will use Moorgate. We just need to find one of them that we can connect to Richard Weaver. I've spoken to them, and none of them seemed like killers to me, but we can ignore that. I think you should go in and talk to them. You might spot something I didn't.'

Wilcox nodded. 'And what we really need is to link Amy to any of our three principal suspects.'

'Yes, that would be the best break. If there's a connection there, we have to find it. I think I'm going to have another chat with Alison Weaver after the funeral – see if there's anything she hasn't been telling us. And now I guess we should move, while I still have some chance of levering my arse out of this deckchair.'

Chapter Thirty-Seven

'I WANTED TO ASK YOU SOMETHING' said Murphy, looking round the Fox and Feathers to make sure nobody was in earshot.

'You mean' said Susannah 'you invited me over here in order to ask me something that you wouldn't want to ask me in front of Simon?'

'Yes, basically.'

'OK, ask away' said Samantha, sipping her gin and tonic. 'You've always been about as tactful as a herd of rhino, so don't change now. I'm glad you didn't pretend it was just for the pleasure of my sisterly company.'

'Well it's that as well of course,' said Murphy, 'but I just wanted to get your take on something. If Simon had stayed with what's-her-name, if he hadn't come back, would you have thought of selling the house?'

'It's Felicity, and no, I wouldn't. I still have the children and it's their home.'

'What about if the children had left home?'

'Is this about you and Jack?'

'No, not specifically. I'm not selling the house because I don't want to.'

'I wouldn't want to either,' said Susannah, 'if I'd managed to move in a pair of domestic gods. The average husband can't compete with that.'

'I had Maisie round the other night,' said Murphy, 'saying she felt sorry for him because he's living in a small flat on his own. While I'm still in the house, was what she really meant. I didn't rise to it, but I did wonder if I'm being a selfish bitch. But really, this is not about me. Tell me, if the girls had grown up and left home and your husband was dead – not making any wishes about Simon, this is purely speculative – would you then sell up?'

'Now there's a question,' said Susannah. 'If my husband was dead, then the house would be all mine, so I wouldn't have to share the proceeds with anybody, apart from the kids at some later stage of course. That would make a big difference to my decision. I mean, a husband who's just absconded doesn't forfeit their property rights, and you might have to agree, as part of the divorce proceedings, to sell up and give them half. If they're dead, no problem. You're not thinking of killing Jack, are you?'

'No, I'd never get away with it. How about if your husband was dead, your children had left home and somebody else was interested in you?'

'Aha.' Susannah took another sip. 'A fortune hunter.'

'Well not necessarily.'

'It all depends' said Susannah.

'On what?'

'On what the house is worth, on whether I want to actually live with this person anyway, like do I actually fancy them? On what their net worth is, as opposed to mine, and on what my children's financial status is.'

'Yes, the children. That's a good point.'

'I mean' said Susannah, 'downsizing would free up some funds which could give your children a deposit, but I'd still want somewhere decent to live that was mine, whether or not I ended up sharing it with somebody else. I think it's not a matter to rush into.'

'That's what I think,' said Murphy, 'and I am speaking for myself here. But the pressure to get on with it can come from all sorts of different directions. There can be other people who have a dog in the fight.'

Chapter Thirty-Eight

RICHARD WEAVER'S funeral was held at St Bartholomew's Church, King's Cross. It was originally a medieval church which had fallen into disuse and been destined for demolition when the expansion of London in the 1850s brought in waves of new parishioners and the church was restored in the Victorian gothic style. This much Murphy had read on the board outside. It was a cold, sunny morning and Murphy was interested to see who would attend. Quite a lot of people, actually.

Standing a little way off, she counted in his work colleagues – Andrew Castle, Parvez Shah and Melanie Thomas, plus another man and a woman. They were followed by the duo, as she had come to think of them, of Adrian and Arthur, and a woman who appeared to be Adrian's wife, then various people who were presumably friends or neighbours, and finally the family.

Alison was wearing the same black suit with a hat and Florence was in a turquoise and cerise dress, presumably on the basis that her father would prefer bright colours. Jake, probably unsure how to fit into the colour spectrum, had opted for black jeans and a navy jacket. They were accompanied not by Tom Finlay, who had slipped in alone earlier, but by another middle-aged couple. Richard's sister and her husband maybe? When it looked as if all the arrivals were in place, Murphy filed in behind them and took a seat near the back.

The vicar spoke about Richard as if he knew him, which he presumably did. This suggested that the Weavers were at least occasional churchgoers. Murphy couldn't think that this information was relevant to her enquiry, but she filed it away anyway, in that part of her mind which housed assorted clutter.

Alison spoke about her husband and his courage in the face of his cancer diagnosis. Arthur Wellesley spoke about Richard and their long friendship. Then, surprisingly, it was Jake who stood up, walked to the front and read the Mary Frye poem 'Do not stand at my grave and weep'. Florence, despite her upbeat attire, was visibly weeping throughout.

The cremation followed the service and was for close family only, to be followed by refreshments at the house in Camden. Murphy couldn't think of a compelling reason to gatecrash the drinks, but it was an opportunity to observe all the suspects in one place. She wanted to see how all these people related to each other – Adrian and Arthur, Tom Finlay, Alison, Florence and Jake.

She went back to her car and sat for half an hour to allow the cremation party to get back and the house to fill up before she put in an appearance. Then she drove the short distance to Camden and parked in the next street. The door to the house was opened by the middle-aged woman who Murphy had pegged as Richard's sister, now wearing a proprietorial apron, who whisked her in without questioning who she was.

Murphy helped herself to a virtuous orange juice and surveyed the various knots of people. The work colleagues made up one little group – Andrew Castle plus another man and Parvez and Melanie. They looked as if they weren't planning to stay long. Tom Finlay was part of a group that included Adrian French and a few other people she didn't recognise. Florence and Jake were nowhere to be seen. They had probably seized the opportunity to disappear to their rooms and she didn't blame them. A middle-aged man suddenly materialised in front of her, hand outstretched.

'David Fulbrook, Richard's brother-in-law,' he said as they shook hands.

'Miranda Murphy,' she replied, hoping he wouldn't ask for further clarification.

'Amanda has taken this very hard,' he said. 'That's why she's taken over in the kitchen, so she can keep busy and not have to talk too much.'

'That usually helps,' said Murphy.

'I guess it would be easier if there were other brothers and sisters,' he said. 'Or if their parents were still alive, but, as I said to Amanda, that's more of a blessing than anything else. Nobody wants to bury their children.'

'She must feel like the last one left,' said Murphy.

'Exactly,' he said. 'And we should have visited more, but we thought he had lots of time yet. It's not as if the journey up from Winchester is so far. And now, all of a sudden, it's too late. It's been a terrible shock. And poor Alison, left to bring up the children alone.'

'At least they're pretty much grown up now,' said Murphy.

He drained his glass and Murphy realised he'd probably

had several drinks already. 'I know, you can say that, but I think some of them need more help at this stage than they did when they were younger. Take young Florence for instance' he cast a swift glance around and evidently decided it was safe to proceed, 'very beautiful girl of course, and very clever in many ways – but with a lot of growing up yet to do. At that age it's all about appearance and they think – girls especially – that they're really sophisticated, but of course, they're not. Richard worried quite a lot about Florence. I know he saw off more than one unsuitable boyfriend. Well, she didn't thank him for that of course. Whoops. Looks like I'm going to be given a job.' Murphy turned to see his wife waving from the kitchen. 'Lovely talking to you.'

He trotted off and Murphy looked around the room to see what her persons of interest were doing. Adrian Finch was having an animated conversation with Alison, while she seemed to be scanning the room as if looking for a means of escape.

Arthur Wellesley and Tom Finlay were talking to Adrian's wife. Tom Finlay suddenly drifted off, picked up a bottle of wine and began going around with it. As he reached Alison, Adrian sidled back to his wife. It was nicely done, Murphy thought. She'll appreciate having this Tom around. Adrian might be trying to persuade her to sell this very nice house, but Tom Finlay would probably rather she hung onto it. Better than the flat in Tufnell Park with no furniture.

Chapter Thirty-Nine

'SHE WAS A FOLLOWER,' said Wilcox, looking up from Facebook. 'She didn't have many people following her. She didn't post much about herself, apart from lots of posing-type shots designed to show off what she was wearing. But she didn't get many likes. There's nothing here that suggests she was having a great time. Not many shots of her having fun with other people, and most of the ones here look old, like college or whatever.'

Murphy flicked a rubber band at the bin. It missed. 'There must be some other people that she was connected to.'

'Just a few. Let's see. There's a Mandy Wells that crops up occasionally, looks like an old school friend, but the last thing she posted was 'Loving my new life here in Oz'. And Amy was followed by her mum of course, and one of her aunts and a cousin by the look of it. And a few other people, but nobody we've come across, nobody from her work. Some of them seem to be based in Enfield, which is where her parents live, so I guess that figures.'

'And who was she following?'

'About fifty people.'

'OK. Go through them all. See if anything interesting comes up.'

Wilcox sat back in his chair. 'It's not likely. I mean I follow Rafa Nadal but I wouldn't say there's much connection between us. He doesn't follow me back, I'm afraid.'

'You need to up your tennis,' said Murphy. 'We can at least learn something about you from who you follow, like you're a tennis nerd, so maybe the same will apply in respect of Amy. So far, she seems like a kind of nothing person, Stella at the office said she didn't make enough of a mark to have any enemies, Isabel said she'd be grateful for any attention, but I'm not buying that. There's more to Amy, we just haven't found it. Somebody somewhere may have felt that she was endangering them. We need to find out what she cared about, what she was looking for. She won't have been unimportant to herself, so something was going on in her head and we have to look for what it was.'

An hour later Wilcox pushed his chair back and rubbed his eyes. 'OK, so here's roughly what was going on. She was following lots of other girls who were probably schoolfriends. They were posting pictures of their perfect lives, their boyfriends, their exciting holidays. She was posting likes and the odd comment. She was also following a dog shelter up in Enfield and reposting their stories. She posted a few pictures of herself with some of the dogs – she was a volunteer dog walker apparently. And there's one event she posted about which was raising money for the dogs. Got quite a few likes for those, actually.'

'See?' said Murphy. 'I like her much more already. If we're lucky the people at the dog shelter might be able to give us some information. What else?'

'Most of the other people she was following were young women posting as themselves and directing people to follow them on Instagram. If we look at who she was following on Instagram, there are hundreds of them, lots of influencers selling all sorts of products. My brain hurts now just from looking at them all. And one in particular.'

He turned the screen around and Murphy recognised Florence Weaver posing with a good-looking young man.

'Flo & Cal they call themselves' said Wilcox. 'And they have a lot of followers – like, a lot. Plus, they are pushing products – tanning creams, hair straighteners, some other things that I don't even know what they are, his and hers underwear. This is well-monetised.'

'Interesting. What clever young things. How many followers do they have?'

'Almost 18,000. Pretty good really.'

'So the fact that Amy Horsfall followed them is not so significant? It was her and 17,999 others.'

He shrugged. 'Yes. Probably coincidence. But interesting.'

'I'm wondering about this Cal,' said Murphy. 'He's the boyfriend her mum and dad hadn't met. Wonder what his real name is?'

Chapter Forty

FLORENCE AND SUSIE were sitting in Costa checking their phones. Florence was drinking black coffee, which made her feel grown-up and faintly intellectual, but she didn't like it much and she was sure it was going to stain her teeth. Still, whatever. She smiled and took a selfie, then felt bad. How could she be posting smiling selfies when her dad was dead?

'He's quite a bit older than you, isn't he?' said Susie, who was sipping a latte.

Florence frowned. 'A bit. So what? He's not exactly cradle-snatching.'

Susie smiled. 'I didn't mean that. It's nice to have a man with a bit of experience.' She winked and Florence laughed. She wasn't going to tell Susie that she had not yet availed herself of much of Cal's presumed experience.

'Cradle snatching' said Susie, 'would be more like Mr Henderson. Remember how we all were? The weird thing, well it seems weird now, is that everybody really did fancy him, even I did a bit. And all sorts of people were putting in extra time in the Chemi' lab – some of them didn't even do the 'A' level in the end.'

'I couldn't have done chemistry 'A' level,' said Florence. 'The GCSE was hard enough. I got a lot of encouragement from Mr Henderson though.'

'Yeah, you and about a dozen others. I think he just liked having lots of girls hanging around him. He didn't have any serious designs on any of us.'

'No, probably not. He'd have gotten into a lot of trouble if he had. Even more so these days. It all seems a bit gross now, fancying teachers.'

'I think it was his part in it that was gross,' said Susie. 'We were just silly girls, he should have known better, treated us with more respect. Imagine meeting him now – he'd be five years older, probably really decrepit.'

'We're five years older too,' said Florence. 'And he probably wasn't that much older than us. But I don't think I'd fancy him now.'

'Well, with somebody like your Cal available, you're not going to be fancying anybody else, are you?'

'Not at the moment, no, but I keep my options open.' They both laughed.

'I ran into Beth last week,' said Susie, 'at that exhibition I was telling you about, at the British Museum. She was never one of Mr Henderson's bitches, was she?'

'No' said Florence. 'She was too uptight, immature, whatever. Mr Henderson would never have noticed her.'

'She seems to be doing very well now,' said Susie. 'She's passed the first lot of her Bar exams and she's doing some research project which might turn into a book. Something on grooming, I think.'

'Yes, I did hear about that,' said Florence. 'Good for her. I think my project's going to make more money.'

'So when are you moving in with him then?'

Florence rolled her eyes. 'His sister's sharing his flat at the moment, so we have to find somewhere else for her. He says she's looking for somewhere, but it's not happening. Don't know why - she has a good job and enough money of her own. Actually, I do know why. She's just one of those needy people, no good on her own, and he's too kind to tell her to leave.'

'You'll just have to find her a man,' said Susie.

'I've thought of that, but it won't be easy. She's old and not that much to look at. Nobody's really going to fancy her.'

'But she can't be that old. What do you mean – thirty? Thirty-five? If she has money and a good job, lots of guys will be interested in her, even at that age.'

'What, just for her money? That seems awful.'

'It's not awful, it's a fact of life. If she's financially secure, that makes her eligible. A lot of guys really fancy older women, they think they have experience, or whatever. And if they have a good job and money, that's a bonus. You should help her out, do her a really good Tinder profile, with some great airbrushed photos. Then give her a makeover, you know all about that. She's bound to attract at least one good prospect. That will solve the problem. Everybody wins.'

'That's not a bad idea' said Florence.

Chapter Forty-One

WILCOX WASN'T EXPECTING any miracle breakthrough to result from a return trip to the Jobcentre, but, having agreed to go, he was giving it his best shot. The supervisor in the too-tight skirt was surprised to be getting another visit.

'I just don't think there's any more we can tell you.'

'Sometimes,' said Wilcox, 'people suddenly remember something ages after the event and these insights can be very helpful. So I'd just like to talk to everybody again.'

'Stella's not in today' she said, 'but you can talk to Romy and Jasmin, if that's any good.'

'That will be great, thank you,' said Wilcox. It wasn't great of course, it was crap, because the only person who knew Amy well was apparently Stella. But he might as well see if he could get anything out of the other two, now that he was here.

Romy shuffled in sideways and sat down carefully as if trying to minimise the amount of space she was taking up. Wilcox found this an interesting contrast to most of the aggressive and opinionated young women that he encountered on a daily basis.

'There's nothing to worry about,' he began. 'I realise Stella is the person who knew Amy best, but she's not here today so I'm hoping you can help.'

She smiled uncertainly. 'I'll do my best.'

'Great,' said Wilcox in what he hoped was a bracing manner. 'Now can you just tell me what Amy's job entailed, to begin with.'

Romy seemed on safe ground here and gave him a detailed rundown of all the backroom and client-facing tasks which the four of them performed on a rotating basis.

'So would you say Amy pulled her weight?'

She hesitated a moment and crossed her long, skinny legs. 'Up to about two months ago, she definitely did, she was often the last to leave in the evening, but I would say that recently she was losing interest. She often complained that the work was boring. Well, it is, to be honest.'

'Do you think she was looking for another job?'

'Yes, I think so. I walked past her desk one day last week and saw a job application form up on her screen.'

'Could you see the name of the company?'

'No, that would have been further up the screen.'

'Could you see what type of job it was?'

'It was one of those fashion jobs. Brand awareness assistant, merchandising junior, something like that.'

'So she wanted to work in fashion?'

'Yes, she was interested in clothes, make-up, all that stuff.' Romy said this as if clothes and make-up had no relevance to her own life.

'Did she talk to you about it?'

'Not much, to be honest. I guess she knew I wasn't that interested.'

'How about social media? Was she following people in fashion?'

'I think that's very likely. She spent a lot of time on her phone.'

'Did she ever mention these influencers?' He brough out his phone and showed her the Flo & Cal Instagram page.

She shook her head regretfully. 'No, not to me.'

'And can you remember anything about that last day you saw her at the office? Did her manner seem different, like she had plans, anything like that?'

'She was just the same as usual. She spent quite a bit of time on her phone and she was in a good mood. I thought maybe she was going for an interview that evening, or a date, but obviously not. It's awful, what happened.'

'That's for sure,' said Wilcox. 'Thank you for your help, Romy.'

'You're welcome'. She flashed him a quick smile and left.

Jasmin was a much more familiar type – a stocky girl in a short skirt and heavy boots who marched in and fixed him with a challenging stare. He wondered whether her parents had named her in the expectation that she would grow up to be delicate and fragrant. So much for that.

'Thank you for your time, Jasmin,' he said. 'I know you saw my colleague a few days ago, but I'm just here to see if you've remembered anything else in the meantime.'

'If I had I'd have got in touch, wouldn't I?'

'I guess that's right,' said Wilcox. 'I'm really here on the assumption that, as one of your colleagues is tragically dead, you would want to give any help you could to the enquiry.'

'Do your job for you, you mean?'

'No. That's not what I have in mind. I don't think you'd

be able to do my job. It demands a certain degree of empathy.'

A few seconds went by as she digested this and then she smiled unexpectedly. 'Sorry,' she said. 'I deserved that. I can be a bit aggressive sometimes.'

'No problem,' said Wilcox. 'Is there anything you can tell me about Amy, or what was going on in her life? She doesn't seem to have had a boyfriend.'

'If she did, she never mentioned him, and I think she would have done. Amy was educated, or educated enough to work here anyway, but not very smart. I don't think she would have been good at picking men. She was the sort of person who would get taken in by a scammer, because it wouldn't occur to her to disbelieve anything she was told.'

'Do you think she spent a lot of time on social media?'

'Yes, of course, but then so does everybody else.'

'Has she ever mentioned these people?' he showed her one of the videos on the Flo & Cal site.

Jasmin smiled. 'Flo and Cal,' she said musingly after a few moments. 'What are they like? Don't they just love themselves? But the dynamic's strange don't you think? I'd say she's keener on him than he is on her. Or his attention's somewhere else. He's going through the motions.'

Wilcox was intrigued. 'How can you tell?'

'I dunno. I guess from how they look at each other. That's how it looks to me anyway. I'm probably just a cynical bitch.'

'A bit of cynicism never goes amiss,' said Wilcox. 'But you never heard Amy talk about them?'

She shook her head. 'No, she's never mentioned them, not to me anyway, but that's just the sort of crappy influencer site she'd have followed. Probably bought the products too. But this wouldn't have anything to do with her death, would it?'

He put his phone away. 'Probably not, but we're looking at all angles. Did you know she was looking for another job?'

She laughed. 'We're all looking for another job. I'm sure she was too.'

'Well, that's all my questions' said Wilcox. 'Thank you for your help.'

She nodded. 'No worries. I hope you get him.'

'You think it's a him?'

'Of course it's a him. Woman don't kill each other.'

'I guess not. Not often anyway. Thank you, Jasmin.'

She smiled and stomped out.

Chapter Forty-Two

MURPHY WASN'T sure how much more information she could obtain from Alison Weaver but, in the absence of any more promising leads, she decided to pay her another visit.

Alison's face when she opened the door reflected the same thought. 'I'm not sure what more I can tell you,' she began.

'Nor am I,' said Murphy. 'But there are a few points you might be able to help me with.'

Politeness demanded that Alison let her in and offer her a seat, so she did. In this respect, Murphy thought, middle-class people were trapped in social norms that prevented them from saying 'Fuck off' and slamming the door. Whereas the people she normally got to deal with had no such inhibitions.

'I wanted to ask you about the funeral,' said Murphy.

Alison slumped back in her seat. 'The funeral. Will we ever get to the end of this? The funeral is usually the endpoint. It's supposed to bring some kind of closure.'

'I think it does for most people,' said Murphy, 'and I'm sorry it's not been like that for you, but I think you deserve to know what happened.'

'I know what happened. He fell under a train. It was probably an accident. If he hadn't fallen under a train, he would have died a painful, lingering death from liver cancer. Maybe that would have been worse, I don't know. He may have been robbed of months of life. Part of me feels angry about that but part of me is shamefully relieved. Because I know the strain and suffering that was waiting for all of us – him, me and the kids – further down the line, and I'm starting to feel grateful that we've been spared that. Sounds awful, doesn't it?'

'No, it sounds completely understandable. Most people in your situation would feel exactly the same.'

'The other point is,' Alison continued, 'that while he was still here, I was never willing to look ahead to the time when he wouldn't be here. I never thought about the decisions that would have to be made.'

'What sort of decisions?'

'Well, when Florence goes there will only be me here and can I really go on rattling around in this big house on my own?'

'Are you thinking of selling the house?'

'Yes. I think if Richard had still been around, we would have sold the house, given some money to the children and just gone travelling. I was really looking forward to it, for however long we had. Now I don't know what to do. I feel I should be making sensible decisions, but in some way I'm not sure what's sensible and what isn't. I don't think either of the children are mature enough yet to be given a sum of money and to be able to do the right thing with it. Although it's true that most young people who have trust funds or whatever gain access at 21, so maybe I'm being unfair.'

'I think,' said Murphy, 'that those sorts of decisions are best postponed. They say, whoever they are, that you shouldn't make major decisions when you are suffering from stress or trauma and a bereavement is pretty traumatic. I just have two simple questions for you.'

Alison nodded. 'OK. Go ahead.'

'The girl who came to Italy with you – Beth – I didn't see her at the funeral.'

Alison shook her head. 'I would have invited her but Florence and Beth seemed to have lost touch with each other. She didn't seem interested in inviting Beth, so I left it.'

'Alright,' said Murphy. 'And here's my other question. At the service, about three rows behind you, there was a group of people from SCB. Three of them I recognised, but there was another man and a woman with them and I thought you might know who they are.'

'The only person from Richard's work that I knew was Roger. I don't know who the rest of them were.'

'In that case Roger must have been the man I hadn't met. Any idea about the woman?'

'No, I don't remember seeing a woman with him.'

'Was Roger a close colleague?'

'I guess he was Richard's boss, really, although they always seemed more like friends. Roger was in charge of the trading floor. So he was Richard's boss before he moved to M&A. Roger Sissons.'

'At that moment they heard the front door opening, followed by murmured voices and then Florence appeared, trailing a young man with a stubble-shadowed jaw and deep blue eyes. Really, thought Murphy, he didn't look bad in the flesh. No photoshopping needed here. Florence's face when she saw Murphy was thunderous.

'Oh, I didn't know you had…' she began pointedly.

Politeness now demanded that Murphy announce that she was just leaving and get up and take herself off. She decided to do no such thing.

'Don't mind me,' she said cheerfully.

'This must be Cal,' said Alison, as if she had not noticed the sudden frosting over of the atmosphere.

'That's me,' he said and advanced to shake her hand, while Florence glowered next to him.

'Miranda Murphy,' Murphy announced and half-rose to shake his hand in her turn.

'OK, well we'll be upstairs,' Florence announced and dragged him off.

'That's an attractive young man,' said Murphy, when she was sure they were out of earshot.

'Yes, isn't he?' Alison replied. 'I'm glad I get to meet him at last.'

'They look happy together,' said Murphy, thinking that Florence had looked anything but happy. 'Did she meet him at work?'

Alison shook her head. 'I don't think so. The only job she's got is in the coffee shop. I don't know how they met. But I think she's planning some sort of business venture with him.'

'They're all very entrepreneurial these days, aren't they?' said Murphy.

'Yes, so many new businesses springing up. That's what I tell my students. There are far more opportunities available now than just those offered by a nine to five job.' She rose and Murphy decided to take the hint this time.

As she headed down towards the tube station she

wondered why Alison Weaver, who dealt with young people all the time, was so unaware of her daughter's presence on Instagram. Or was she? Maybe it was something she didn't want to enquire into. One thing was for sure. If her father had taken a good look at that site, he'd probably have had something to say about it. And something to say about Cal too.

Chapter Forty-Three

MURPHY HADN'T SEEN Amy Horsfall's parents since her initial meeting with them and, seeing them now at the inquest, she was struck by the physical change they had undergone. Both of them looked thinner and more insubstantial and she watched with compassion their slow, hunched progress towards the nearest seats.

This was what losing a child did to you, she thought, experiencing the momentary pang of guilt common to all those whose children are safe and well. This was a good enough reason to make damn sure she brought this one to justice.

The only evidence was being given by officials. There were no other interested parties. She was worried to note that the journalist in attendance looked familiar. It was the same one that she had seen at Richard Weaver's inquest. What were the odds that he would tie the two cases together? It was a possibility, due to the Rohypnol. Hopefully, he'd attended a number of other inquests in the interim, and with a bit of luck he'd get tied up in his game.

The first evidence came from a member of the river police, who described finding Amy's body and bringing it out of the river, with her handbag still attached. Murphy saw Sandra Horsfall's shoulders heaving and knew that she was crying.

Linda Fleming had sent along her deputy, a dour young man called Frank, who told the coroner that river water had been found in the lungs. It was not possible to say what section of the river the water had come from, but the cause of death was definitely drowning. He acknowledged that the Rohypnol would have made it much harder for her to swim – that and being fully clothed. The newshound perked up at this. Murphy swore under her breath.

Wilcox then took the stand and explained that police enquiries were still ongoing. The coroner returned an open verdict, which was, Murphy acknowledged, all he could do in the circumstances.

Murphy caught up with Sandra Horsfall in the corridor outside. 'I'm sorry we don't have any closure for you yet' she said, 'but I want you to know that we will find the person responsible for this. Sometimes it just takes a bit of time.'

Sandra nodded and her husband squeezed her shoulders. 'I don't know whether knowing who did it will make it any better' she said. 'But at least we can bury her now.'

'That's right,' said Murphy. 'We'll be in touch.'

She left the building and immediately saw the journalist leaning against the wall and stabbing at his phone. The pressure would be on now.

Chapter Forty-Four

MURPHY WAS PLEASED to get another chance to go up in the lift at the Gherkin. 'Otherwise, we'd have to pay to get in here,' she told Wilcox. 'If we just came as members of the public.'

He nodded. 'Goes up at six metres per second,' he told her. 'Forty-one floors.'

'Pity we're only going to Floor 10' she said, as the lift stopped and they stepped out.

James Sisson's office was in the centre of a large open-plan area, full of desks and people sitting at laptops. He was a well-built man in late middle-age and Murphy remembered his back view from the funeral.

'So this is where millions are made and lost' she said.

He nodded. 'Not so much of the lost, I hope – or not on my watch.'

'You knew Richard Weaver for a long time,' said Murphy.

'Yes. About twelve years. I poached him from Credit Milan and it was the best deal I ever did.'

'He was a good trader?' said Wilcox.

'He was a phenomenal trader. Nerves of steel. And he had a lot of contacts. People don't make friends much in this industry, but he did. Nobody ever refused his calls.'

'So you must have been sorry to lose him,' said Murphy.

'Very sorry,' he said. 'Sorry because for me he was a friend, we knew each other's families. We lost him initially when his cancer was diagnosed and he moved to M&A. But then we lost him again- permanently. For all of us here it's been very sad.'

'Do you think it's possible,' said Wilcox, 'that he committed suicide?'

'Definitely not. He had a lot of courage; he would have seen it through to the end. Apart from anything else, suicide would have invalidated his life insurance, and he would have thought about that.'

'How do you think his family coped with his diagnosis?' asked Murphy.

Roger Sissons shrugged. 'I don't really know. I didn't see so much of him after he transferred to M&A and when I did see him, we didn't discuss his illness. He really didn't want to talk about it. I asked after Alison a few times but he just said she was fine.'

'How about his children. Do you think he worried about them?'

'I'm sure he did, and he probably wondered if they would be OK after he had gone, but he never said much about it. Actually, I'm sure he thought they'd be OK – they both had a good education after all.'

'You were at the funeral, I think,' said Murphy.

'I was, yes. Were you there? Yes, I suppose you would be. I was very impressed by Jake – his dad would have been proud of him.'

'Yes, he did very well,' said Murphy. 'You were with a woman, I think. Was that your wife?'

He smiled. 'Oh no, that was Janice. Janice Fuller. She's our office manager. Janice has known Richard as long as I have, so she wanted to be at the funeral.'

'Could we speak to her?'

'Of course. I'll go and find her.'

He returned a few moments later with a conservatively-dressed middle-aged woman and tactfully withdrew, shutting the door.

'Thank you for seeing us Ms Fuller,' said Murphy. 'We're investigating Richard Weaver's death, so we're talking to everybody who knew him.'

'Of course,' she said. 'I'm happy to help.'

'Mr Sissons said you knew Richard Weaver a long time,' said Murphy. 'Do you think you knew him well?'

'Oh no, well I mean I knew him well as a colleague, so yes, in that respect. He was very well thought of.' Her hands came to rest in her lap and Murphy thought she could see them shaking, just slightly.

'It must have been a shock for his friends when his cancer was diagnosed.'

Janice Fuller nodded emphatically. 'It was, for all of us. And very sad for him. And his family.'

'When you first heard about his death, did you think he had committed suicide?'

'No, of course not. He wouldn't have done that.'

'Why not?' said Wilcox.

'Well ... he was more... resilient than that. He had plans.'

'Plans?'

She swallowed. 'He wanted to go travelling. With his wife. That sort of thing. Visiting countries that they'd never been to. He told me that. He wasn't just waiting to die.'

'Understood,' said Murphy. 'Did he have any enemies that you knew about? People angry with him over deals, anything like that?'

'No, nobody. This is a very competitive environment but all's fair among dealers. Everybody knows that. It doesn't give rise to personal animosities.'

'And no information from M&A finds its way over here?'

'Absolutely not.' She frowned. 'Has somebody made that allegation?'

'No, not to us. But it's something we have to ask about.'

'As far as I'm aware it's not an issue. We have very robust protocols.'

'That's good,' said Murphy. 'Is there anything else you can tell us about Richard, what was going on in his life, anything like that?'

She hesitated and then shook her head. 'No, I can't think of anything else.'

'Well thank you for your time' said Murphy and they headed back to the lift.

'So she was in love with him,' said Wilcox, as they shot down at six metres per second.

'I would say so,' said Murphy. 'But that might not mean very much. It would only be relevant if it was reciprocated.'

Wilcox shook his head. 'It couldn't possibly have been reciprocated. His wife is really good-looking and this woman is – well you just wouldn't notice her, would you?'

'But it's not just about that,' said Murphy. 'He would have noticed her, because he worked with her every day. And even if you're married to somebody very attractive, they appear a lot less attractive after twenty years. I'll tell you that for nothing.'

'You really think he could have been having an affair with her?'

'Well it's a possibility I'm not discounting for the moment.'

'I NEED you to write up a progress report for the DCI' said Murphy, as they entered the station. 'He demanded it yesterday and I've been putting it off.'

Wilcox pulled his chair out and slumped into it. 'On the case? What am I going to say?'

'Anything that will keep him off our backs for a day or so. Use your initiative. No lies, but maybe a few long technical words that he won't understand. If that cub reporter suggests any link between the two deaths, stuff will start hitting the fan, so we need to demonstrate that we're getting somewhere – even if we're not.'

He nodded and went back to looking at his phone.

'What are you looking at?'

'Flo & Cal' he said. 'Jasmin at the Jobcentre said that Flo was keener on Cal than he was on her, so I'm just looking at their latest video.' He handed her one of the earbuds and they looked together. 'The video I showed Jasmin was from a few months ago' he said. 'It was just one I picked at random. It looks to me as if he's a bit keener on her now, and she's looking a bit stroppy. But that could just be a temporary thing, like she's pissed off about something.'

Murphy nodded. 'Yes. I wouldn't think it takes a lot to piss her off. It's a good idea to monitor these two, although I can't see how they fit into everything.'

Wilcox tapped it off. 'I had a thought' he said, 'after seeing Amy's mum at the inquest. She mentioned speed dating and so did somebody else. We haven't looked into it.'

'That's right, we haven't,' said Murphy. 'But how do we know which one she went to?'

'Bank records' said Wilcox. 'People book and pay online.'

Within minutes he had tracked it down to the Revolution Bar on the Goldhawk Road. 'The event is run by DateLondon,' he said. 'Every Wednesday night.'

'That's tonight,' said Murphy. 'You can go along and check it out.'

Wilcox's face froze. 'What? Me?'

'Yes, you. You're the right demographic. You can learn how to chat up a girl in four minutes, it will be good practice for you.'

'That's sexist.'

'OK we'll send one of the female PCs with you. You can take Amy's picture and see if you get anywhere. I'll ask Avril, she'll appreciate the overtime.'

'They won't be the same people who were there when Amy went' said Wilcox, who appeared to be regretting his burst of initiative.

'Probably not, but the organisers might remember her. It's a long shot, but I agree that we should pursue it. I'd like to see you being a bit more enthusiastic about this. You can put the drinks on expenses.'

Chapter Forty-Five

WILCOX COULD SEE that police constable Avril Daley was delighted to be getting a free night out and the chance to do a bit of what she described as 'undercover work'.

'It's not undercover' he told her repressively. 'We're not hiding the fact that we're police. We're just making a bit of an effort to blend in. Why I'm not sure,' he added, looking at Avril's tight T-shirt and distressed jeans.

'We're making a bit of an effort to blend in because that gets us more co-operation from the organisers,' Avril told him. 'If we went clodhopping in there in uniform it would put the punters off. You don't seem very enthusiastic about this Kevin. We need to give it our best shot.'

'Right' said Wilcox, leading the way down the stairs with a confidence he didn't feel. He was annoyed with Avril, for no good reason that he could work out, and he felt as if he was turning up without his authority. It wasn't the lack of a uniform; he was plain clothes anyway. It was the 'blending in' bit. If he was with Murphy there would have been no chance of blending in, she was really not a blender. They'd just have been there as cops and that would have been fine. Although Murphy would have thrown herself into it in a way that he felt unable to do. The visit may have yielded something or nothing – probably nothing – but Murphy would at least have extracted a bit of enjoyment out of it.

At the bottom of the stairs, they were engulfed by dim lighting, background music and a lot of bodies crammed into a small space. Wilcox hoped all the fire regs were being complied with. The organiser was called Daisy and when they enquired behind the bar they were directed to a large woman in a kaftan with pink hair, who shook her head as they approached.

'I'm sorry' she said. 'This event is only for people who have booked in advance. They should have told you that at the door.'

'They did,' said Wilcox, showing his badge.

She immediately ushered them through a doorway. 'What is this?' she hissed. 'A raid? We've haven't broken any laws.'

'We're not aware of any laws being broken here,' said Wilcox. 'We're here to ask for your help.'

He handed her a picture of Amy. 'This young woman came to two of your events here, and we are now anxious to trace any contacts she may have made.'

'Has something happened to her?'

'Yes. She's dead.'

She was silent for a moment. 'You're thinking this may be something to do with somebody she met here?'

'It's just a possibility we're looking into.'

She pulled out chairs and they sat down. 'Let me tell you how this works. When people book, we have their email address and phone number. The people who meet here do not have any of that information about each other. The name badges just have a forename – that's all they know. Afterwards they let us know if they would like to link up with anybody they met. If we get a mutual request, that's a match and we give the parties concerned each other's contact details. Otherwise, we don't give out those contact details to anybody.'

'But you will have a record of matches' said Avril.

'That's right,' said Daisy. 'There aren't so many of them. We have twenty people in tonight and I'd expect about two or three matches. You want to know whether this girl was matched with anybody? What's the name?'

'Amy Horsfall.'

'OK. Let's have a look.' She powered up a Macbook, and they stared over her shoulder. 'Here she is. She was at two events a fortnight apart. Actually, you can see here that we did get a request from her regarding one of the men she met, but no request from him, so no details were passed on. That's it.'

'Well thanks for your help,' said Wilcox. He turned to Avril. 'OK, I think we're done here.'

'Poor Amy,' said Avril on the way out. 'The guy she fancied probably wasn't up to much anyway.'

'No,' said Wilcox, watching fascinated as the buzzer rang and the contestants moved around the circle to their next allotted encounter. 'But maybe if she'd had a boyfriend, any sort of boyfriend, things would have turned out differently.'

'Does no good to think like that,' said Avril robustly as they emerged into the night air. 'Didn't DI Murphy say we could put drinks on expenses?'

Chapter Forty-Six

AMY HORSFALL'S funeral took place the following morning in the Enfield parish church near where her parents lived. Murphy had come alone; Wilcox having arrived at the office just as she was leaving and looking very much the worse for wear. It didn't seem respectful to bring somebody to a funeral who looked like they'd already been at the wake and drunk all the supplies.

Murphy was surprised to see such a large turnout; enquiries so far having given the impression that Amy had very few friends. The church was almost full. Some of the people there must be relatives, she decided, some of them looked like schoolfriends and some of them wore T-shirts bearing the name of a dog shelter.

The vicar opened the service by recalling that Amy had been a member of the church choir. Her father spoke about his daughter and how much they would miss her. Then a woman from the dog shelter spoke about how much help Amy had given over the years and how much the dogs loved her. Murphy found herself really wishing Amy Horsfall had stayed up in Enfield, where people cared about and valued her, rather than drifting down to London where she seemed to have been regarded as something of a sad case – a girl with no boyfriend and no street cred.

Following the cremation there was a gathering at the Horsfall house, which Murphy decided to attend. The idea that a murderer would attend the victim's funeral was always a possibility, but she hadn't seen anybody in the church who fitted the bill. Although what was the bill? Anybody could push somebody else in the river; this perpetrator would look no different to anybody else. Nonetheless, there might be some information to be picked up from the attendees.

Despite her grief, Sandra Horsfall, had managed to lay on an impressive amount of food and drink. Murphy hoped she'd had lots of help. The first person she managed to engage in conversation was the woman from the dog shelter, who was juggling a plate, a fork and a cup of coffee and was therefore in no position to escape.

'The sad thing is' she said, 'Amy was actually a good swimmer. She did a sponsored swim for us a few years ago.'

'I think being fully dressed would have made it a lot harder,' said Murphy. 'And there are dangerous currents in the river.'

'It's just a tragedy,' said the woman. 'She always stayed in touch, even after she left home. We're always short of funds and she promised to help promote the shelter, get us some publicity. I'm sure she would have done too. I just hope they get whoever did it.'

'Yes, so do I,' said Murphy.

BACK IN THE CID room Wilcox was staring intently at his screen.

'So, are you feeling any better?'

He grunted. 'A bit.' He shook his head. 'Avril can really put them away.'

Murphy laughed. 'Yes, she'll go far. A woman who can hold her beers. So did you learn anything?'

'Nothing useful. Amy was at two events. Nobody asked for her details, so they were not supplied to anybody. She asked for one guy's details, but he didn't ask for hers, so no details were passed over. And we know she was alive for at least a week after the second event, so it's not a case of somebody following her from it or whatever. These contact details are kept securely of course, GDPR and whatever, so we'd need a good case to get a court order requiring them to hand over details for everybody who was present at these two functions. And I can't see that there's any connection.'

'No, maybe we hold that in abeyance for the time being. There were a lot of people at the funeral and she was highly thought of, she sang in the choir, helped at the dog shelter. There are always more aspects to people than the ones we get to take into account. Anyway, what are you doing now?'

'I'm checking to see whether this Cal has come across our radar before,' he explained. 'Obviously we don't have a name, but I'm checking mugshots in London, Caucasian, in the right age group. It's a bit of a long shot, nothing so far. The system couldn't match his face up, but a lot of these faces are obscured by beards and there are some features he could have changed.'

'You mean he could have had Botox?'

'Well maybe not that, but he could have changed hair colour, eye colour, added tattoos, whatever. Actually, yes, I think he could have had Botox, apparently some men do.'

'Fascinating,' said Murphy, remembering a beautician telling her that most men couldn't even cope with waxing.

Wilcox carried on scrolling through them, the bad, the worse and the ugly. 'Wait. Stop' said Murphy. 'What about him?'

'He doesn't look anything like Cal.'

Murphy squinted. 'But there's something about him, that expression, that sort of 'aren't I great?' look.'

'Well, they all have that,' said Wilcox. 'Standard criminal attitude. Look, if you compare it to the Instagram picture, there are too many differences. Look at the nose – this guy's nose has a kink.'

'Nose job,' said Murphy.

'And this guy has light brown eyes, our Instagram pin-up has blue ones.'

'Contact lenses.'

'OK. Look at the skin. It's quite rough, blackheads, whatever. Not like smooth-skinned Mr Instagram.'

Murphy smiled. 'I'll tell you why. Mr Instagram is wearing make-up.'

'No way.'

'I tell you he is. Remember I've met this guy and his eyes are very blue but his skin in the flesh is not matte and flawless – it's just like in the mugshot.'

'You really think this is him?'

'I'm certain of it. I'm good on faces. What's his name?'

'Derek Fletcher. Age 30. That means he'd now be 32. Looks younger than that on his Instagram profile.'

'Yes, well he's had work done, we can see that. What do we have him on file for?'

'Let's see. Something two years ago. Looks like he was investigated over the death of a girlfriend. She died of an overdose. He was not charged over the death, for some reason, but he was convicted of supplying her with drugs, which is why we still have him on file.'

'That's interesting,' said Murphy. 'Nothing like a bit of previous to get the grey cells working. Let's get all the details.'

Chapter Forty-Seven

FLORENCE LOVED the flat in Shoreditch. It was just off the Bethnal Green Road, near to Brick Lane, surely the hippest part of London right now – cool bars, music venues, street food. And, of course, the flower market in Columbia Road, which was her favourite place to visit on a Sunday. She wandered slowly past the stalls, sipping a coffee, stopping to grab an armful of sunflowers that were being sold off cheap.

Cal's flat was in a converted warehouse which had previously been a vinegar factory. Florence loved the heavy front door but hated the fact that she had to use the entryphone. Surely, she should have a key? Cal answered immediately and Florence remembered that Lindy was away for the weekend. So that was all good.

She ran up the stairs, kissed him and went to get a vase for the flowers. Sunlight was streaming through the full-length windows and the sunflowers looked amazing against the exposed brickwork and the pale grey floorboards. She put one between her teeth and took a quick selfie. The flat behind her looked so cool. The only problem with the place was, she wasn't living in it.

'OK, let's get these pictures done and then we can go out for lunch' said Cal, giving her a hug.

Florence picked the bits of leaf out of her mouth and got changed, while he arranged the background.

'Did you think any more about what I said?' she asked as she posed with weights in leggings and a sports bra that was so difficult to get into that she would probably have to be cut out of it. How did people with big tits wear these things? With a lot of discomfort, probably.

Cal was fiddling with his lenses. 'What you said about what?'

'About me moving in here. About Lindy moving out.'

'It's all in hand,' he said, attaching a filter. 'We just need the money to start coming in and then we can put a deposit down on a flat for Lindy.'

'I would have thought the money for the TantoGo campaign should have come in by now,' said Florence. 'You signed the contract, I made two videos about the product, as agreed. Lindy will have invoiced them. What more do they need? They should have paid us.'

'It doesn't work like that, babe. They had to send us a purchase order and then we sent them an invoice and then that has to be approved for payment their end. That probably takes a few days, then their payment policy could be payment after 60 days, or even 90 days and after that time they will pay, but it might have to wait a fortnight or longer for the next payment run. In big organisations all this stuff takes a lot of time.'

Florence didn't know what to say. Who knew that Cal knew so much about payment procedures? Then something else slid into her brain.

'But surely Lindy can afford her own deposit?'

His expression hardened. 'Lindy has invested everything she has in the business – our business.'

Florence picked up the dumbells and held them over her head. 'So eventually we'll have to buy her out?'

He smiled. 'Exactly. We'll all have lots of money by then. Buying her out won't be a problem. Now lean towards me and pout. And again. That's good! OK, we're done with that. These are good shots.'

'You may have to help me out of this bra.'

'I can probably do that.' He put his arms round her and they fell backwards onto the bed.

Chapter Forty-Eight

WILCOX YAWNED. 'OK, here it is. Finally. I think indexing procedures back then were really not up to scratch. Two years ago. A girl called Kelly Wilson died towards the end of a night clubbing. Club called Voodoo Cave in Walthamstow. Collapsed and died in hospital. Post-mortem found a large amount of MDMA in her bloodstream – about the equivalent of six ecstasy tablets. Not necessarily fatal but, in her case, combined with quite a lot of alcohol and several hours energetic dancing in a hot club, it unfortunately was. Catastrophic impact on the heart.

She was with her boyfriend, who had also taken ecstasy, but a much smaller amount. He said he bought the drug, just two tabs and they took one tablet each. He had no idea why she had such a large amount in her bloodstream. So he said. One Derek Fletcher. All the police could charge him with was supplying an illegal substance. Her parents wanted him charged with manslaughter, but that was never going to fly. It doesn't explain why. I'd have thought they'd have had a good case.'

'Who was the investigating officer?' asked Murphy.

'One DS Shirley Fraser. Looks like she's now based in Harrow.'

'Give her a ring. See if we can come and see her.'

DS SHIRLEY FRASER was a sharp-suited woman in her early 30s. Graduate intake and a healthy dose of ambition to have made DS so young, Murphy surmised. Which meant the failure to get anybody into court over the death of Kelly Wilson must have really rankled.

'So here he is again,' she said with satisfaction, looking at the picture of Derek. 'He's scrubbed up a bit, but I always felt he'd be a person of interest again at some point.'

'What made you think that?'

'His attitude, I guess. I mean nobody was suggesting he had to be desperately in love with her, but she was supposed to be his girlfriend. And he didn't seem particularly upset that she was dead, all he was upset about was the possibility that he might be held responsible. Kelly's parents wanted him to be charged in connection with her death, and so did I, but the CPS weren't convinced they could bring it in. I really felt we let her family down.'

'So the evidence wasn't good enough?' said Murphy

DS Fraser shook her head. 'He said he bought two tabs and they had one each and he stuck to that. We couldn't go after him for spiking her drink because it turned out they only had one drink each and she bought them. The barman remembered her; they'd exchanged a few words.'

'The cheapskate,' said Murphy.

Shirley Fraser smiled. 'Of course. As far as I remember she was the one with the job and he described himself as a freelance photographer, or something like that – effectively unemployed.'

'Were there any other suspects?' asked Wilcox.

'Not that we could identify. By the time she fell ill, some of the punters had already left and those who remained couldn't tell us much – off their faces, most of them. One or two of them thought they remembered noticing her earlier and at least one said they'd seen her chatting to other girls, presumably while Derek was in the loo, but none of these girls who apparently chatted to her were around when we arrived and nobody knew who they were, if they even existed. Drug dealers don't hang around for the dancing. Once everybody's sorted, they're off, so we could never find the source of the drugs she took. Basically, nobody there could tell us anything useful. It was a mess.'

'So it could possibly have been someone else who slipped the drugs into her drink?' said Murphy. 'If we were playing devil's advocate.'

'It could, I suppose, and it could even have been Kelly herself, if she decided she wanted to get really high and didn't understand how dangerous it was. Those were the possibilities that freaked out the CPS. Plus, there was a heart condition. You'll see that in the case notes.'

'Well, our enquiry is probably not going to obtain any justice for Kelly,' said Murphy, 'but we'll definitely be giving him our close attention in respect of Amy.'

'Go for it,' said Shirley. 'I hope you turn something up.'

'I HOPE we turn something up too' said Wilcox as they drove back, 'but he seems like the sort of guy that's good at wriggling out of things. And what if we're wrong, and it's nothing to do with him?'

'If it's nothing to do with him, he sure has a way of innocently cropping up in the middle of things. I'm not a big believer in coincidence, so I'm assuming he's involved somehow. He might look prettier these days, but he's still the same lowlife that Shirley Fraser couldn't stick anything to. Now he's recreated himself as Cal – photographer, influencer, wearer of Bondego His'n Hers jeans and lifestyle pioneer. And there's probably a few other tasteless things we can add to the charge sheet. Do we have any grounds for outing him to anybody – like Alison Weaver?'

Wilcox shook his head. 'You know we don't. Florence is old enough to do what she likes, whatever her parents say, and if we approached him, he'd whine about police harassment. That would just buy them more followers, wouldn't it?'

Murphy nodded. 'Maybe. But there's a lot of substance abuse here isn't there? Kelly Wilson, Richard Weaver, Amy Horsfall. Can we tie them all together?'

'Cal is connected to Kelly Wilson and to Richard Weaver through Florence – even if he and Richard never met. Can we connect him to Amy? Can we connect him to the tube station?'

'We might be able to,' said Murphy. 'Let's go back and see Winona Francis.'

Chapter Forty-Nine

THE MOTORBIKE WAS STILL PARKED in the hallway at Winona Francis's house, but a sizeable part of it appeared to be missing. Venturing further inside, they saw the missing section reclining on the kitchen table on a bed of newspapers, being worked on by a well-built young man in oily jeans.

'Gasket?' said Wilcox, and the young man nodded ruefully.

'Take up more space than a baby, motorbikes' said his mother, coming in behind them. 'And they make more noise.'

'I'm sorry to interrupt your evening,' said Murphy. 'But can we just show you a few pictures?'

'Of course. Come next door.'

They sat on the sofa and Wilcox produced the police mugshot and the Instagram feed.

'Looks like two different people,' said Winona. 'You're sure this is the same person?'

'We're satisfied it's the same person,' said Murphy. 'But,

as you can see, he's upgraded his appearance quite a bit. Now if you passed him in the street he wouldn't look quite as good as he does on Instagram. The complexion might be a bit more like in this picture here.'

'Wait, let me get my glasses.' She fetched them from the top of the TV. 'Ok, now they look more alike, they have some of the same features, and the expression is the same.' She stared for a few more minutes. 'It is the same person, I can see that now, and he does look familiar. I've seen him somewhere.'

Murphy forced herself to remain silent as Winona stared at the images. Finally, after what can only have been a few seconds, she looked up.

'Yes, he was there.'

'At the tube station?'

'Yes. It was definitely him.'

'Whereabouts did you see him?'

'He was standing quite close to me when it happened. I think he had been one of those people trying to shove their way to the front, but it was impossible, there were too many people. So I suppose he had given up and stayed where he was.'

Murphy tried to keep the disappointment out of her voice. 'So he wasn't near where it happened?'

'No, he was several rows back.'

'And he wasn't the person in the hoodie who bent down?'

'No, they were two different people.' She looked at them both. 'That wasn't the answer you wanted, was it?'

'Well, I guess we did get our hopes up,' said Murphy. 'But the facts are the facts and that's what we have to work with. Thank you for your help, Winona.'

They walked out slowly and Wilcox unlocked the car. 'It

might not be what we wanted, but it does get us further in one respect,' he said. 'We have now made the connection between our friend Cal – sorry Derek - and the third victim. They were both on the platform at Moorgate. So he's now connected to three substance abuse death cases – no degrees of separation.'

'LET'S start with the Kelly Wilson case' said Murphy, 'as that was his first appearance. What other details do we have?'

Wilcox sent her the link and they both read through the case notes.

Kelly Wilson was working in a bar and saving up to travel round south east Asia. This was explained to the police by her sister, Julie Wilson. She was planning to go with Derek Fletcher, who was working in the same bar. Derek Fletcher was the son of a single mother who had little interest in him, so he effectively had no family. Kelly Wilson lived with her mother and father and younger sister and they were a close family. Kelly's parents didn't like Derek (or so they claimed after she died) but Kelly was very keen on him and wouldn't listen to any criticism.

Why didn't they like him? Murphy wondered. Nobody seemed to have asked them that question.

Kelly's sister said that for a about a week before her death Kelly had been depressed and short-tempered and Julie had thought that she had split up with Derek. Then it seemed as if everything was fine again and she went out with him for the last time.

Witnesses at the club hadn't really noticed her until she collapsed. One of the clubbers was a paramedic and she performed CPR and put Kelly in the recovery position while they waited for the ambulance. She was interviewed afterwards and said that the boyfriend seemed distraught and went with her in the ambulance. Kelly was taken to the emergency room but died a few hours later.

The pm found severe damage to the heart and her parents later confirmed that she had had rheumatic fever as a child. The pathologist told the inquest that the weakness of the heart due to rheumatic fever, coupled with the overdose of MDMA and the unusually heavy exertion had combined to produce the fatality. He was unable to say whether death would have occurred if there had been no history of rheumatic fever. The finding was death by misadventure.

Kelly's family had not been satisfied with the verdict and had asked if they could bring a civil case against Derek, but were advised that this was unlikely to yield any kind of positive result. Derek had applied to have his DNA record destroyed and that had been done.

'Strikes me' said Murphy, 'that this would be a pretty risk-free way of getting rid of somebody. You slip them a drug overdose. If it doesn't kill them, maybe they get ill and recover, nobody's going to say you were trying to kill them. The person in question won't suspect you of anything. If it works and they die, it will be very difficult to prove. It's one of those cases where we would pay a lot of attention to motive. But what motive could anybody have for wanting to get rid of Kelly Wilson?'

'Or Amy Horsfall, for that matter,' said Wilcox.

'That's right. It could only be perhaps because of something that they knew. Or something that somebody thought they knew. First of all, we have to confirm that Derek is Cal. I think we should have a word with Kelly Wilson's sister. She'll probably be a better bet than the parents, she'll have more idea what was going on. Do we have any contact details for her?'

'Nothing on file. She was at Manchester University two years ago. She might still be in that area. Let's look for her on Facebook. Loads of Julie Wilsons. I'll narrow it down to Manchester.'

He carried on scrolling while Murphy went to make a cup of tea.

'Any luck?' she asked as she wandered back.

'No... yes! I think this is her. Living in Salford. Do you want me to ring her?'

Murphy nodded and got on with drinking her tea. It would be nice to take her shoes off but they could be back on the move anytime.

Wilcox switched his phone off. 'She's a nurse now. Comes off shift at 7 tonight. She's happy to talk to us. Can we get there for 7?'

'Check the train times. I don't feel like doing the drive. Train will probably be quicker this time of day.'

Relief spread across Kevin Wilcox's face. He stabbed at his phone. Train at 4.30. Shall I buy two tickets.'

'Yes, do that,' said Murphy. Maybe she could have a quiet doze on the train.

THEY HAD RECKONED WITHOUT HALF-TERM. The first sign was the crowds massed on the platform at Euston Station.

'I suppose we don't have first-class tickets' said Murphy hopefully.

Wilcox looked shocked. 'Didn't you read that directive about travel expenses?'

'You know very well I didn't. When have I ever read any

of those bloody things? What did it say? That we have to travel on foot or by bicycle at all times and repair our own punctures?'

'Something like that.'

'Perhaps we can get into the quiet coach. Which one is it?'

'I don't think there is one. They scrapped them. Apparently, people didn't want it.'

'OK. Have we at least booked seats?'

'Yes. This way.' Wilcox swung into action and Murphy followed him down the platform cursing under her breath. So much for the nap.

By the time the train was ready to depart the noise level was such that it was impossible to speak. Wilcox produced a pair of oversized headphones and gratefully clapped them over his ears. When Murphy spoke to him, he smiled and mouthed something. When she snarled, he briefly lifted them and explained that they were noise-cancelling, so he couldn't hear anything she said. For a moment she considered pulling rank and demanding that he hand them over.

By the time they left Milton Keynes, Wilcox seemed to be gently dozing. Murphy made a point of falling against him every time the train swayed, just to keep him awake, but after a while that seemed to be a bit childish. And surely there must have been times when she took her children on trains and they drove other people mad? That being so, she should have more patience. At what point did she become a miserable old bat? In the end there was nothing to do but surrender herself to the noise, so that was what she did. Interestingly, the children were now doing like Wilcox and falling asleep and the voice that rose above all the others was an adult one located in the seat that backed onto hers.

'... I tried to tell her that, of course I did, but she won't be told. She's like, he loves me, and I'm like, Dawn, get a grip, he loves money and that's all it is. And when it's all gone you won't see him for dust. She's not having it. She thinks they're going to spend their lives together, go travelling the world, whatever. I'm like, well don't complain to me when it all goes tits-up. Gotta go, babes, getting off in a minute…'

This going travelling business, Murphy thought. Everybody was at it, or at least planning to be at it. Mentally she ticked them off. Richard and Alison Weaver, Florence Weaver, Jack and Tracey, Kelly Wilson. But none of them had actually made it out of the country yet. Was that significant?

Who the hell knew, thought Murphy, as she belatedly dropped off.

Chapter Fifty

JULIE WILSON WAS a few minutes late. 'Sorry,' she said, 'the handover took a while tonight.' She was a stocky girl with blonde hair in plaits and no-nonsense boots.

'No problem,' said Murphy, 'we're just grateful to you for agreeing to speak to us. Where should we go? I'm afraid we don't have a car here.'

Julie hesitated and then seemed to make up her mind. 'Let's go next door to the pub.'

The Queen's Head was half empty and they were able to find a table in the furthest corner. Wilcox went off to get the drinks and Murphy shuffled out of her jacket. She liked pubs, a much more grown-up venue than the coffee shops that littered every high street, with their milky-sweet aroma and the posers with laptops. Unfortunately, her working life didn't involve much in the way of meeting snouts in pubs, and the free time she could devote to socialising was minimal and usually spent catching up on the laundry.

'How long have you been nursing?' she asked.

Julie took delivery of her coke and smiled her thanks at

Wilcox. 'Just over a year. It was after what happened to Kelly. I went to the inquest and one of the paramedics gave evidence. She was about Kelly's age and she'd tried to save her life. I decided then that it was what I wanted. I wanted to be a useful, competent person, able to do something like that.'

'That sounds like a good decision,' said Murphy. 'We wanted to talk to you about Derek Fletcher, because he's cropped up again in connection with another case.'

'Another girl, you mean?'

'Yes, it is another girl. Can we just show you these pictures, make sure we have the same person?'

'That's him alright,' said Julie, looking at the police mugshot. 'I'd recognise that nose anywhere.'

Wilcox showed her the Instagram stills. Julie stared. 'Are you saying this is the same person? This is still him?'

'We think so, yes,' said Murphy. 'Calls himself Cal now. Of course, he's had a nose job and there's probably a certain amount of photoshopping gone on.'

Julie nodded slowly. 'And a lot more tattoos.'

'Do you remember any tattoos he had as Derek?'

Julie hesitated for a moment. 'I may still have a photo of him on my phone.' She began scrolling back. 'Here he is, with Kelly. I would only have kept that photo because of her. Wouldn't really want photos of him.'

They stood together against a wall with the sea at their backs, smiling at the camera as Derek held his arm out to take the selfie. 'In Spain, from what I remember,' said Julie. 'She would have sent it to me.'

'Looks like the Mediterranean,' said Murphy. The sky was blue and the sun glinted off a large watch on Derek Fletcher's wrist. 'Luckily for us, he's got his top off.'

They zoomed in on what looked like a small dragon in

the centre of his chest. Wilcox then zoomed in on the Instagram shot. A lot more tattoos, as Julie had said. And there, in the middle of them, was the same small dragon.

'Looks like that confirms it,' said Wilcox.

Julie nodded. 'Yes, I can see it now. He's really recreated himself, hasn't he?'

'Surely has,' said Murphy. 'He's love's young dream now.'

'And this girl he's posing with,' said Julie, 'she's very pretty. They have a lot of followers.'

'That's right,' said Wilcox. 'They'll be making lots of money.'

'It was clear during the investigation' said Murphy, 'that your mum and dad didn't like Derek. Do you know why?'

'My dad said he was a chancer,' said Julie. 'Only out for what he could get. He didn't seem to have a proper job, or not one that Kelly could tell them about anyway. Dad said she was probably subsidising him. Then he seemed to have finished with her and she was devastated, stopped eating, crying all the time. I think she was following him around. Just when we thought she might get over it, suddenly they were back together. And a week later she was dead. Dad said he'd probably been a drug dealer all along, but the police weren't prepared to prosecute. It was really hard on mum and dad.'

'What was Kelly's job?' said Murphy.

'She was a copywriter. I think she was quite good and she enjoyed her job. She wasn't paid a lot, but she was still learning. She worked for Anson Barnes – they're one of the big advertising agencies.'

''Do you know how she met him?'

'As far as I could gather, he'd turned up at some photographic shoot – photographer's assistant, rather than the actual photographer. But Kelly told mum and dad he was a photographer.'

'That seems to be how he's describing himself now,' said Murphy. 'That and lifestyle guru.'

Julie rolled her eyes. 'I think his lifestyle is sponging off women.'

Chapter Fifty-One

IT WAS POURING with rain when Murphy skidded into the car park the next day. She slammed the car door and then almost garrotted herself by shutting her scarf in it. Two uniformed PCs standing outside smoking were unable to keep their faces straight and she heard the laughter after she'd gone past.

Oh well, she'd brightened their morning, if not her own. They'd managed to miss the fast train back to London the previous evening, resulting in an hour waiting at Manchester Piccadilly and a journey back on a train that stopped at a multitude of places Murphy had never heard of – stations at which nobody got on or off. By the time she eventually got home she was too tired to sleep – too many thoughts and theories swirling round in her brain.

Wilcox was at his desk, looking keen and well-rested. How the hell did he manage it?

He looked up as she slumped down beside him. 'Remember I told you last week that I had an idea about that missing jewellery? Look at this.'

He pulled up an Instagram account. It showed a young woman smiling in skimpy underwear with an unmade bed in the background.

'Look at what she's wearing round her neck,' said Wilcox. 'Compare it with the photos we have here, of the stolen goods.'

Murphy frowned. 'Yes, it does look like the same piece. But it can't be. Nobody would be stupid enough to post a picture of stolen property on their Instagram page.'

'Actually, I think some people are that stupid. But she might not know it's stolen. Maybe it's just the latest gift from her boyfriend and she doesn't know it's stolen. But he wouldn't have stolen it just to give to her, he must be selling it on. Maybe he just let her borrow it to pose in, then he sold it on.'

'If somebody had lent me an expensive piece of hardware to be photographed in, I'd have at least put a decent dress on,' said Murphy. 'I wouldn't have tried to show it off in my knickers. Or does that brand me as very old?'

'I'm afraid so,' said Wilcox. 'The knickers are very much Instagram territory.'

'And how did you find this picture?'

'Well, I started looking on Instagram last week and I found a few bits I thought might be right, but they weren't. Then when I started looking through the people Amy was following, there it was. Wandagirl.'

'Can we get Wandagirl's name and address?'

'I already have. She's called Shirley Beesley and she lives in Brentwood.'

'We could pass it on to Essex police, but Bellweather will be more likely to shut up about it if we bring it in ourselves. OK, let's call her up and arrange to see her. First, we'll go along to Anson Barnes.'

ANSON BARNES OCCUPIED the first floor of a modern building in Covent Garden and they were walked through it by Samantha Wells, the HR director, a woman somewhere in her mid-30s with a whip-thin figure and blonde hair tied in a short ponytail. She was wearing trousers and a jacket which, while being baggy, still served to emphasise her slenderness. It was good tailoring, Murphy decided.

The space occupied by Anson Barnes consisted mostly of a large open-plan area with 'breakout spaces'. These were furnished with comfortable sofas, floor cushions and tables on which were laid out enormous glass jars full of confectionery. Murphy blinked. Confectionery? She spotted at least three coffee stations with proper machines *and baristas* and a sign pointed to the Play Room.

'We're in the wrong business' she told Wilcox, as they passed a breakout space in which three people were lying on the floor, all staring at one laptop.

'You're right. Unfortunately, we're in public service.'

Samantha Wells seemed delighted by their reaction. 'We've done everything we can to make the office environment happy and comfortable' she said. 'People work better that way.'

'Well, the police force is missing a trick here' said Murphy. 'Are those really marshmallows?'

'Yes, marshmallows are very popular. Would you like a coffee?'

'Yes please,' said Murphy, who thought she'd never ask.

The HR office was more akin to a normal environment, well it had to be Murphy realised, all those confidential records.

'Now you wanted to talk about Kelly Wilson?' said Samantha Wells, when they were seated at her desk.

'That's right,' said Wilcox. 'We're investigating another

case and some aspects of it might link back to Kelly's death.'

'I'm sure Kelly's death had nothing to do with her work here,' said Samantha. 'She had no problems at work, nobody was bullying her, nothing like that. We have very strict policy around bullying.'

'There's no suggestion of that,' said Murphy. 'We just want to talk to people who knew her. We spoke to her sister yesterday and she told us she had been working here. We would just be grateful if you could tell us a bit about her, and maybe there are other people here she was close to.'

Samantha nodded. 'I didn't know her well personally, only in my capacity as HR director, but she was a valued employee and we were all very shocked by what happened. Unfortunately, the person she reported to has since left. But I think she worked quite closely with Trevor. I'll go and see if he's in.'

She left the room and Murphy frowned. 'Well, she got her disclaimers in fast. I guess that's part of the HR job.'

Trevor was wearing a boiler suit and had multiple piercings, including one in his tongue, which flashed as he was speaking. He led them out to one of the breakout spaces.

'Thank you for seeing us, Trevor,' said Murphy as she sank gingerly into the sofa.

'I'm not sure I can tell you anything, to be honest,' he said. 'But I was very sorry to hear what had happened to Kelly. I liked her a lot.'

'Can you tell us a bit about her, what sort of person she was?'

'She was good at her job, very bright. And we had a lot of laughs. You have to have a bit of imagination, writing copy. Some of what you write gets used, some of it gets rejected, and you have to accept that and all the criticism that comes your way. I think we coped OK. But I don't think her personal life was going all that well. She'd be up one day, down the next and towards the end her work was suffering. I had to take over one of her accounts, they were threatening not to pay. I asked her several times if things were OK, but she didn't want to talk about it.'

'Did you meet her boyfriend?'

'Yes, he came along once or twice. We used to go for drinks a couple of times a week, a whole bunch of us, bosses and all, and he would join us. At one point I heard he might be coming to work here, but nothing came of it. Nice enough guy, but I think he must have been messing her around.'

'Do you remember his name?'

He frowned. 'Dave...no, Derek, that was it.'

'This guy here?' Wilcox showed him the police mugshot.

'That's him. Has he been arrested for something?'

'He was arrested for supplying drugs, but it was dropped.'

'When you said he was messing her around' said Murphy, 'what can you remember of that?'

'There were quite a few times when I thought she was phoning him and he wasn't picking up. Once I heard her leaving him a message asking why he wasn't returning her calls.'

'Do you think he had somebody else?' said Wilcox.

Trevor smiled. 'That's usually what it is, isn't it? That's what I thought anyway. He stopped appearing and I figured he was out of the picture.'

'And were you aware of him coming back into the picture?'

'The last week she was here,' he said. 'She was happy again. I didn't know whether she was back with him or whether she'd met somebody else. But something had changed.'

'Yes, it had,' said Murphy. 'What was the name of your boss – the one that left?'

'Charlie. Charlie Westonholme,' said Trevor. 'He was a good guy, I liked him a lot. He retired. I think they wanted him to retire. He was too old, over 50 anyway. They're still interviewing for replacements.'

'Are they indeed?' said Murphy grimly. 'Thank you very much for your help, Trevor.'

'No worries.' He smiled and sauntered out.

'Let's go and ask for Charlie's contact details,' said Murphy, trying to remember where the HR office was, without looking like she was lost.

'This way,' said Wilcox, striding ahead.

'I can give you his home address,' said Samantha Wells, 'or the last address we have for him anyway. But I don't think he'll be able to tell you much.'

'Probably not,' said Murphy, 'but we'll have a chat with him anyway.'

Chapter Fifty-Two

'I WONDER if it was a good idea to call ahead,' said Murphy, looking at the traffic moving sluggishly in front of them on the A13. 'It's a lot of time wasted if she's not there.'

'She said she'd be there,' said Wilcox, 'so if she's not, that's a suspicious circumstance in itself. Anyway, I didn't suggest that we suspected her of anything, just that she might have some information which could be helpful to us.'

'At least Bellweather won't be questioning why we're making this trip,' said Murphy. 'If we can wrap this up quickly, maybe we can get back to the important stuff. I know thieving's wrong and it's our job to stop it, but I'm far more concerned to find the perp who threw Amy Horsfall into the river.'

'Here we are,' said Wilcox, pulling up in front of the Wheatsheaf, a concrete structure with PVC windows and none of the rural pretensions implied by the name. 'Not very attractive, is it? Probably replaced an older pub from the days when this would all have been fields.'

'Two pubs in two days,' said Murphy. 'I'm starting to feel like one of those 1970's cops. I wonder why she wanted to meet us here?'

'Probably lives with her mum and dad,' said Wilcox. 'Doesn't want them to know what she gets up to.'

Wilcox was right. Shirley Beesley entered furtively and came over when Wilcox waved at her. She looked about 16, but was able to produce evidence of being 17. It was clear that much photoshopping and many filters had been applied to her Instagram pictures.

'Thanks for coming to see me here,' she said, taking a large glug of coke. 'My mum and dad would have asked lots of questions, it would have done my head in. What do you need my help with anyway?'

'We came across your Instagram page as part of another investigation,' said Wilcox.

Shirley sat up and smiled. 'Oh, right. Glad you liked it. It's doing quite well, my page.'

'Yes, it's very good,' said Wilcox. 'What we wanted to ask you about is this.' He showed her the picture of her posing in the necklace.

She nodded. 'Yes, that's quite a good shot.'

'Can you tell us where the necklace came from?'

'My boyfriend lent it to me.'

'Lent it to you?'

'Yes, he said it was quite valuable. He'd been able to buy it cheaply and he was going to sell it at a profit, but he let me use it for a shot.'

'So you don't still have it?'

'No, I only had it for that evening.'

'Shirley,' said Murphy, 'can we have your boyfriend's name and address?'

'Why? He's done nothing wrong.'

'He may have done nothing wrong, but he may know somebody else who has done something wrong, so we would like to speak to him.'

'I can't give you his name without his permission.'

'Yes, you can and you have to, because this is a police matter.'

'I don't understand.' Shirley was now starting to sniffle.

'I think you do,' said Murphy. 'I think you may have suspected that this boyfriend was handling stolen property, but you decided not to think any more about it. Well now you have to think about it. If you are not willing to give us his details, we will come back with a search warrant to search your house. I think your mum and dad will then be asking lots of questions.'

Shirley was now openly sobbing. 'I don't want him to get into trouble. He'll be mad at me.'

'I think he'll be too busy dealing with us to get mad at you,' said Murphy. 'And he won't know the information came from you. Here – write it down for us. Name, address, phone number.'

Shirley took Wilcox's pad and wrote the details down in a rounded childish scrawl. Wilcox went off to make the phone call.

'How did you meet Rod?' asked Murphy.

Shirley sniffed. 'In a club, in Basildon. He was with a mate and I was with my friend. He said I had really good legs, I could make money on Instagram.'

'So your Instagram shots were done at his place?'

Shirley nodded. 'He has a flat in town. I couldn't post shots from home.'

'Does he know where you live?'

Shirley shook her head. 'No. He wouldn't have liked my house much.'

'I understand,' said Murphy. 'I guess he's a bit older than you.'

'He's twenty-five,' said Shirley, proudly. 'Boys my own age are so stupid. And Rod said I'm very sophisticated for my age.'

'I bet he did,' said Murphy. 'How long have you been together?'

'About six months,' said Shirley. 'We met just before my birthday.'

'And have you made much money on Instagram?'

She shook her head. 'Not yet, but Rod says we just have to build up our following.'

Wilcox reappeared and nodded.

'OK Shirley,' said Murphy. 'You can go home now and we'll give you a lift. I want you to stay away from Rod. Stop going to his flat, stop with the Instagram. Stick with the friends your own age. Otherwise, if he ends up getting arrested, you could be an accessory. He might have friends you wouldn't like much and you could be in danger from them. It's good he doesn't know your address. Change your phone number. Hang out with your family and friends, not on your own. And if you get worried, if anyone threatens you, call me straight away.' She handed over her card.

Shirley took it. 'I'm going to stick by him anyway,' she said. 'Whatever he's done.'

'I think you may find,' said Murphy, 'that he won't want you sticking by him. Your usefulness is probably at an end. It's time for you to ghost him.'

'GROOMED,' she said to Wilcox, as they got back on the road after dropping Shirley off. 'Met him when she was 16, and I bet he's more than 25. I'm worried about her. If she was still 16, I'd talk to her parents, but how far can they protect her, anyway?'

'I think we should stay in touch,' said Wilcox. 'See what's happening with friend Rod and then maybe give her a ring.'

'The thing is,' said Murphy, 'she thinks she's clever and grown up because she's reeled in this cool twenty-something – she thinks – guy. But the fact of the matter is that she's managed to attract him because he thinks she's stupid and immature – stupid and immature enough to be taken in by him. A woman in her twenties probably wouldn't look at Rod. I could be wrong of course, he could be gorgeous, but I'm guessing not.'

'He might have made himself gorgeous,' said Wilcox.

'You mean he might have had work done? I do hope so. I'm looking forward to seeing him, checking out his nips and tucks. There are certainly similarities between him and young – or not so young – Cal. And Florence Weaver, granted she's older and better-educated than Shirley, but she's still probably gullible in the same way. The groomer makes them feel grown-up and sophisticated and they swallow it all. There was some talk a while back about how critical thinking should be taught in schools and I think that would be a very good idea. Because I'm sure, for both of these girls, there would have been moments when they wondered if something was a bit off, but they just brushed those thoughts aside.'

'It's all just about the profile,' said Wilcox. 'They want to look grown up and sophisticated.'

'Yes, but they need to know that in a few years' time these older guys won't be doing anything for their profile. I know somebody called Tracey who could explain it all to them.'

Chapter Fifty-Three

RODNEY BOWLES' flat was in a high-rise block with a lift that didn't smell too good.

'Floor fourteen,' said Murphy. 'Bugger. At least it's not forty-four. I guess it can be my exercise for the day.'

'I read something yesterday' said Wilcox, as they toiled upwards, 'some new research. They said that going uphill is a less useful exercise for the body than going downhill. Apparently going down is better for the muscles.'

'Well, that makes me feel good. Sometimes I wish these people kept their research findings to themselves. Remind me of that again on the way down, I might appreciate it more.'

The door to 14C was opened by a young man in jeans and a vest holding a can of caffeine-reinforced soft drink in his other hand. A large dog of indeterminate breed growled behind him.

'Rodney Bowles?' said Wilcox.

'Yeah. That's me. Who the fuck are you?'

Murphy pulled out her badge. 'Police. We'd like a word.'

'About what? I don't have to let you in.'

Murphy sighed. 'You can make things hard for yourself if you want to, Rodney. You can let us come in and have a chat or you can have us hang around here for all the neighbours to see while we wait for reinforcements to arrive with a siren and a search warrant.'

He turned on his heel and walked down the hallway followed by the dog, still growling. Murphy and Wilcox followed at a safe distance, although Murphy knew no distance would actually be safe if the dog decided to spring at them. Wilcox, to her surprise, crouched down, whispered something and held out a fist. The dog stopped, padded back, looked at him for a minute and then rubbed its large muzzle against the fist.

'Good boy,' said Wilcox, scratching it behind the ears.

'It's a girl,' said Rodney contemptuously, 'and she's probably got fleas.'

They followed him into a sitting room which consisted of a sofa and two armchairs squatting attentively in front of an enormous TV which showed two men pretending to kill each other. Rodney picked up the remote and switched it off.

'Don't suppose you've come to watch the wrestling,' he said.

'No, we see enough of that every Saturday night in Hackney,' said Murphy. 'We've come to talk about stolen goods.'

Rodney's face immediately set like concrete. 'Yeah, well I wouldn't know anything about that,' he said.

'In which case you won't mind us having a look around, will you?'

'Yes, I will…' He was interrupted by the doorbell.

'I think that will be the Essex police with the search warrant,' said Murphy. 'Do you want me to let them in?'

'Do what you like.' The fight seemed to have gone out of Rodney. Murphy opened the front door to admit a detective constable and two members of the uniform branch, who pulled on gloves and began going through the place.

'What I would like to know, Rodney' said Murphy, 'is who is bringing you the stuff? And who are you passing it onto? You're obviously the smallest and most insignificant cog in the operation. It's all the other players who make the money isn't it?' She looked around at the threadbare carpet and, through an open doorway, the unmade bed which had featured so artistically in Shirley Beesley's Instagram post.

'No comment,' said Rodney.

'Well, that is one option,' said Murphy, 'but it leaves you as the fall guy while the others, who probably made more money than you, go on their way rejoicing. Doesn't seem quite fair, does it?'

He folded his arms. 'I'm saying nothing.'

At that moment the DC emerged with items of jewellery in plastic bags and other plastic bags containing white powder.

'I think they've got you bang to rights, Rodney,' said Murphy. 'Tell them everything you know, it's your best option. We're leaving you for the time being. Essex Constabulary will be taking care of you.'

'OK,' she said to Wilcox, as the front door shut behind them. 'Now for the health-giving benefits of stumbling down fourteen flights of stairs.'

'It's interesting,' said Murphy, as they clattered down. 'Rod is a reasonably cool name, or it was in my day, but Rodney is about as uncool as you can get. I guess he could be called Roderick, but that's not much better. Maybe he was just christened Rod. Maybe I'll shut up now, and concentrate on getting down these stairs.'

'I think he's a pound shop version of Cal,' she said as they reached the fifth floor. 'He wouldn't be bad looking, at least when he's had a shower and shave, but he wouldn't have been able to hook Florence Weaver. She would never have walked into that flat. I didn't want to ask him about the Instagram page as that would have directed his attention to Shirley. We need to keep her out of it.'

'I think,' said Wilcox, as they emerged at the bottom, 'that the Instagram page was not really about making money, even if Shirley thought it was. The money was in the stolen goods. He could have been using Instagram to advertise what he had for sale. He was using her to display the merchandise.'

'So if we go through Wandagirl's Instagram followers, some of them will be Rodney's customers?'

He nodded. 'Definitely worth a look.'

Chapter Fifty-Four

ESSEX POLICE APPRECIATED the tip-off and were happy for Murphy and Wilcox to observe the questioning of Rodney behind one-way glass.

DS Wilberforce was a solid-looking man who would probably have described himself as an 'old-fashioned copper', a soubriquet not highly-regarded in today's police force. What he had in spades was the ability to sit and stare at the suspect as if he had all day to waste and he used it as soon as the first 'no comment' was aired. The duty solicitor was obviously used to this and looked as if he might be using the opportunity to have a nap, but Rodney was looking increasingly agitated.

'You can't just keep me here all day,' he threw in eventually. The solicitor sat up and looked across at Wilberforce, who smiled benignly at Rodney.

'That's exactly what we can do, lad,' he told him.

How Murphy wished she could address suspects as 'lad', but she knew it wouldn't sound right. You needed to be male, and preferably Northern.

'Let's look at some pictures of the objects we found in your flat, shall we?' said Wilberforce in avuncular tones. 'Then you can tell me where they came from, how they found their way into your flat and where they were heading. I think that will be a good start.'

Rodney folded his arms and looked away.

'I understand the problem,' said Wilberforce. 'You can't tell me any of this, because you don't know. You're just the dumb klutz that they use to warehouse the stuff, aren't you? You don't actually know anything about the clever stuff, the operational details. They don't tell you anything, probably think you wouldn't understand. Unfortunately for you, you're the one in the frame.'

Four hours later Murphy and Wilcox left Brentwood Police Station. Faced with taking the rap for the whole operation, Rod had eventually chosen to cooperate and the story that emerged was fascinating.

'We have to admit,' said Wilcox, manoeuvring through the traffic, 'it's quite a clever ruse. Who do you not notice on the street these days? People delivering packages. They're everywhere. Fake van signwritten to look like a courier company, with a fake registration plate. Fake parcels with fake names and addresses on. If the householders are in, sorry wrong house, honest mistake. If they don't answer the door, slip round the side like you're going to put it in their safe place, then effect entry with whatever tools you have at your disposal, whisk round the house grabbing anything small and valuable, dump the parcel in the bin and come back out without it, just in case any nosy neighbour is watching. You have to be bold and fast, and you have a beard and a hoodie to deal with any cameras.'

'Yes, it's pretty good,' said Murphy. 'You have to hand it to them. And I wonder, if they managed to effect entry without doing any damage, how many people never even realised they'd been done over? Missed some piece of jewellery and thought they'd just misplaced it. To be honest, that would be my first thought, not that I have much proper jewellery. But I do tend to misplace things.'

'Let's hope a night in the cells persuades Rod to hand out names and contact details' said Wilcox. 'Otherwise, we'll have to send the uniforms out looking for these guys and bang goes the overtime budget again.'

Chapter Fifty-Five

KELLY WILSON'S ONE-TIME BOSS, Charlie Westonholme, lived in a large terraced house in Wimbledon with his wife and three dogs. He explained this as he let them in and shooed the dogs into the garden.

'Children have left home,' he said. 'Packed the last one off two months ago. We thought it was a great result at the time, but now we really miss them. No noise, no mess, no worrying about where they are.'

'And now no job, I gather,' said Murphy, sitting at the kitchen table.

'That's right' he said, waving the coffee pot for emphasis. 'The only way now is down. I guess I should be feeling depressed, but I can't quite summon it up.'

He was a slim, academic-looking man, to Murphy's eye, with greying hair and a direct gaze. And she had to admit that, no, he didn't look depressed.

'Advertising was an exciting business to be in when I started' he said. 'Could you craft the killer slogan that would make sales take off? Could you come up with something that sounded better than what the competition were claiming about themselves? It was a challenge. But those days are gone. The big advertising companies are having to adapt to a new environment now. TV and magazine advertising still happen, but more and more money is now going into digital campaigns, tracked by analytics. And if a manufacturer can get their product promoted to thousands of the right demographic by some influencer, why should they pay megabucks to an ad agency? So, for me, the writing was on the wall. It was time to go. Plus, to be honest, Anson Barnes was happy to let me go. I didn't fit into the corporate demographic any more. Time to take off and go travelling, I think. We're making plans.'

Jesus Christ, another one was Murphy's immediate thought, quickly suppressed.

'We wanted to talk to you about Kelly Wilson,' she said.

'Kelly, yes. That was tragic.' He shook his head. 'She was so young.'

'What do you know about what happened?'

'Practically nothing. I heard that she died of a drug overdose in a club. That's all anybody could tell me.'

'Did you know her boyfriend?'

'I wouldn't say I knew him. I don't think we were ever introduced, but I did go along for a drink one evening and somebody pointed him out to me. They thought he might be coming to work with us, but that was probably just a rumour. Kelly seemed very keen on him. Although, I gather, she was with him the night she died and he had bought the drugs.'

'Yes, that seems to be the case,' said Murphy. 'What can you tell us about Kelly herself?'

'She had started at the bottom as I remember, some junior admin role. But then somebody left and they gave her a trial writing copy. And she was good at it. Both her and Trevor were good, because they were clever and they were also young. So they knew the right phrases to reach a young audience, and they kept up to date with it. They were both, well of course Trevor still is, the sort of people Anson Barnes needs to retain.'

'So they could have made it as influencers?'

He laughed. 'I don't know about that. I think it requires some liking for self-exposure, for putting yourself out there. I could see Trevor being up for that more than Kelly, she wasn't really a self-promotion person.'

'Was she happy at Anson Barnes?' asked Wilcox.

Charlie crossed his arms and sighed. 'Yes, as far as I know. Or as far as I knew at the time. She was doing well; I was very happy with her work. And it's quite an employee-centred place to work, Samantha Wells has made sure of that.'

'Oh yes,' said Murphy. 'The marshmallows.'

'Exactly. I've never been persuaded that sitting in breakout spaces eating sweets contributes much to job satisfaction. I'd have said it contributes more to tooth decay, but what do I know? People seem to like it. So, I don't think Kelly had any problems at work – or not ones which were to do with work, anyway.'

'Ones which weren't to do with work?'

'Maybe. I saw her looking a bit upset a few times, but I didn't like to pry. Perhaps I should have. Then it seemed to resolve, so I was glad I hadn't stuck my nose in. I knew from my own kids that young people don't like interference, I've learned that lesson.'

'I don't think interference from you would have made much difference,' said Murphy. 'As far as we can make out, she had a falling out with her boyfriend, which is probably when you noticed her looking upset, and then they were back together just before she died. So it's him we're mostly interested in.'

'I can't help you much there. I only saw him twice, and not to speak to.'

'What was your impression of him?'

'Seemed like a sociable sort of bloke, he was mainly talking to Kelly, but I saw her introduce him to Trevor and Samantha and a few other people. I was sitting a bit further away, so I didn't get to meet him. He must have been devastated about what happened.'

'Maybe,' said Murphy. 'But he's probably gotten over it.'

Chapter Fifty-Six

'SO LET'S look at where we are,' said Murphy the next morning, dumping her bag on the desk.

'We are in a good place' said Wilcox, looking up from his coffee and croissant. 'Essex police found all sorts of interesting stuff at Rod's place, in addition to what we saw, and sounds like they got plenty of information out of him this morning, including names and addresses. I'm looking at the Instagram page now, going over the followers. It looks like we can roll up the whole operation. We have the middleman, he's giving access to the sellers, who are the perps we're supposed to be after, and Instagram should give us a lead on the buyers. And Bellweather smiled at me this morning.'

'Well I'm glad it was you. The day he smiles at me I'll know something's seriously wrong. Let's look at where we are on these deaths, that's what I'm interested in.'

'We have our prime suspect,' said Wilcox. 'Can't we just bring him in and lean on him?'

'You've been watching too much *Life on Mars*. Leaning is no longer permitted. What we need is evidence.'

'He's been clever there – or lucky.'

Murphy frowned. 'Yes, he has. One or the other, or both. The only place where we know he was at the same time as both victims is the tube station. There's something we've missed. Let's go back and look at that footage again.'

Wilcox pulled the tape from his bottom drawer where it was nestling between a copy of the professional guidelines and his spare cycling shoes.

'We've looked at it so many times already,' he said.

Murphy shrugged. 'I know, but let's give it one more run through.' She led the way to the video room and Wilcox slotted it into the machine.

The grainy footage looked no clearer than it had on any previous occasion. There was the back of Richard Weaver's head, lined up with all the other heads, and then the shocking moment when it disappeared from view, followed by a swirling movement in the mass of shadowy shapes around him.

Murphy felt as though she could predict every second – and none of those seconds told them anything. But something was suddenly stirring in her brain.

'Just a minute, stop.' Wilcox stopped the tape and looked across at her. 'Go back a few frames – there.'

He froze the picture and waited. She stood up and walked towards the screen. She was too close, everything was blurry. She took a few steps back and the picture resolved itself.

'There.' She pointed at the head next to Richard Weaver's.

'But that's not Derek,' said Wilcox. 'Nothing like him.'

'No,' said Murphy. 'It's a woman's head. It's Janice Fuller.'

'How can you tell?'

'It's the back of her head,' said Murphy. 'I saw it at the funeral.'

'Are you sure? It's not very distinctive. All these heads look very similar.'

She nodded. 'I'm sure. That's her. If she'd worn a hat to the funeral, I wouldn't have been able to pick her out, but luckily for us she didn't.'

Wilcox looked unconvinced. 'Well, if you're sure…'

Murphy smiled. 'We'll go and see her and find out, shall we? If I'm wrong and she screams harassment, I'll make sure your reservations are communicated to the IPCC.'

JANICE FULLER DIDN'T LOOK like a woman about to scream harassment. She just looked sad as she listened to Murphy explaining quietly why they thought she'd been at the scene. At the end she just nodded and Murphy was sure she heard Wilcox sigh with relief.

'Can you just tell us how you came to be there Janice,' said Murphy.

Janice hesitated and then drew a breath. 'We were having an affair,' she said. 'Surprising, I know. I've seen his wife.' Murphy was silent and Janice carried on. 'I said to him once that him falling in love with me was like that Depardieu film where he dumps the beautiful wife and runs off with the not-beautiful temp.'

'*Trop Belle Pour Toi*,' said Murphy. Wilcox frowned and shook his head.

'Exactly.' Janice smiled sadly. 'He didn't agree of course. He said I was much better-looking than Depardieu's love interest, which was gallant of him. And he didn't feel that his wife was too beautiful for him. She's attractive, but she's not Carole Bouquet.'

Wilcox was now rolling his eyes and staring at his phone.

'But he was in love with you,' said Murphy.

'Yes, he was. Unbelievably. We'd been working together for years, so we knew each other very well. I never expected it to turn into anything else and now I can't even remember how it happened, but – it did.'

'How long were you in the relationship?'

'About two years. We were very discreet. No texts, no emails, no phone calls, no evidence. At first, we agreed that it would not endanger his marriage. He loved his family, and I respected that. In fact, I wanted to keep it compartmentalised even more than he did. I had been alone for five years, since my marriage broke up, I had a good salary and my life was pretty much the way I wanted it. I wasn't looking for any kind of upheaval. But nothing stays the same. What we had was going to either fizzle out or become stronger. It had to go one way or the other. After about six months we realised we were both in love. Up to that point we could probably have called it off without too much damage, but after that we didn't want to.'

'How did his diagnosis affect your relationship?'

Her smile died. 'It changed everything. We had talked about being together. We would leave work and just take off somewhere. Richard thought his wife wouldn't be difficult about granting him a divorce. The children were grown up and he said that he and Alison were leading very separate lives. But when he got the diagnosis that was the end of it. He said he could no longer offer me any kind of future, he wanted me to be free, to meet somebody else. Not likely at my age and I didn't want anybody else, I just wanted him. Well, apart from that, he felt he should devote his remaining months to his family. It was logical and I understood how he felt, but I found it hard to bear. And then he was transferred to M&A, so I wasn't even seeing him at work anymore.'

'So you followed him to the tube station.'

Janice nodded. 'Pathetic, isn't it? I just wanted to see him, to be near him. I knew where he went on Monday nights, he'd been going there for years. The Ropemakers Arms. I peered through the window and there he was. I could just see his head through the crowd. I knew he never stayed long. I loitered outside the pub and caught up with him on the street after he'd left the other two. We walked to the tube station together. Then Richard spotted one of the juniors from the trading floor, so we entered the tube station separately. He didn't want me to become the butt of jokes after he'd died. I caught up with him on the platform. Everybody was so tightly packed down there that nobody would know who was with anybody else. We stood there and held hands.'

'At the moment when you looked through the pub window' said Murphy, 'did you notice anybody standing close to him?'

Janice was silent for a moment. 'There were the two friends he always went drinking with. I had seen them before so I recognised them. I've never been introduced to them and I wouldn't have wanted that, as I know they are also friends of his wife. But I didn't notice anybody else particularly. The place looked very crowded.'

'OK. And at the tube station, how did it happen?' said Murphy.

Janice closed her eyes for a moment. 'His knees suddenly started to buckle' she said, 'or that's what it looked like to me. He was fainting. I grabbed his arm, but he was falling towards the tracks and at the last moment he looked straight at me and shook me off.'

Her shoulders were shaking. Murphy gave her a moment. Wilcox had wandered off to look out of the window.

'Was there anybody else down there that you recognised, Janice?' Janice shook her head.

'Or anybody behaving suspiciously, maybe standing close to Richard?'

'No nobody. We were all close to each other anyway, so I probably wouldn't have noticed. Certainly, nobody pushed him, if that's what you're thinking.'

'OK' said Murphy. 'That was one possibility we wanted to eliminate.'

'It wasn't suicide,' said Janice. 'I know it wasn't.' Her mind had clearly made the jump to the next possibility.

'No' said Murphy. 'It wasn't suicide. Somebody had given him a drug that caused him to collapse, so in my book that's murder, whatever the CPS might say.'

'A drug?' said Janice.

Murphy nodded. 'Rohypnol.'

'The date rape drug? But why?'

'We're still investigating. But it may have been what caused him to fall. And he wanted you to survive.'

'I've thought about it so many times,' said Janice. 'Seeing the final look on his face and wondering what he was trying to tell me. And I think that's why he shook me off. He knew he was going over and he didn't want to take me with him.'

Murphy nodded. 'He was a good man.'

'He certainly was,' said Janice, as they both stood up and walked towards the door. 'Will his wife have to know about this? There's no point causing her any further pain. That's not what he would have wanted.'

Murphy turned back to her. 'Don't you think it's possible she knew? Or guessed?'

Janice's eyes widened. 'That never occurred to me.'

'I don't know whether we'll need to tell her,' said Murphy. 'I wouldn't tell her unless it was necessary. But I don't think she's the sort of woman who'll come after you. What I'm concerned with is finding the person responsible for his death.' She led the way out of the room. 'So, if you think of anything else, please get in touch.'

Janice escorted them to the lift and they watched her walk slowly back to her office.

'She could have pushed him,' said Wilcox.

'Yes, she could,' said Murphy. 'She's number one in the means and opportunity stakes. But motive, not so much. I'm inclined to give her the benefit of the doubt for now.'

'So we're no further forward.'

'On the face of it, no. I'd like to say something cheering, like we're a bit closer to establishing the truth, but we're no closer to apprehending a perp, so we'd better keep swerving round Bellweather, if we can. In some way, I was glad to hear that Richard Weaver was having an affair.'

'Were you?' Wilcox looked puzzled.

'Didn't you feel,' said Murphy, 'that he was a bit too good to be true? Naturally nobody wants to speak ill of the dead, we're used to that phenomenon and very annoying it is too, but I got the impression that all these people would still be telling me how wonderful he was if he was still alive. He does seem to have been a genuinely good bloke, but nobody's that perfect. So I was pleased to discover that he may have passed on price-sensitive information and that he had a mistress. All of a sudden, he's become somebody I can believe in.'

'Do you really think Alison knows about Janice?'

Murphy stopped and thought for a minute. 'She's certainly never given that impression. They're both people with busy jobs, so maybe she never questioned how often he was working late, or however he arranged his love life. And both Alison and Janice say that he was planning to spend his last few months with Alison and his children. So she may never have known. On the other hand, she may have known and kept it to herself. She doesn't strike me as the type to go in for screaming and recriminations. From what Janice says, if he had not been dying, he would have left Alison and gone away with Janice. I wonder if Alison knows that? I wonder if it's true?'

'Alison wasn't at the station,' said Wilcox. 'Richard would certainly have spotted her if she was anywhere near him. The person best placed to have pushed him was Janice. And if we accept her statement that nobody pushed him under the train' said Wilcox 'then how do we account for Amy Horsfall?'

'We know Derek and Amy were both in the tube station. Derek wouldn't have known Amy Horsfall, but she may have recognised him – she follows him on Instagram.'

The lift slid noiselessly to the ground floor and the doors opened.

'Amy wanted to get into fashion' said Wilcox as they headed through the revolving door to the street. Murphy strode ahead too enthusiastically and ended up having to go round twice.

'That's right' she said, as she emerged on the second circuit. 'She wanted to get into the fashion business. She may have thought Derek – or Cal – could help her with that.'

'Though they seem to be more about underwear and accessories than fashion,' said Wilcox.

'Well Amy's wardrobe wasn't exactly classic, quality pieces,' said Murphy. 'Most of it was cheap stuff, so she probably thought what Flo and Cal were selling was pretty good. Maybe she thought she'd rather be working for a couple of influencers than doing her boring job.'

'But I doubt they needed or could afford an employee,' said Wilcox. 'And she didn't look like influencer material.'

'That's right,' said Murphy. 'I can't see Florence Weaver wanting to be BFFs with Amy Horsfall. But what if Amy Horsfall had some leverage? What if she sent Cal a private message saying I saw you at Moorgate? She wasn't accusing him of anything, because, as far as we can make out, he didn't do anything. But it could just be some kind of fangirl message like *I love your site and we were both at Moorgate, what a coincidence! What do you think happened?* So Amy didn't actually have leverage, that's not what it was – or not leverage that she was aware of, anyway. What she had was an opening. What if she used it?'

They had arrived at Moorgate. 'Here we go again' said Murphy, as they made their way through the automatic gates and onto the escalator. For once, she was prepared to stand on the way down.

'The thing is, if he did nothing nefarious here, at this station' said Wilcox, 'why would he be bothered about anybody having seen him?'

'Maybe he didn't want it known that he had been here because there was somebody in particular who might wonder about it. Who would that be?'

'Florence,' said Wilcox.

'I think so,' said Murphy. 'I'm sure she wouldn't have suspected him of killing her dad but, from his viewpoint, it's best she doesn't make any connection at all. Then he gets a message from this naïve girl who's planning to spill precisely those beans.'

'She stayed to talk to us so that she would have something to tell him,' said Wilcox. 'For her, it was a bit of excitement. I don't think she was blackmailing him.'

'No, of course not. She wasn't that type and she didn't think he'd done anything wrong anyway. She just wanted to hustle her way into his orbit. Probably thought she could even get some publicity for the dog shelter, poor kid.'

A train pulled in and they stepped aboard. All the other passengers were sitting so they stood by the doors.

'He wouldn't have seen it like that' said Wilcox, keeping his voice low.

'No, he wouldn't have. He's not bright enough to appreciate the distinction. He thought she was threatening him. Which means there was something over which he could be threatened.'

'Maybe' said Wilcox, 'he intended to push Richard under the train but couldn't get close enough. That would tie in with what Winona Francis told us.'

'That seems plausible. And maybe he was worried she'd tell the police she'd seen him. That might have led to them speculating exactly as we are now.'

'He would have made an appointment to meet her' said Wilcox, 'to find out what she'd said to the police, whether she'd mentioned his name. As soon as she'd told him she hadn't, it was safe to get rid of her.'

'This is all speculation of course' said Murphy. 'No

proof, no evidence. We have to find something. I think it's back to the pubs.'

They left the tube at the next stop and crossed to the other platform, to get on a train going back into the City.

Chapter Fifty-Seven

STAN WAS busy changing a barrel when they walked into the Ropemaker's Arms.

'Well, if it isn't Cagney and Lacey,' he said, stopping and resting his meaty forearms on the bar.

'Hello again, Stan,' said Murphy. 'When you've finished that, we'd like to show you a few more photos.'

'Sure thing. Just give me a minute here.'

A period of thumping and swearing followed and then he reappeared above bar level.

'Ok, that's that. I'm all yours.'

Wilcox brought out the two photos – the police mugshot and the Instagram still. Stan squinted at them.

'No, I don't recognise either of these guys.'

'It's the same person,' said Murphy.

'No! You mean he's had a makeover?' He looked more closely. 'Yes, I can see he's had his nose fixed, but the skin... Is this off Instagram?'

Wilcox nodded.

'That's it then,' said Stan. 'It's all done with filters.' He pointed at the Instagram still. 'If this guy was to walk in here now, he'd look nothing like that.'

'That's partly true,' said Murphy. 'I've seen him, and his complexion is not that flawless, but he looks a lot better than this original version.'

'Hmm.' Stan looked again. 'Of course, these days most of us grow whiskers to hide our grotty skin.' He rubbed his beard apologetically. Murphy held her breath and waited.

Stan sighed. 'Well, I'd like to be of help, but I've never seen this guy. He hasn't been drinking in here, or if he has, he hasn't been up here at the bar buying the drinks. I've a good memory for faces, but he's not ringing any bells.'

Murphy smiled. 'That's OK. Thank you for your time. It was just an off-chance that you might have seen him.'

They made their way out. 'Bugger' said Wilcox.

'It is that,' said Murphy. 'For some reason I trust Stan's eyesight. Maybe Derek's not our man. Really, what would his motive be?'

'Maybe Richard would have stopped Florence going out with him.'

'I don't think so,' said Murphy. 'He might have put off some of her previous boyfriends, but Florence is now old enough to do whatever she wants, and she looks like a pretty tough customer to me. Murdering your girlfriend's father seems like a pretty extreme reaction.'

'The problem is,' said Wilcox, 'what motive would anybody have? The poor guy was dying anyway. If we accept that nobody pushed him under the tube, maybe the Rohypnol was some kind of accident.'

'Like somebody tripped and stuck the needle in the wrong leg?'

'Well now you put it like that…'

'But we come back to Amy Horsfall' said Murphy, stopping to grab an Evening Standard outside the tube station. 'She was definitely murdered. Maybe we should pay Derek a visit. In the meantime, let's see if the trawls of pubs along the embankment have turned up any sightings of Amy or Derek.'

'NOTHING' said Wilcox, scrolling through the reports. 'Nobody recognised her, nobody recognised him. But she had a distinguishable amount of alcohol in her bloodstream, so it seems fair to conclude that the Rohypnol was administered in a drink.'

'What was the alcohol?' said Murphy.

He scrolled up to the toxicology results. 'Rum, just a moderate amount, and citrus juice, probably lime.'

'Mojito' said Murphy. 'And you can buy that ready-mixed in a can. Much cheaper and much easier to spike. Drop a few tabs into somebody's can and they'll never be seen.'

Wilcox put his hands over his face. 'So now we have to trawl off-licences, supermarkets and corner shops?'

'Yes, we do. We'll send everybody back out tomorrow. Bit heavy on the budget, but not much we can do about that.'

'Bit cheapskate buying her a canned drink,' said Wilcox.

'Well he's a cheap kinda guy isn't he? He got Kelly Wilson to buy the drink that killed her. And I rather think poor Amy wasn't difficult to impress. He could even have told her they had some deal to promote canned booze and got her to pose with it. She'd definitely have fallen for that.'

'Do you think Florence would have known about this?'

Murphy shook her head. 'Probably not. Young Florence is not as clever as she thinks she is. And we can't say anything to her about it, because we have no proof or evidence. It's all just a product of our diseased and fevered imaginations.'

Chapter Fifty-Eight

FLORENCE AND LINDY were sitting in the Trapeze Bar on Shoreditch High Street drinking margaritas. Florence was wearing her new cool dungarees and was disappointed that so few admiring glances were being cast in her direction. That was the trouble with these hipster types. They were too busy admiring themselves to take any notice of women. Not that it mattered. She and Lindy were serious women, here to discuss business.

'Here's another one.' She scrolled up Rightmove on her phone and passed it across to Lindy.

'That's a really nice place,' said Lindy. 'Love the balcony and all that glass. But can you afford it Florence? It's not just the mortgage, you know. Most of these blocks have ruinous service charges. And they can put them up whenever they like. There's nothing you can do about it. You should see how much we're paying.'

Florence opened her mouth to explain that she wasn't looking for herself, the idea was that Lindy should find a place of her own, but nothing came out. Somehow, she just couldn't say it. Either Lindy had no idea what she was on about and would be hurt and offended at the idea that she should move out in favour of Florence, or Lindy knew exactly what she meant and was being deliberately obtuse. It was looking more and more like the latter.

'I think you would be better off looking in a slightly cheaper area, Flo,' she said now. 'Maybe something further out in the suburbs. That's where most first-time buyers are heading, and then you can move back in when you're making more money.' Florence opened her mouth to respond, but Lindy was still talking. 'I've been talking to Ada Page. She has seventy-five thousand followers and she's making good money now. She has a lot of contracts coming up. I promised to introduce her to Cal, I'm sure there's stuff we could collaborate on.'

OK, thought Florence. Message received and understood. If I piss her off, she'll cut me out. And Cal will do whatever she says. He thinks all the business comes from her. Time to move onto the other issue.

'I've been wondering when I might get some money,' she said. 'We've done the promotions for the fake tan, the underwear and the spot cream. I've been providing content for my followers every day. Surely by now somebody must have paid us?'

Lindy sighed deeply; the picture of patience sorely tried. 'What you need to understand Flo, is that this is a business. It's not like you doing a shift in the coffee shop and then they pay you at the end of the month. When we complete a contract for one of our clients, we have to establish that they are satisfied with the service, then they give us a purchase order. Then we invoice them and that invoice then has to go through an approval process. This can involve a bit of back and forth between us and them and it may involve people higher up in the organisation for final sign-off. Then it's approved and it goes onto the next payment run, which can be weeks away, or even longer. Maybe they only pay at the end of ninety days – that's three months. And when we get some money in, it's not like we immediately get it in our hot little hands and we can rush off to Primark or wherever.' Florence opened her mouth to protest at this, but Lindy swept on. 'When you're running a business, especially a start-up like this, there are business costs that have to be met and that is the priority. Only after all the expenses have been paid can we look at taking money out of the business, and there are strict limits to how much we can take. Otherwise, we would just be depleting our working capital. And that's before we've even begun to think about the tax implications. I won't bore you with that, it's very complex. Basically, I think you should regard your work on the platform as an investment, not a current income source.'

Florence drained her margarita and forced herself to put the glass down gently.

'I understand all that, Lindy,' she said. 'I did a Finance for Entrepreneurs module at uni.' Lindy looked like she curled her lip at this, but Florence decided to ignore it. 'The point I would like to make is that these were all my followers originally. We've attracted some new ones, of course, but most of our followers were my followers to start with, so I should have some input into decisions.'

'Of course you should,' said Lindy. 'And when there are decisions to be made, we will listen to what you have to say. But you must admit, you may have had all these followers, but had you monetised them? No, you hadn't. I think, if you're short of money, the best short-term solution is for you to get an additional job. Maybe you could fit in another coffee shop, or a bit of telesales?'

Lindy sat back and smiled. Job well done. Florence was about to start arguing, but realised just in time that this was the reaction Lindy was primed for. She wanted to provoke a tantrum and she wanted to provoke it particularly because Cal was now weaving his way towards them. Immediately she forced herself to relax and look up at him and smile.

'Hello girls.' He kissed them both on the cheek and sat down next to Florence, who put her arms round him in proprietary fashion and smiled across at Lindy. Maybe she could still score the next point.

'I've been thinking' she said, mostly to Cal. 'about a dog. One of those lovely labradoodles. They look lovely in photos and we'll want to have one with us when we take off.'

'We can't have a dog in the flat' said Lindy at once. 'And who'd end up walking it?'

'Well initially it won't be in the flat because we'll be travelling,' said Florence. 'I guess we'll be in the flat when we come back and then I'll be walking it. I'm fine with you staying in the flat while we're away, Lindy.'

Cal cut in hastily. 'I think we're getting ahead of ourselves here. And those poodle crosses are bred for sale, probably mostly by criminals. If we want a dog, we should go to a dog shelter and adopt a homeless dog.'

'Yes, you're right' Florence decided. 'That's a better look - compassion for animals. That's far more in line with who we are.'

Chapter Fifty-Nine

'I'M WONDERING if we should just get him in for a chat, or maybe visit him, rattle his cage a bit' said Murphy, after the morning briefing. The uniformed branch had been sent off to trawl the alcohol outlets and the lack of enthusiasm was palpable.

'I'm not sure we even have an address for him,' said Wilcox, accessing the database. 'The address on file when he was detained over the Kelly Wilson death was in Lewisham. I wonder if he's still there.'

'Didn't Alison Weaver say something about Florence planning to move in with him?' said Murphy. 'That means Alison must have some idea where he lives. Although I would peg Florence as one of those girls who doesn't tell her mum any more than she has to – that's how I was at her age.'

Wilcox gave her a look that suggested that any idea that she had ever been that age was inconceivable.

'I think it would do no harm to alert her mum to the fact that we're looking into him,' he said.

Dead Cool

'Good point.' She shrugged her jacket on and felt for her car keys.

'I've brought mine in today,' said Wilcox hurriedly.

'Good man. You can chauffeur me. I'm getting a bit sick of London Underground.' She dropped the keys into her handbag and followed him out.

THERE WAS INITIALLY no answer when they knocked on the door in Camden.

'Alison must still be at work,' said Murphy. 'Guess we should have called first.'

They were just turning away when the door was slowly opened and Jake took shape behind it, wearing a T shirt and tracksuit bottoms and sporting what Murphy had seen referred to as 'bed hair'.

'Hello Jake,' she said. 'Sorry to disturb you. Can we come in?'

He seemed to hesitate for a moment and then turned wordlessly and led the way through to the kitchen.

'So you're down from Leeds,' said Murphy as she sat uninvited at the kitchen table.

'Reading week,' he replied, shuffling from foot to foot as if wondering what to do with these unwelcome guests.

'Here, come and sit down,' said Murphy. 'No need to make us tea.' Jake's face immediately betrayed the fact that such a thought had not occurred to him. 'We were hoping to ask your mum for a bit of information, but you can probably help us.'

Jake sat down gingerly. 'My mum will be back later this afternoon,' he offered, 'and I don't really know...'

'Of course you don't,' said Murphy, comfortingly. 'But

sometimes people know things that they don't even know that they know, if you get my drift.'

He shrugged. 'I guess.'

'How old are you now Jake?'

'Nineteen.'

'Excellent. Tell me, have you seen much of Florence's boyfriend?'

'What, Cal? No, I've only seen him a few times.'

'And he lives in Lewisham, is that right?'

He shook his head. 'Shoreditch, one of those new blocks with a gym and everything.'

'I don't suppose you know the name of the block or the number?'

'Nah.'

'No problem.'

Jake frowned. 'What do you want to see him for?'

'Oh, just a few questions we want to put to him.' Murphy flapped a hand. 'Nothing serious. Actually, there was something else I wanted to ask your mum. I've got some friends moving to Camden with a daughter about to start secondary school and I said I'd ask your mum which school Florence went to, because I seemed to remember her saying it was good.'

Jake looked bemused at this change of tack and then probably decided to humour her.

'Florence didn't go to school in Camden, she went to St Cecilia's in Marylebone. Don't know about good, Florence always said it was pretty crap.'

'Ah, my mistake,' said Murphy. 'Well, it was worth asking. We'll leave you in peace now.'

Jake shot up and led the way out. The front door was shut as soon as they were through it.

'Do you think he's hiding something?' said Wilcox as he unlocked the car.

'I think he's hiding masses of things, but probably none of them of any interest to us. He's just a typical nineteen-year-old boy. But talking to him did remind me of something. Remember last time we spoke to him and he mentioned Florence's school reunion, and she cut him off?'

Wilcox nodded. 'Yes, she was the one with something to hide. Also probably nothing relevant to our investigation.'

'But interesting, nonetheless. A best friend called Beth, who's no longer a best friend. I'm always interested in that sort of thing.' Wilcox rolled his eyes and pulled away from the kerb.

ST CECILIA'S School for girls had a website and a Facebook page on which past pupils posted pictures of their enviable lives and the current crop posted pictures of their enviable weekends.

'Not much sign of Florence Weaver here,' reported Wilcox, dragging himself away from the latest video of girls jumping up and down, screaming and waving their GCSE results. 'There was none of this sort of thing at my school.'

'Did you go to a boy's school?' asked Murphy and he nodded. 'That explains it then. Anybody looking pleased about their GCSE results would probably have been beaten up behind the bike sheds.'

'Something like that,' he admitted. 'What about your school?'

'I went to school back in the Dark Ages,' said Murphy. 'Jumping up and down waving your exam results hadn't come into fashion. In fact, we were generally given to understand that we were unimportant and should be seen and not heard. Hearing national news reporting on GCSE and A' level results would have sounded completely weird to us. But times change.'

'I don't think anything useful is coming up here,' said Wilcox. 'Although I've seen a couple of interesting recipes.'

'I think the website is going to be more useful,' said Murphy. 'And here it is. Reunion for class that graduated in 2014, held two months ago. Quite a posh venue, dinner and cocktails. They had to pay for the tickets of course and the real purpose of the evening would have been to get them to open up their online banking apps in favour of the school. They were probably all wise to that, but it would still have appealed to a lot of them - £50 for a smart meal and the chance to get smashed in company with your old mates – even the ones you didn't like much. We know Florence was there. Now, who is Beth?'

'And does she matter?' said Wilcox. 'It's hard to see what this has to do with anything.'

'Maybe not, but mention of it made Florence uncomfortable, so I think it's worth just a small amount of investigation. I'd like to get something to talk to her about, something that might unsettle her a bit. She seems to be the only person who knows where to find Cal, and we may need to persuade her to tell us.'

Chapter Sixty

MRS EVANGELINE WORTHY, headmistress of St Cecilia's, was a tall woman with a formidable embonpoint and a very untidy desk. Her MacBook rested on a stack of assorted paperwork from which HMSO publications on health and safety and the provision of safe spaces in schools poked out as if wedged into place. Murphy, having fought her way past the gorgon in the outer office, was pleasantly surprised to discover that her facility for reading upside down had not deserted her and to see that government directives were being put to good use.

Mrs Worthy fixed her with what was probably meant to be a penetrating stare and Murphy dragged her attention away from a bust of Catullus, who was sharing his plinth with a half-eaten banana.

'Thank you for seeing me Mrs Worthy,' she began, in time-honoured fashion. Mrs Worthy inclined her head as if to give her permission to continue. 'We're currently investigating a case and it's possible a couple of your alumnae may be able to help us. They are not themselves in any trouble and I won't burden you with any further details. One of them we are in contact with but we have been unable to trace the other young woman.'

'Well, I don't see how I can help you with that,' Mrs Worthy batted back. 'We don't keep tabs on our girls after they have left and, if we did, that would be personal data. I'm sure you are aware of the GDPR provisions.'

'Indeed,' said Murphy, who had so far avoided doing the police GDPR module and was receiving regular threats from HR. Her opponent was not as scatty as she looked. 'And I would not of course wish to put you in a compromising position. Perhaps you could simply furnish me with a list of attendees at the reunion held back in March. I don't think that would be regarded as personal data, as you will probably be putting it in your school magazine.'

Mrs Worthy seemed to be considering this. 'OK, I don't see the harm in that,' she said eventually and she opened the door. 'Eunice,' she shouted at her gatekeeper, 'can we have a copy of the guest list for the last reunion.'

Eunice, who was probably still annoyed by her failure to send Murphy on her way, frowned and grunted something. Unlike Mrs Worthy, she had a very tidy desk and after a few mouse clicks the document in question slid silently out of the printer.

'Here you are then,' said Mrs Worthy, and Murphy made a conscious effort not to snatch it.

On the way out she passed what looked like the school caretaker chatting to a couple of teachers. He sprang in her direction. 'Can I ask what you're doing on school premises?' He looked her up and down. 'Are you here for the governors meeting?'

'No' said Murphy, giving him her best smile as she swept past. 'Ofsted. Unannounced inspection.'

'THERE ARE TWO ELIZABETHS,' said Wilcox, scanning the list. 'Webster and Allardyce.'

'Check their Facebook pages,' said Murphy. 'One of them will be the girl in the photo.'

'I think it must be this one. The other one has curly blonde hair and she's about two stone heavier.'

Murphy slid her chair across and looked intently at the features. 'Wish I had a copy of that photo they had in the frame. She's several years older now, quite a lot could have changed. How far back do the photos go? Here, click on 'older posts'.'

Wilcox scrolled down a dozen screens and stopped. 'Here's the oldest available.'

Murphy squinted. 'Yes, that looks much more like the girl in the photo. Less scrubbed up. I think we've found her. Elizabeth – or Beth – Allardyce. Go back to the recent stuff and let's see where we can find her.'

'No home address, I'm pleased to see,' said Wilcox. 'Clever girl. Not one of those over-sharers. Might have more luck searching for her work. Let's try LinkedIn.' For a few seconds there was silence as Wilcox searched LinkedIn and Murphy read the reviews for a serum which claimed to banish crow's feet overnight.

'Here we are,' he said. 'Junior solicitor at Waterfords. Started this year.'

Murphy frowned. 'Waterfords? Where have we come across that before?'

'Arthur Wellesley. We went to see him there,' said Wilcox.

She nodded. 'Yes. Arthur Wellesley. There are a few things I want to talk to him about. Time to pay him another visit, though for the life of me I can't see how any of this connects up.'

Chapter Sixty-One

ARTHUR WELLESLEY WAS with a client when they arrived. His secretary looked them up and down and then claimed he would be tied up all afternoon.

'No problem, love. We'll wait.' Murphy settled herself comfortably in one of the armchairs facing the desk and grabbed a copy of the FT laid out on the coffee table. Wilcox put his earbuds in and connected them to his phone. After fifteen minutes the secretary returned to say that Mr Wellesley was now free.

'I really don't understand why you are here again,' he began, as soon as his secretary had closed the door. 'I appreciate of course that what happened to Richard was awful, but there's no more I can tell you.'

'We have been looking into share dealings involving companies which were being advised by Richard's firm,' said Wilcox. 'I wonder if you can tell us anything about that.'

He shrugged. 'I'm afraid not.'

Wilcox consulted his notes. 'You bought shares in

Canavan Ltd just before the takeover. Just before their shares shot up.'

Arthur Wellesley stared at him. 'Are you accusing me of something?'

'We're interested in whether you may have received price-sensitive information from Richard Weaver.'

'And you have some proof of this?'

'No, but we're looking at anything Richard could have been involved in prior to his death.'

'Well the answer is no, I did not receive any price-sensitive information from Richard. I did buy some shares. I bought a number of other shares at about that time. I was diversifying my portfolio.'

'Thank you for explaining that,' said Murphy. 'I also wanted to ask you a bit more about the history of your relationship with Richard, as you'd known him for such a long time. Can you tell us how Alison and Richard met?'

'I think you should ask Alison that question, although I can't see for the life of me how it can have anything to do with your enquiry.'

'As you can probably appreciate,' said Murphy, 'we are trying to spare Alison as much as possible.'

He nodded. 'Yes, of course.'

'So, humour me please. As I understand it, Alison was originally your girlfriend. Is that right?'

He rested his elbows on the desk. 'Yes, we were together for a short time.'

'And then what happened?'

'She came to visit me at Durham and met Richard. The rest, as they say, is history.'

'So how did you feel about that?'

'I was upset, of course, but these things pass. I met Sue – my ex-wife – and we all stayed friends.'

'Very civilised,' said Murphy.

Arthur Wellesley stared intently at her, as if looking for any sign of sarcasm, but he appeared to find none.

'To be honest, there was a lot of switching around of partners going on in our year. We all kind of took it in our stride. Nobody was up for any kind of emotional trauma.'

'That was a good thing,' said Murphy. 'The resilience of the young. There's something else you can help us with,' she added. He turned to face her.

'Elizabeth Allardyce,' she said. His face cleared. 'I gather she works here.'

'Beth? Why do you want to speak to her?'

'She is – was – a friend of Florence Weaver's and she's working here with a friend of Richard Weaver, so we're bound to make connections.'

'But there's nothing sinister in that. Richard recommended her to me but she went through the same recruitment procedure as everybody else. We have nothing to hide. What connection can she possibly have to Richard's death?'

'We don't know yet,' said Murphy. 'Probably nothing, but we'd like to speak to her.'

He was silent for almost a minute, and Murphy fancied she could see the consequences being thought through.

Eventually he seemed to make up his mind. 'I'm sure that will be OK. Wait here a minute.'

He was back a few minutes later, followed by a young woman that Murphy recognised from the Facebook page. She wore a white shirt, a dark pencil skirt and ballet flats and her hair was gathered into a neat ponytail. It was not hard to see that she and Florence must have parted ways at some point.

'You can use this office,' said Wellesley. 'I'll be in Sandy's office if you need me, Beth' he added, before withdrawing.

'He thinks we're going to beat you up,' said Murphy to Beth, 'but we're not allowed to do that anymore.'

Wilcox rolled his eyes. 'We've never been allowed to do that' he stressed.

Beth laughed. 'If you beat me up, I'll scream and Valerie will come rushing in' she said, pointing to the outer office.

'OK, we won't give Valerie any excuse to chuck us out,' said Murphy. 'Now sit down and we'll tell you how you might be able to help us.'

'I guess it's about Florence's dad,' said Beth. 'I was so sad when I read about it in the paper. I sent flowers to the funeral and I texted Florence but she never replied.'

'So you were quite close to the family?'

She nodded. 'Florence and I became friends in Year Seven, we met in the first few days at St Cecilia's. I didn't have a very good home life, my mother died when I was very young and my father had remarried, so I used to spend a lot of time at Florence's house. Her parents were very good to me.'

'You went on holiday with them to Italy,' said Wilcox, 'when you were both about sixteen.'

'That's right. It was a lovely holiday. Until Jake had the accident, of course. Did you know about that?'

'Yes,' said Wilcox. 'He showed us his scar.'

Beth smiled. 'He was quite proud of that scar. Although it was scary at the time.'

'What happened?'

'He hired a scooter and had a collision with a lorry. He was very lucky.'

'You said it was a lovely holiday until the accident,' said Murphy. 'How did that change the holiday?'

'The atmosphere just changed. We were all naturally

very concerned about Jake and, once the adrenaline had worn off, he was quite bored because there are lots of things you can't do with your arm in plaster.'

'But you and Florence were still getting on well?'

'I guess we weren't getting on quite so well after that. She was kind of ignoring me, and I felt I'd done something wrong, but I didn't know what it was.'

'And how did you get on with her father?' asked Murphy.

Beth's face suddenly tensed and she looked at the floor.

'Were you having an affair with him?'

'No! Of course not.' She looked straight at Murphy. 'He wasn't that sort of man at all. He was more like a father to me. I guess I liked that, because my father took no interest in me. I think sometimes Florence felt that he paid too much attention to me and not enough to her.'

'Maybe you and he had more interests in common.'

She nodded. 'Yes, it was something like that. I guess I was a bit of a swot at school, whereas Florence wasn't interested, so he could discuss school subjects with me, we both liked crosswords, stupid things like that.'

'What happened Beth?' asked Murphy. 'You haven't been in touch with the family for years. What happened between you and Richard? If it wasn't an affair, what was it?'

Beth stood up briefly and straightened her skirt. 'It's more embarrassing than anything else' she said. 'I was so stupid.'

'We get to listen to lots of embarrassing stuff,' said Murphy. 'Some of it you wouldn't believe. And if it's not relevant to our investigation, it goes no further.'

'OK.' She drew a deep breath and sat down. 'When the ambulance arrived for Jake, they would only take two other people, so Florence and her mum went off in the ambulance. That left me and Richard and I guess, with nobody else around, we got round to discussing things we wouldn't usually talk about. He asked me about boyfriends and ... I was involved in a sort of relationship. It was a relationship nobody else knew about, but I suddenly had the urge to tell somebody about it, so I told Richard.'

Murphy said nothing and after a few minutes of silence Beth carried on. 'There was this teacher at school, Matthew Henderson, he taught chemistry. A lot of the girls fancied him, there was always a lot of gossip about him. He was attractive and he had some sort of ... I don't know ... charisma.'

'Yeah, charisma,' said Murphy, nodding. 'Such a useful characteristic. So what happened?'

'For some reason, he was interested in me. I don't know why. I wasn't one of the girls who hung around him, I wasn't one of those who rolled up the waistbands of their skirts or wore makeup or heavily padded bras, I wasn't pretty or sophisticated, I wasn't even much good at chemistry.'

'You were probably more interesting than the more overt contenders,' said Murphy. 'You were unlikely to boast about your conquest and, if your parents weren't up to much, you probably appreciated the attention.'

'Yes, I did. He wanted to know about me and what I thought about things. I guess he made me feel important, I'd never felt that before. It was just about to get physical – I think – when the Italian holiday happened.'

'So you never actually slept with him?'

'No, but I guess I would have done. I was sixteen, so it wouldn't have been illegal.'

'No, he'd have thought that one through,' said Murphy. 'And you told Richard. What did he say?'

'He hit the roof,' said Beth. 'He said I was being groomed. He said he'd seen Matt at parent's evenings and thought he was probably a slimy bastard, and now he knew he was.'

'How did you feel about that?'

'I was horrified, angry. I told him I was in love with Matt and he had no right to say he was grooming me. I said I was old enough to make my own choices. I probably said a lot of other stupid stuff, as well.'

'What did he say to that?'

'He said that if I didn't end it, he would report Matt to the school. I think I got a bit hysterical at that point. I remember screaming that there was nothing wrong with it because Matt wasn't married and the age gap was only ten years. I remember him saying that it was wrong on Matt's part because it was a fiduciary relationship. I said I didn't even know what that meant. He said 'Look it up' and walked off.'

'So that killed the holiday atmosphere?' said Murphy.

Beth smiled. 'Well, it certainly did for me. When the others arrived back, we had to pretend everything was normal but Richard and I avoided each other after that. I don't know if anybody else noticed, I hoped they didn't.'

'So did you carry on seeing this teacher?'

'As it happens, no. When the term started again, he seemed to have lost interest in me. I think now he'd probably found somebody else, although I did wonder if maybe Richard had been in touch with him. It was a bit shattering when it ended because, while I was seeing him, it was like I had some exciting secret that the popular girls didn't know about. They fancied him, but I had him, and they didn't know. When it was over, I realised that they were smarter than me after all, they would never have taken him that seriously, and my secret wasn't exciting, it was just sordid and embarrassing. But I did one intelligent thing. I looked up 'fiduciary' and then I understood what Richard meant. And that's when I decided to do law.'

'So how did your relationship with Florence proceed after this?'

'Florence started freezing me out. I no longer got invited round. We never had any kind of confrontation, but we just drifted apart.'

'Do you think Richard said anything to her?'

Beth shook her head. 'I'm sure he didn't. I saw him once after that, at a graduation event when we all left school and I told him and Alison I had a place to read law. He smiled and said 'Good for you, Beth' and sort of winked and it was like an acknowledgement of the disagreement we'd had and a sort of closure. He would never have said anything about it to anybody else.'

'And you saw Florence again recently at this school reunion,' said Wilcox.

She turned to him. 'That's right. We were all pretty hammered by the time we were able to circulate and actually talk to each other. And we'd never been together in that state before. We'd had the odd few illicit beers in the sixth form common room, but we'd never been drunk. So I can't even remember half of the conversations I had, but I do remember talking to Florence. She was telling me about her Instagram business and how many followers she had and her cool partner – I don't know if he was her boyfriend or her business partner, I think probably both. She said they were going travelling and they'd put pictures from all around the world on their Instagram page and make lots of money from product advertising. Sounded like a fun way to make a living, more fun than anything I was doing.'

'Was she interested in what you were doing?' asked Murphy.

'Not really, I don't think so. Florence was always mainly interested in her own stuff, not other people's and nothing I was doing sounded that interesting. I had my job here, which I like a lot, but I couldn't make it sound exciting, not like her roaming round the planet stuff. Then somebody else came along, somebody else who was in a law firm and said they'd heard about the case I was involved in. It's a grooming case, quite a shocking one. A games teacher grooming a girls hockey team – well, not all of them at once, but you know what I mean. I told them a bit about it, but obviously I couldn't say much at that time, because it was still in progress. It had made me very interested in grooming and I had started working on a book about it, because I felt it was something young people should have more awareness about. I guess the business with Matt Henderson had shown me how easily it can happen, but I wasn't going to tell Florence anything about that. I had an agent and several publishers were interested. I'm sure I mentioned that to Florence, but she'd lost interest by that point. She was much more out of it than I was. And that's the last time I saw her.'

'Did she tell you much about her boyfriend?' said Wilcox.

She shook her head. 'She showed me his picture on her phone. He was pretty nice-looking and she said he was a really cool photographer, but I don't remember her saying anything else much about him. I can't even remember his name.'

'Cal' said Wilcox.

'Yes, Cal, that was it. I remember wondering what it was short for, but I couldn't think of anything.'

'I don't think he even knows what it's short for,' said Murphy. 'Calculating, maybe.'

'You think there's something wrong with him?' asked Beth.

'We have our suspicions,' said Murphy, 'but that's all they are at the moment. Just one more question. Have you ever met a girl called Amy Horsfall?'

Beth started shaking her head and then stopped. 'I've heard of that name. She's the girl they found in the river, isn't she? That's so dreadful. No, I've never met her. Why would I have done?'

'No reason really,' said Murphy. 'It was a long shot. We're dealing with a number of different events, and we're just trying to see if there's any way in which they all tie up. I didn't seriously expect you to have met Amy, but it was worth asking.'

'No, I never met her, but I hope you find whoever did it.'

'We will in the end' said Murphy, demonstrating a confidence she didn't currently feel. 'Thank you for everything you've told us, it's cleared up a few things. If you have any more thoughts, about Florence, or her dad, or anything else that might be relevant, please give us a ring.'

'WELL, THAT WAS ALL BLOODY USELESS' said Wilcox, as they got back in the car. 'It doesn't get us any further forward in any direction.'

'No, not really. Just closes off another couple of lines of enquiry. I think Arthur Wellesley did get a tip from Richard Weaver, but we can't prove it and he knows we can't prove it, so that makes it a pretty unconvincing motive for murder. I think it's likely there was quite a lot of animosity involved in Richard taking his girlfriend but, as he pointed out, they've stayed friends all these years. And if he wanted to kill Richard and get her back, which is a somewhat outlandish idea, why would he choose to do it when Richard was dying anyway? He's a very intelligent man and I can't see any rational reason for him to be responsible for any of this.'

'And nothing Beth told us seems particularly relevant,' said Wilcox. 'We're not treating her as a suspect, are we?'

'No' said Murphy, 'I think we can put her to one side. I was just interested in the relationship between her and Florence, but I think, from what we've seen of Florence, that what Beth told us is pretty credible.'

'So we're back where we started.' He was sounding despondent and Murphy reminded herself that she was to some degree responsible for the morale of her juniors, him being the only junior she had.

'We just have to keep going,' she said. 'Every bit of information we get moves us nearer to the truth, although it doesn't feel like that right now and I would hesitate to suggest such a proposition to DCI Bellweather. We can now accept that Richard Weaver was not pushed, but he was drugged, so whoever drugged him was responsible for his death. In the case of Amy Horsfall, she was drugged and almost definitely pushed. I just can't fathom that there can be more than one person doing this, but the connection between Richard and Amy is tenuous at best.'

'Tenuous is right,' said Wilcox. 'It could just be a coincidence that they were both in the tube station at that moment on that night — so were hundreds of other people. It's really a coincidence that Amy followed Florence on

Instagram – so did thousands of other girls. There are far more coincidental events that take place every day than we know about, because nobody's even aware of most of them. If Amy Horsfall hadn't made herself known to us in the tube station, we wouldn't even be looking for a link. She might still have been there and she might still have been killed, but we wouldn't be running around chasing some possibly non-existent connection.'

'I can't argue with that,' said Murphy. 'What we need is a sighting of Amy at some time that night. Perhaps the teams will have uncovered something.'

'Let's cling to that hope,' said Wilcox, as they pulled into the police station car park.

But no bartender had been found anywhere along the river who admitted to seeing either Amy or Cal. Enquiries were still going on at supermarkets and convenience stores.

'It's a big nothing,' said Wilcox, scrolling through the reports.

Bellweather materialised and jerked his thumb in the direction of his office.

'So what have we got?' He bared his teeth and Murphy forced herself not to stare at them.

'Not a lot so far sir, but we are still pursuing a few lines of enquiry.'

'Not a lot' he snarled. 'And what are these 'lines of enquiry'? Sending half the uniform branch round every supermarket between here and Gravesend? Do you have any idea what the overtime bill is looking like?'

'We know Amy was poisoned, sir. We are trying to find out how that was done.'

'Don't you have any bloody suspects?'

'We have one that we are attempting to locate,' she said.

''Attempting to locate'? Find the bastard and bring him

in. This girl's parents want answers, I want answers, pretty soon the bloody press are going to want answers.'

'He's right,' said Murphy, as they headed back to the car park. 'We need to find bloody Cal and question him. Then we can either eliminate him or dig a bit deeper. Let's go and see Alison Weaver, she should know where he lives.'

Chapter Sixty-Two

FLORENCE AND CAL were curled up on the sofa in the Camden house, going through the Auto trader listings, looking at vans. Florence was very keen on this, but had detected a bit of reluctance on Cal's part (maybe he couldn't drive? Surely that couldn't be it).

'I'm thinking VW microbus,' she said, pointing to a bright yellow one.

'That's one of the old ones, from the 1960s,' he said.

'I don't mind if it's old,' said Florence airily. 'We can paint it. It will be cheaper than the new ones. They're really ugly.'

'No, it's not cheaper than the new ones,' he said, as though trying to explain to a stupid person. 'It's a classic motor vehicle. That means it's much more expensive than the newer models. It will also be less reliable, the parts will be more expensive and it will be harder to drive. Probably no power steering or ABS.'

'It will look great, though,' said Florence. 'We can get it fitted out with lots of stuff and it will look really cool.'

'It will look just like the vehicle every other Instagram World Travelling tosser is posing in front of.'

Florence backed away. 'What is the matter with you? Did you just call me a tosser?'

'No, I wasn't calling you a tosser. But the point is, we have to be ahead of the curve, not behind it. The moment for driving round the world in a beat-up vehicle with a pet of some sort and posting pictures has passed. There are about a hundred people already doing it. How would we be any different?'

'We'd be different because we're us and we have our own followers and we'd have our own adventures and our own take on things. I thought you were as keen on it as me. What's happened to you?'

'Nothing's happened to me. I just think we should consider things more carefully. We can't afford to spend £30,000 on an old van. No matter how cool it looks.'

'Well what can we afford? How much money have we made? Nobody tells me anything. I tried talking to Lindy about it but she was just stonewalling me. What's going on? Are we no longer an item?'

'Sure we're an item.' He gave her a perfunctory hug. 'We're doing great work, but it takes time to build up the business and get in the money and we can't just go out and spend it.'

'Why not? What else do we need it for?'

'Working capital' he said importantly.

'Oh.' That again. What the fuck was it anyway? Florence was unsure how to proceed.

Cal shut the MacBook, as if that discussion was now over, and turned to her. 'The good news is that we've got another possible new contract. There are a couple of other influencers bidding for it but we have a good chance, we just have to come in a bit under them. Eyelash curlers.'

'You think my eyelashes need curling?'

'No, I think your eyelashes are fine, but I think yours would look better curled than mine would.'

Florence laughed. 'I don't see why. Men are now using Botox and moisturisers and make up – why wouldn't they curl their eyelashes? We should demonstrate it together.'

Cal was saved from having to reply by the sound of the doorbell. 'Are you expecting anyone babe?'

Florence shook her head. 'No, mum won't be back for hours. Maybe it's Amazon. I ordered some new trainers.'

'OK. Here I go.' He got up from the sofa and headed into the hall.

Florence did a stretch and loosened her neck. Important to avoid the dreaded double chin. Cal was taking a long time to come back with the Amazon delivery. What was going on?

When he shuffled back into the room followed by the police goons, she found herself suddenly speechless. What the hell?

'Hello again Florence,' said the old cow. She sat down in an armchair without being asked. 'It was your mum we wanted to see, but I'm glad of the opportunity to have a chat with you.'

Florence glared. 'Why? What about?'

'We were talking to one of your friends' said the other one, the nerd.

'Oh really? And why were you talking to my friends?'

He shrugged. 'Part of our enquiries. We had a good chat with Beth Allardyce. Remember her?'

'Yes, of course I bloody remember her. So what?'

'She's a clever girl,' said the old cow. 'High-flying career, getting a book published. On grooming.'

'Really? I wouldn't know anything about that.' Florence hoped that sounded suitably dismissive. Her hands were shaking so she slid them under her thighs. Bloody Beth.

'She told us about a case that took place years ago,' the woman continued. 'It was while you were both at school. Did you know anything about that?'

'No, I certainly did not,' said Florence, fighting hard to keep the tremor out of her voice, 'and if you want to question me any further you can do it when my mother's here.'

'That's fine with us,' the woman said. 'It's actually young Cal we'd now like to talk to. Do you mind if we take him away with us?'

Florence shrugged. 'Whatever.'

Cal looked helplessly from her to them. 'Come along son,' said the old woman. 'We won't keep you long.'

A few minutes later the front door shut behind the three of them. Florence burst into tears.

Chapter Sixty-Three

FOR ONCE, in fact for the only time ever, Wilcox was glad that Murphy was driving. He was sitting in the front which was pretty alarming, but he had been through this particular ordeal quite a few times and it had lost its edge for him. Cal, sitting in the back, looked positively horrified. At one point, when it seemed inevitable that they would go into the back of the van in front, Wilcox saw him hunch up and close his eyes. Checking the mirror, he saw Cal slowly open his eyes again, as if surprised that he was still alive.

He turned towards him. 'Make sure your seat belt's fastened,' he said. 'Do you know how many deaths are caused by people in the back seat flying through the windscreen and knocking out the people in the front on the way?'

'No... I mean yes... it's fastened,' Cal stammered. When they arrived at the police station, he seemed keen to get out of the car and into the building. Really, as a softening-up procedure, it couldn't be beat.

Murphy led the way to the most dismal of the interview rooms. Wilcox was starting to feel sorry for Cal now.

'Would you like a coffee?' he asked him and Cal nodded. He'd look less grateful once he got a look at the canteen coffee, but it was the thought that counted.

'We've invited you here just for a chat' said Murphy as the beverage in question arrived. 'And we appreciate your willingness to help us with our enquiries.'

Cal started to nod, then shook his head, then took an ill-advised mouthful of coffee. Poor bugger doesn't know what to think, thought Wilcox.

'We're calling you Cal, because I understand that's how you refer to yourself these days. Am I right?' Murphy began. Cal nodded.

'Only we have you on record as Derek Fletcher. And we don't have a current address for you.'

He sat up and crossed his arms. 'So I changed what I call myself. Lots of people do that. And I don't have to give you my address. I've never been convicted of anything.' Cal was now recovering a bit of his mojo.

'No, you haven't, have you?' said Murphy, managing to make it sound as if such an outcome was now overdue. 'Although, actually we're both wrong about that. You were convicted of supplying drugs to Kelly Wilson.'

'Yeah. Supplying one tab. That's all. It had nothing to do with her death.'

'Well, seeing as she died of a drug overdose, the amount you supplied to her would have been a contributory factor, don't you think?'

'Nah. Nothing to do with me.'

'I wonder if Florence would agree with that. Does she know about your previous incarnation as Derek?'

'She wouldn't care. Nothing to do with her.'

'How well did you know Florence's father?' asked Wilcox.

Cal shrugged. 'Never met him.'

'But you and Florence are an item, isn't that right? Or are you just business partners?'

'Yeah, we're an item. But I never met her dad. What's this about anyway?'

'Moorgate underground station' said Wilcox, consulting his notes. 'Twenty-fifth February, about seven pm.'

'What's that about?'

'It's about death, Derek. Florence's father died that evening.'

'Yeah, I know about that. She told me. She was well upset. But what's it got to do with me?'

'You were there weren't you?'

'Course I wasn't.'

'CCTV says you were.'

'Well then the CCTV is wrong.'

'You were also identified by a member of the public who was there that night.'

'How would some member of the public know who I was?'

'Derek.' Murphy leaned forward confidentially. 'You're Cal now. You're no longer just some uneducated saddo called Derek.' Cal opened his mouth to protest at this, but she continued on. 'You're a celebrity, you have a public profile. Thousands of people with nothing better to do follow you on Instagram. They want to know all about you, Derek. They want a piece of you. I'm surprised you can still walk down the street unnoticed and you should prepare yourself for the fact that one day you won't be able to do that. People will accost you on the bus, in the pub, in the supermarket. They'll look at what's in your trolley and post pictures of it. They'll want selfies with you, they'll want your opinion on things that matter to them, they'll want you to help them out with money, to make donations to causes. Pretty soon you'll understand why the big influencers have bodyguards, and you'll have to have them too. And, between you and me, I don't think they come cheap. So tell me, what is the chance that one of your besotted fans sees you in a tube station and doesn't even recognise you? Pretty much nil, isn't it?'

Cal smiled briefly 'I guess so.'

'Exactly.' Murphy sat back and stretched. 'So, on that basis, we can take it that you were there. What were you doing there?'

'Waiting for a tube.' He looked pleased with this response.

'Does Florence know you were in the tube station when her dad died?' Wilcox enquired.

Cal suddenly looked less pleased. 'Why would she? Nothing to do with me. Hundreds of other people were there.'

'The thing is Cal,' said Wilcox, 'we're starting to notice you turning up on the scene when people die. Do you think you're a harbinger of death maybe? Or perhaps it's a more obvious connection than that. After all, if we were to do a Venn diagram with all the people in that club when Kelly died as one group and all the people in the tube station when Richard Weaver died as another group, I think the overlapping sub-group of people present at both would have just one element – you.'

'That's rubbish. It's just coincidence.'

'Tell us about Amy Horsfall.'

'What?'

'Amy Horsfall. You were there when she died. Tell us what happened.'

'I don't know what you're talking about.'

'Amy Horsfall was one of your fans. She followed you on Instagram. Got a bit close, did she? Made a bit of a nuisance of herself?'

'I don't know what you're talking about. I'm saying nothing else without a lawyer present.'

'You can have one if you want, but I don't think there's any need for that at this stage,' said Murphy. 'Unless you have something you want to confess to? No, I thought not. All we've been doing here is having a chat, and you've been very helpful. You see, when we come across all these links, it makes us curious, we want to know how they're all connected, so we look for the common factor and bingo! There you are.'

'So I can leave now?'

'Yes, of course,' said Wilcox. 'Do you want us to run you back?'

'No!' The response was immediate. 'I'll make my own way.'

Wilcox escorted him outside and came back to the CID room.

'He's not very clever, is he?'

'No' said Murphy, 'but we shouldn't underestimate him. He's managed to attract Florence Weaver, who's pretty and well-educated and has a much higher intellect than he does – although maybe that's not saying much. But she is in many ways not that bright, or she wouldn't be with him, and I think he's probably clever in other ways – which is why we haven't yet nabbed him.'

'He may be innocent of anything,' said Wilcox.

'He may' said Murphy, 'but I'm not really buying it. He's cropping up all over the place.'

'But no evidence.'

'No evidence that we've yet found. But it's there somewhere. If he killed Amy Horsfall, I'm going to nail him. We never did get to see Alison Weaver. Tomorrow we'll go back and look for her again.'

Chapter Sixty-Four

ALISON WEAVER CAME to the door wearing glasses and with a pen between her teeth. She stared at them for a few seconds and then removed the pen.

'Hello again. I don't know what further help I can be, but I'm glad you're still on the case.'

'We would just appreciate a few minutes of your time,' said Murphy.

Alison held the door open. 'The reason I'm inviting you in is because it's given me an excuse to stop what I'm doing,' she said, as she led the way into the sitting room. 'You're acting as a displacement activity.'

'What's the activity you're escaping from?' asked Murphy.

'Marking,' said Alison. 'It's kind of better these days because they do everything on laptops, so we don't have to grapple with the handwriting, but it's still mind-numbing in every other way.'

'I'd be no good at that,' said Murphy, sitting down. 'I

can't sit still for hours on end, not unless it's a really good film. I wanted to ask you a bit about Florence's boyfriend.'

'Cal? What about him?'

'How well do you know him?'

Alison frowned. 'Not particularly well, but then it's none of my business. Florence is over the age of consent and she seems to like him. That said, I'm quite glad she hasn't moved in with him yet. She's still a bit young in many ways. Why? Is there something I should know?'

'It's really more a case of what you might be able to tell us,' Murphy said. 'Do you know anything about his background, what he does for a living, where he lives, anything like that?'

'If you have any suspicions about Cal, I think you should share them with me,' said Alison.

'I'm sure you understand' said Murphy, 'that we can't go around making unsupported allegations. But you said you were glad she hadn't moved in with him, so you must have some reservations of your own. Can you tell us what they are?'

Alison sat back and folded her arms. 'I don't know, and that's the truth. I'm used to dealing with young people, so I'm not fazed by any of the usual attitude and behaviour issues – I get all of that from Florence. But there's something different about this guy. He's more sort of – knowing. Florence and her friends and the young people I teach, they can be a pain in the arse when they want to be, but they're basically innocent. I just don't feel that about Cal. He's very polite and all the rest of it, but it's like he knows how to deal with me. I just feel there's some other agenda at play. And Florence is much quieter when he's around, so I wonder if there's some kind of pressure being exerted – even subliminally. As if she's being groomed or something like that. I don't know his age but I know he's older than her. Maybe that's all it is. He just seems more like an adult. I really wish Richard was here. He'd know what to do, or he'd tell me I'm just being a neurotic mother.'

'I don't think he'd tell you that,' said Murphy. 'I think he'd be asking some questions of his own.'

'Yes, he would,' said Alison. She hesitated a moment. 'I'm glad we've had this conversation. I did have my own reservations, but I thought I was probably just being unfair.'

'No, I think you should hang onto your reservations,' said Murphy. 'And if we get any firm information, we'll let you know. Do you happen to have Cal's address by any chance?'

Alison frowned. 'I wonder. Not his full address, I don't think, but Florence did show me a picture of the block. It's one of those new blocks in Shoreditch. Let me see if I can find it.' She crossed to the laptop, sat down and began scrolling.

'Here it is. I'm sure this is the one. Hornbeam House. It looks posh from the outside, doesn't it? I asked Florence where she was proposing to move to and she showed me this. I guess she figured showing me how smart it was would shut me up. She was pretty much right.'

'That's a pretty expensive rent and service charge,' said Wilcox. 'Aimed at 'the young professional'. The young professional with plenty of money. I guess young data scientists or programmers. Or young influencers.' He looked at Alison as he tagged on the last bit.

'Influencers, yes,' said Alison. 'That's how Florence thinks she's going to make money. Certainly not what we would have wanted for her.'

'If Florence is still living at home right now,' said

Murphy, 'then is Cal living alone in this luxury flat and paying for it all by himself?'

'That's what she gave me to understand,' said Alison. 'And to be honest, I don't know how much Florence will be able to contribute to the rent. She's not earning much at the moment.'

'Interesting' said Murphy. 'Do you know the flat number?'

Alison shook her head. 'I didn't worry about that because I would have insisted on helping her move in, and then I would have known where she was.'

'No problem,' said Wilcox. 'We can find out.'

Murphy stood up. 'Thank you for your time, Alison. If you think of anything else, do give us a ring.'

'Of course.' She opened the front door and let them out.

'Well, I think that was as much as we could do,' said Murphy, as they walked slowly down the street. 'Ideally, I'd like to have told her that we suspected him of at least passing involvement with three deaths, but I wouldn't like to give him any grounds for suing the police.'

'So what's our next move?'

'Blowed if I know. There's some missing thread here that I'm just not getting hold of. I think I'd like to talk to Beth Allardyce again. I have a feeling that she knows more than she realises. Give her a ring, let's see if we can see her. It must be about her lunchtime.'

Chapter Sixty-Five

BETH ALLARDYCE WALKED TENTATIVELY into the Queen's Head and looked around.

'Cheer up' said a voice behind her, making her jump. 'We're not planning to arrest you,' said Murphy. 'Or not on any evidence available to us at the moment.'

Beth dropped her shoulders and smiled. 'I guess I should be getting used to talking to the police, if I want to continue a career in law.'

'Yes, definitely you should. You should start by talking to that young policeman at the bar and giving him your order.'

When Wilcox had returned with the drinks, he took out his notebook.

'Now,' said Murphy, 'I want to talk again about that school reunion where you saw Florence, and this time I want to know word-for-word what passed between you, as exactly as you can recall it. I don't want a replay of what you told us last time, I want you to get the feeling of actually being there.'

Beth frowned. 'Well, OK, I'll do my best. I didn't get to speak to Florence during the dinner because we were on different tables, but I was hoping I'd have a chance to talk to her afterwards, because, well, we used to be best friends. About half an hour after the mingling time started and people were moving around, there was an empty seat next to me and she came and sat in it. We both said how good it was to see each other again, all that sort of thing. We'd both had a bit to drink, and we hugged and kissed, which we probably wouldn't have done if we'd been stone cold sober.'

'Good,' said Murphy. 'So what happened next?'

'I think I must have asked what she was doing, I expected to hear about what career she was pursuing, something like that. She told me all about her profile and all her followers, and her boyfriend and the lucrative contracts they were being offered. It was all a bit surprising to me. I'd heard of influencers of course, but I never imagined somebody I knew becoming one. I asked about her family and she told me Jake was at university and they were still at the house in Camden. I had very happy memories of that house. She told me her dad was ill, but she said they were hoping he would go into remission. That was a shock. I was very sorry to hear that. Anyway, after a bit she asked what I was doing and I told her I'd done my pupillage and I had a job at Waterfields, and she looked kind of pitying as if that was dead boring, which I guess it was when compared to the influencer lifestyle, or whatever. But at that point Leonora, who was also at a law firm, she leaned across and told Florence that I was a much bigger cheese than I was letting on – she did say cheese. She said that I had been on the team for the Havelock grooming case and that I was writing a book about grooming based on the case. I wouldn't have told Florence any of that, because she didn't seem very interested in my job, but now she did look interested. And I wanted her to know that I felt grateful to her family, so I told her that I had experienced grooming a long time ago, without realising it at the time, and her father was the first person who had made me aware of it, and what it was. I didn't tell her that it involved Matthew Henderson, of course. That would have been too embarrassing.'

'OK,' said Murphy. 'Now tell us exactly, word for word, how you said that last bit.'

Beth frowned. 'What did I say exactly? I said 'Well, it's due to your family really because I experienced grooming a long time ago and your dad was the first...' She stopped. 'Oh no. I never got to finish the sentence. Just at that moment Beverley pushed in between us with fresh drinks. She said 'Here you are girlfriends. Drink up. The next round's arrived.' So we both had another swig of our drinks and then Beverley started taking pictures and Florence said she wanted a good shot for Instagram and then several other people were posing with us and we were in a group shot. Florence was in the middle of a crowd after that, they were all looking at her Instagram profile and asking her how she got all these followers. I didn't get to speak to her again.'

There was silence for a few moments. Then Beth looked up. 'Do you think she thought I meant that her dad had groomed me?'

'She may have done,' said Murphy. 'She's the sort of girl who doesn't pay too much attention to other people. I think that includes not listening properly to what they're trying to tell her.'

Beth shook her head. 'Oh no. That's awful. I can't bear it if she thought that. And if he died with her thinking that. Do you think she told him?'

'No, I'm sure she didn't,' said Murphy.

'SHE TOLD SOMEBODY ELSE' she said to Wilcox after Beth had gone back to her office. 'She told somebody who was as stupid and ill-informed as her. Then they both agonised about what it would do to her social media profile if her dad was outed as a groomer.'

'Didn't they understand that those would just be libellous allegations with no supporting evidence? That they would have ended Beth Allardyce's career?'

Murphy sighed. 'They probably thought that her being a lawyer made it worse, that she would definitely be believed.'

'So would that have seriously been a motive for getting rid of Richard?'

'I'm sure Florence was not involved in any plot to get rid of her father. She loved her father. She probably thought Cal would come up with an idea for scuppering Beth Allardyce's book. Can't think how she thought he would do that, but I think she rather expects him to sort out problems for her. And Cal probably told her not to worry about it, he'd see what he could do. And he thought it would be easier to deal with Richard than to take on Beth.'

'But he didn't do anything.'

'Well he didn't push Richard under the train, but somebody spiked him with Rohypnol, so the end was achieved.'

'It doesn't seem worth killing anybody for. And he was dying anyway.'

'I think the fact that he was dying anyway made it seem not so bad, it was just pushing him ahead by a few months. And there was also the possibility that he might not die of the cancer. Florence would have told Cal that her dad had been lined up for the new drug trial. They figured that once he was dead, Beth would let the matter die and leave him out of things. Not speaking ill of the dead and all that. Or at least once he was dead, Florence would be less tainted by him than if he was still alive.'

Chapter Sixty-Six

FLORENCE WAS GETTING near the end of her shift at the coffee shop when her phone buzzed with a message.

'Wanna come round for pizza?'

She smiled. Lindy wanting to patch things up. Well, why not?

'6.30?' she texted back and received the confirmatory emoji.

There were very few customers left and no more coming in. People were now intent on getting home or getting drunk. It was the time for pubs and bars, not coffee shops. Florence and Katya, a flamboyant barista from Poland with nose and eyebrow rings (Florence quite fancied the eyebrow ones, but maybe not while she was still at home…) concentrated on cleaning the machine and clearing up the last few cups and saucers. Kimi, a middle-aged Filipina, would be in later to clean the floor and the bathrooms. Florence put the chairs on the tables. Kimi had lots of places to get round, so it was worth doing something to help.

At 6.15 they stepped outside and locked the door. Katya

set off for the tube station and Florence headed off in the direction of Cal's flat. When she arrived Lindy buzzed her up, which was expected, but she was surprised to find that Lindy was alone.

'Cal had to meet somebody at short notice' Lindy explained, as they sat on the sofa. 'He'll catch up with us later. And I've made us passion fruit mojitos. How about that?'

'That seems pretty good to me' said Florence, picking up her glass and taking a long pull on the straw. Perhaps this was the détente she'd been hoping for. Maybe they could be friends after all.

'I've had a go with those eyelash curlers' she said. 'They're a bit of a nightmare and they made me look like a panda, or Bambi after a heavy night. Why does anybody want to bother with curling their eyelashes?'

'Remember' said Lindy, 'not everybody has big eyes like you do. Some people have small eyes or deep-set eyes or eyes set too close together. They want Bambi lashes to make their eyes look bigger or more beautiful, or whatever. Don't think that's the effect they achieve, but it's what people believe that matters. We're just here to point them at the products. I think the important point with these curlers is to make it look very easy. So maybe you'll need to practise a few times before we make a video. And perhaps we'll show your face before the curling with no makeup and put some subtle makeup on for the after-curling shot. That will make it look as if the curly eyelashes made a big difference.'

'Yes, I guess that's right' said Florence, sinking further into the sofa and sliding her shoes off. 'If people are going to curl their lashes anyway, they might as well buy the kit we're recommending. I'll have to give it a few more tries.' She checked her phone. 'Melanie Katz still has badly-swollen lips, in fact they're looking a bit worse, and her followers are going up and up.'

'I don't think we'll be endorsing that product,' said Lindy.

'And I had a thought about Charlie and Bill,' said Florence. 'How come, if they're sleeping in a tent and washing in streams, that Charlie's hair and makeup always look so good? I wonder if they're secretly staying in hotels.'

There was a buzz at the intercom. 'That will be the pizza,' said Lindy, heading for the door and returning a few moments later with the familiar flat box.

She deposited it on the low table and set out two plates. 'Margarita with olives and capers. Our favourite' she said with a smile. 'Let me top up your drink.'

Florence handed over her glass and helped herself to a slice of pizza. She felt a bit faint, probably because she hadn't eaten much all day. The pizza would fix that.

Lindy reappeared and handed her a glass. 'These are really good mojitos,' said Florence. 'I'm feeling quite woozy.'

'I used to be famous for my mojitos,' said Lindy. 'Learned to make them at the beachside bar in Paxos. Have some more pizza. We need to soak up the alcohol.'

'This is such a lovely flat,' said Florence, pulling her feet up under her and positioning a cushion under her head. That was better. 'I'd love to be living here.'

'I can understand that,' said Lindy. 'It's very hard for young people these days to get a decent place to live. We had to work hard to get a deposit together for this place. And the service charge is just ruinous.'

'And I love what you've done with it,' said Florence. Especially these soft furnishings, she thought, that I could just go to sleep on. Her eyes kept trying to close and she had to concentrate on keeping them open. Dropping off in front of Lindy would be quite rude, especially as she had provided the food and drink and was being really very hospitable.

'I'm a big believer in Farrow & Ball,' Lindy was saying. 'I like genuine, earthy tones, the sort of colours you get in nature. I'll just get rid of this detritus.' She picked up the pizza box and the plates and took them into the kitchen. God, had they really eaten all the pizza? Florence didn't even remember herself having a third piece, but she must have done.

'Just had a text from Cal,' said Lindy, coming back from the kitchen. 'He'll meet us in Max's Bar in ten minutes. Come on girlfriend, let's go and get a nightcap.'

'Gosh, I'm so tired,' Florence slurred. 'I'm not sure if my legs will work.' She felt herself giggling, but somehow she couldn't hear it.

'What you need is fresh air. You'll feel much better when you get outside,' said Lindy briskly, handing Florence her jacket and switching off the lights. Florence was having a bit of trouble with the jacket. It seemed to have too many sleeves, and were they inside out? She put her arm through one of them, but the thing now seemed to be on back to front, like a straitjacket.

'Here.' Lindy took the jacket from her and held it for her to get into. That was better. She probably couldn't have managed that on her own. She held onto the rail as they went down in the elevator and tried not to look at her face in the mirror. It looked very pale and kind of blurry. Was that really her face? Maybe not.

Outside there was quite a strong wind whipping around and, despite what Lindy had said, the fresh air wasn't doing much to wake her up. And she used to think she could hold her alcohol. Oh well. She wasn't sure she wanted Cal to see her in this state, but it was too late to worry about that now. Her knees felt really weak. Lindy took Florence's arm and draped it over her own shoulders. That was better. She could lean on Lindy. Lindy was a good sort really. The sort of girl who looked after her drunk friend. They shuffled together down the street like survivors of a hen party.

Chapter Sixty-Seven

WILCOX HAD DONE a good number on the managing agents of Hornbeam House and obtained a list of tenants. It had taken threats of unannounced health and safety inspections, routine maintenance checks on all the gas boilers and cross-referencing to HMRC, but eventually they had given way.

There was no Derek Fletcher on the list and googling all the male names turned up nobody who looked anything like Cal.

'He must be living in one of these places,' said Murphy. 'Florence has been there. She wouldn't have been lying to her mum about that. Would she? It must be in somebody else's name. Just a minute. What about that name there?'

Wilcox was dubious. 'Really? You think so?'

'Let's go and find out. You can drive.'

'You know' said Murphy, as they threaded through the traffic, 'I think Stan was right.'

'Stan?'

'The barman at the Ropemakers Arms. You remember

he said that he would only recognise somebody if they had been up at the bar buying drinks. If somebody else was buying the drinks, so you never went to the bar, the staff wouldn't ever see you. Especially those pubs by the river where people sit outside. The only person likely to see you is the person who comes round collecting the glasses, and they'll have their attention on empty glasses, not people.'

'So there was another person involved?'

'Had to be. Somebody much smarter than Cal. Somebody with their own game plan. Look here's a space. And look who we have.'

Wilcox pulled in smoothly and Murphy shot out of the car and accosted a man coming hurriedly in their direction on the pavement.

'Mr Finlay. Now what would you being doing here?'

'On my way to an appointment,' he said. 'And I'm late, so if you'll excuse me…'

'Well I'm minded not to excuse you,' said Murphy, planting herself in front of him. 'This is the block in which Florence's boyfriend lives and moves and has his being, so to speak. What are you doing hanging around in front of it?'

He sighed. 'Look, I'm keeping an eye on Florence.'

'Oh really? In loco parentis, is it?'

'I just feel Alison needs some support. She's been worried. And I think it was something you said to her, if you want to know.'

'So you're supporting her by following her daughter?'

'Well she followed me, so I'm returning the compliment.'

'OK, and have you found out anything?'

He shuffled from foot to foot. 'I saw her go into that block about an hour and a half ago. When she didn't come out immediately, I went next door to the pub and sat by the window. She came out a few minutes ago being supported by another woman and looking like she was drunk. I was just getting after them, when you stopped me.'

'Let's get after them then,' said Murphy. 'Which direction?'

Chapter Sixty-Eight

FLORENCE WAS ALMOST ENJOYING the floppy, flappy feeling. It was as if she had moved a bit outside of her body and she was trying to work it from a distance. Her head was floating but it was very hard to keep her legs under control. There weren't that many people around now. It was getting dark and most people were probably at home. The few people they did pass looked disapprovingly at them. Florence heard one woman say to her friend something like 'disgrace'. A couple of guys she didn't like the look of stopped and asked if they needed help, but Lindy told them to piss off. Good old Lindy. Florence could just imagine the sort of help they had in mind. Cal had never seen her drunk like this, she hoped it wouldn't put him off. She must try to sober up before they got there. She put her shoulders back and concentrated on putting her feet down in the right place.

They were stopping now. They were crossing the road. Now she was being brought to a halt again. They were on an island in the middle of the road. It was a very narrow island. And there might not be many people around, but there was a load of traffic – buses, taxis, minicabs, motor-bikes, bicycles. Maybe they should have taken a minicab to this bar, or an Uber. If she had known it was going to be so far to walk, she would have suggested it to Lindy. She wouldn't have minded paying for it, though of course Lindy had far more money than she did. But Lindy had paid for the pizza, and provided the drinks. She couldn't remember eating the pizza, but she wasn't hungry so she must have done.

They seemed to have been standing on this island for ages, but it probably wasn't that long. Sometimes it took a long time to get a gap in the traffic. Lindy had taken Florence's arm from round her neck. Did she think Florence had now sobered up and didn't need supporting anymore? Florence wasn't too sure about that. Her knees felt as though they really wanted to give way. She might have to grab onto somebody. No, there was nobody else on their island. She'd have to grab onto Lindy if her knees started wobbling.

A bus was coming, really fast. Obviously, he was behind schedule. Buses that were behind schedule were great, as long as you were sitting on them. Buses that were ahead of schedule were a right pain in the arse, dawdling at every bus stop, even if there was nobody getting on or off. She wished she was sitting on this bus; it would be great to sit down. Suddenly she was flying in the direction of the bus and he wasn't going to stop for her.

Chapter Sixty-Nine

MURPHY WAS PLEASANTLY surprised by Tom Finlay. He was a fast walker, just like her. He had described the two girls as staggering down the street, so they couldn't be travelling at speed. Surely, they must catch them up soon.

'I think we'd better run,' said Finlay, after a few minutes. 'They must be further down here. There's nowhere else much to go.'

Murphy let the men go ahead. Fast walking she was good at, running at a slow pace was OK, even short sprints she could do, but there was always the point at which your oesophagus felt all dried up and she wasn't convinced that jiggling your internal organs up and down like that was really desirable. Wilcox, she was pleased to see, was keeping up, Wilcox who she had always berated for his slow walking speed. Tom Finlay was obviously a man who did marathons or at least park runs, or something like that. But should they be running down the road at his say-so? Did she really trust him? This could all be a wild goose chase.

Finlay stopped suddenly and Murphy cannoned into the

back of him. 'There they are,' he gasped. Murphy looked in the direction in which he was pointing and saw the two small figures on the traffic island, surrounded by vehicles. A bus was bearing down on them. Finlay was doubled up trying to breathe. Maybe not a parkrun man, then. Murphy left him and ran in the direction of the traffic island. She was never going to make it. Like an unfolding slow-motion disaster movie, she saw the smaller figure falling in front of the bus and there was nothing she could do. She put on a spurt and suddenly saw another figure fly across the road into the path of the bus.

Chapter Seventy

FLORENCE'S PAIN was all concentrated around her neck. Somebody was trying to strangle her. She put her hands up to relieve the pressure and suddenly found herself sitting on her backside on the ground. Lindy was sitting next to her and somebody was sitting on top of Lindy. Oh God, it was one of the police goons, the nerd. That was sexual assault, surely. She wanted to tell him to get off Lindy, but her throat was really aching, it was hard to talk. The bus had stopped and the driver was coming over. He'd be even more behind schedule after this, he'd be well mad. The other goon, the woman goon had arrived. She waved her badge at the bus driver and said something to him and they chatted for a bit and then she scribbled something in a really very tatty notebook. After a few minutes the bus driver looked across at Florence, shook his head and got back on his bus.

Tom Finlay seemed to be here now. Where did he come from? Florence blinked. Was she imagining it? How many more people could they fit on this traffic island? The woman police officer (maybe she should stop calling her a goon) was now addressing Lindy.

'So, Miss Wells,' she said. 'On your way to fetch some more marshmallows, were you?'

Florence was sure Lindy's name wasn't Wells (actually, what was it?) and what was that stuff about marshmallows? Were the police really that stupid? It was doing her head in. She needed to sleep. Maybe when she came round it would all have resolved itself. She rested her back against the traffic light pole and closed her eyes just as the ambulance drew up.

Chapter Seventy-One

'I'M QUITE LOOKING FORWARD to having a poke round this place,' said Murphy, as they went up the stairs and let themselves into the flat. Hope SOCO hasn't made too much of a mess.'

'Bit better than Amy's place,' said Wilcox, looking at the fashionable bare brick walls, flamboyant artwork and floor to ceiling windows. 'Good light for making videos or whatever they were up to.'

All the surfaces and doorknobs were covered in powder marks. They might show up some matches apart from the occupants, including presumably Florence, but Murphy wasn't expecting much. It was unlikely that Amy Horsfall had ever been here.

'This place would have cost a bit,' said Wilcox, looking at the steel and granite kitchen and the leather sofas. 'No expense spared. Derek had done well for himself, romancing his way in here.'

'Proceeds of crime,' Murphy grunted. 'Two bedrooms. I'll take hers.'

Samantha Wells had a king-sized bed, a walk-in wardrobe and an ensuite bathroom. The bed linen was top quality. Murphy flicked her way through the hangers in the wardrobe. Some designer pieces, some upmarket high street, all neatly hanging. The shoes were all paired off and aligned. A professional woman's wardrobe. No cheap frippery bits. One of the suits caught her eye, a mulberry-coloured linen. Pity nobody would be wearing it for a while, moths would probably get it.

'Have you found anything?' Wilcox was standing in the doorway and Murphy jumped.

'No, how about you?'

'Not much. He was obviously the lodger. He got the small room. Wonder how he explained to Florence that his 'sister' got the big bedroom with the ensuite.'

Murphy rummaged through the ensuite bathroom without finding anything significant. Electric toothbrush, epilator, toners and moisturisers, a box of ibuprofen. No street drugs or unknown substances. She moved on to the kitchen.

'I have this theory,' she shouted to Wilcox, 'that money lavished on kitchens and kitchen equipment is in inverse proportion to the amount of cooking carried out. Here there's a massive space with state-of-the-art everything, but the cupboards are bare and the bin has nothing but take-away containers. All these people really needed was a fridge and a microwave – the rest is just furnishings.'

Wilcox didn't seem to have heard. He was busy turning out drawers in the living area and exclaiming at the amount of clutter that had been stashed away.

'I hope,' she said, emerging from the kitchen, 'that we have enough evidence to make sure she won't be coming back here. '

'I think there'll be enough on her phone and laptop to see to that,' said Wilcox. 'Let's just a have a rummage through the CDs.' He pulled a handful off the shelf and something behind them fell over. He reached up and brought it down. A phone in a pale blue case.

'Looks like SOCO missed this. Battery's probably dead' he said, but he switched it on anyway. After a few seconds the screensaver came up. Two dogs panted next to each other, looking as if they were smiling, tongues out, posing for the camera.

Chapter Seventy-Two

'HUMAN RESOURCES,' said Murphy, as they started the tape. 'HR. Everybody takes the piss out of the HR department, don't they? It's very well-paid of course. But it's always outside of the mainstream of the business. If the business is something a bit buzzy and sexy like advertising, well HR has nothing to do with the buzzy and sexy bits. It's just HR. So it's not surprising that somebody who's never going to break out of HR starts to look for something else.'

'Is all of this going somewhere?' asked Samantha Wells' lawyer.

'We are definitely going somewhere,' said Murphy, 'don't you worry. I'm just warming to my subject. Where was I? Now, an HR director in an advertising agency may not be part of the action, but she sees enough to know that the writing is on the wall for the big agencies, some of whom will actually be going to the wall. Because the money is being diverted to platforms like Instagram and Pinterest, maybe even TikTok. That's the action to get a piece of, but how to get in on it? Then she meets Kelly Wilson's boyfriend, a chancer called Derek. Derek doesn't have much going for him, but he does have a few ideas. Charlie Westonholme told us that he thought you were offering Derek a job, but you'd had a much better idea, hadn't you? Derek could be given a makeover and used to snare one of these young influencers. The only obstacle in the way was Kelly. Derek was quite taken with you and your exciting plans, and happy to ditch Kelly. Unfortunately, Kelly wasn't happy about it. She was mooning around at work, continually calling Derek, practically stalking him, she was going to take a bit of getting rid of. Finally, you told Derek to take her to a club and buy her one tab of ecstasy and he did just that. Putty in your hands, wasn't he? You were there too and you got chatting to Kelly (what a coincidence, seeing you here) and you managed to slip another bunch of tabs into her drink. Maybe you told her you'd guard her drink while she went to the loo. Might have worked, might not have worked, but it was pretty risk-free, so it was worth a try, wasn't it? Derek probably didn't know what you'd done, but the suspicion fastened on him. In the event it worked brilliantly. No more Kelly.'

'That's crap,' said Samantha. 'You have no evidence for any of this.'

'Bear with me,' said Murphy. 'The best bits are to come. Now that Kelly was out of the way, it was full steam ahead. You repackaged Derek – new nose, new eyeballs, new complexion, probably new gym-toned body. By the end, he was looking so good you fancied him yourself. And he was a sucker for an experienced older woman. You moved him into your flat. His life was really looking up, wasn't it? Bye bye Derek, hello Cal. Now you looked for a profile to hook onto. And there was young Florence Weaver, just waiting to be grabbed. Florence was well impressed by Cal and his new body and his cool flat. You were presented as his sister, and the exciting business venture got going. Flo and Cal. All going swimmingly. Then Florence went to a school reunion and met an old friend who told her, Florence thought, that she had been groomed by Florence's dad when they were at school. That was not at all the message her friend was trying to convey, but Florence is not that good at listening to other people, so she never got Beth to finish what she was trying to say. And ideas, suspicions get mangled when they are passed on by people who are a bit sloppy about facts. Florence told Cal (we'll call him Cal at this point shall we, now he's undergone his metamorphosis?), she told him that her dad had groomed one of her friends who was now a lawyer and was going to name him in a book. Cal's not that bright, as you probably know, so the message he passed on to you was probably that Florence's friend was a lawyer and was going to bring an action against him for grooming her. He probably forgot the book bit. Because as an HR person you probably know a bit of law, and you would have realised that you can't go round libelling people in books. Anyway, he said enough to convince you that here was a problem. Apparently, her dad had a terminal illness, but then he was going to be given some new drug, so he could be around a lot longer. You didn't want to take on a lawyer, so you decided it would be easier to get rid of her father. You knew that he went to the same pub every Monday. Florence probably told Cal, without knowing the information would ever have any particular significance. The plan was that you would slink in through the crowd in the pub and spike him and Cal would follow him and push him under the tube. Poor man, terminal illness, it would be a shoo-in for suicide. You did your bit quite successfully. The barman remembered a number of women being around, but at that time we thought we were looking for a man. Silly us.'

Samantha Wells yawned loudly. 'Whole thing sounds silly to me. I was home all evening. Watching TV.'

'Well, we've been hawking your mugshot around' said Murphy 'and we've had a few results already, so the TV alibi might not hold too much water. To continue, you carried out your assignment, but Cal had a bit of trouble with his. To start with, somebody else caught up with Richard and accompanied him to the station, then the station was packed, I mean Northern Line packed, so Cal couldn't get up next to Richard and elbowing his way to the front might have made him the focus of too much attention. And really, I don't think he tried that hard. I don't think he had the bottle for it. So, imagine his astonishment when Richard falls under the train without Cal having to do anything. Result! He goes on his way rejoicing. You're pleased with him because you think he did it, and he's too scared to tell you he didn't. And of course, he would hate Florence to find out that he had any involvement at all. So he's withholding in two different directions – that would have been really scrambling his brains. Then he gets a private message from a fangirl who saw him at the station, so amazing for me to see you there, yadda, yadda, would love to hear from you, whatever. Now this is a problem for Cal, because he doesn't want her posting something on Instagram about seeing him there. At the same time, he doesn't want you to know that he didn't carry out his assignment. You were definitely the dominant partner there, weren't you Samantha?'

Samantha crossed her arms and stretched. 'No comment.'

'Cal tells you about this problem and you immediately

assume that she saw Cal commit the act – because you still think he did it. Really, as an HR director, you should have appreciated the importance of communication. Cal was too scared to tell you the truth – that's not much of a basis for a relationship, is it? So now you have somebody else to get rid of – see how these things mount up? Getting rid of Amy Horsfall was pretty nifty. You both met her at one of those outdoor pubs. You bought the drinks and made sure hers was well-doctored. Then a walk along the river. Cal asks for her phone to take a few shots of her posing on a parapet – bit more to the left – then you come in from the side and give her a good push. Amy was actually a good swimmer. If she hadn't been drugged and fully clothed, she would probably have survived. So, you were lucky there. So far, so good.'

'So far, so fictional, as far as I can see,' said the lawyer. 'Do you have any evidence for holding my client?'

'The evidence is being compiled as we speak,' said Murphy. 'We've had some interesting chats with Adonis next door.'

'He's lying,' said Samantha, but she looked worried for the first time.

'We'll get back to him in a minute,' said Murphy. 'First of all, I want to just round off our story here. Now, having got rid of Amy Horsfall, you probably thought nothing else could go wrong. But it's at this point that Florence starts to become a bit troublesome. She thinks you're Cal's needy older sister, who needs to be sent on her way, so that they, Cal and Florence, can cohabit in peace in your very expensive flat. And she has some idea that she and Cal will go travelling the world as influencers, dragging their followers after them and leaving you behind. Well, this is all a bit galling, isn't it? And the worst bit is that Cal is now becoming smitten with Florence, he's drifting over to her team. That's what he's telling us anyway. Nothing if not ungrateful. For you, this getting rid of people lark is getting easier all the time, so Florence is next on the list. Obviously, you can't involve Cal in this one, but it's a good solo effort, frustrated only by the amateur sleuthing of a chap called Tom Finlay that you've probably never heard of, the death-defying athleticism of DC Wilcox here and the superhuman reflexes of the bus driver. Quite a few witnesses there. And I have to tell you that, while he may have been party to the earlier escapades, Cal is not at all happy about this one. He's definitely turning state's evidence, as they say in the US. So, let's leave you to mull all this over while we go for lunch. We'll send you something from the canteen. You probably won't like it much.'

Wilcox switched off the tape and they left the room.

'I still don't understand how you did it,' she said, as they headed out into the sunshine. 'You're the slowest mover I know.'

'That's because I only go fast when it matters,' he said. 'I don't rush round everywhere like you do. Actually, I've been practising for a Tough Mudder, it came in handy.'

'Here comes Bellweather,' said Murphy. 'Too late, he's seen us. And God help us, he's smiling.'

'Off to lunch with the Chief Constable,' said Wilcox, as they watched him wave and climb into his car. 'Davina told me. Last-minute entry to the diary. He'll be top of the class now – burglaries tied up, Amy Horsfall's murder tied up and also Kelly Wilson's, which had been left unsolved by another team. What a clearup rate. They might even promote him.'

'They might promote him out of here,' said Murphy, 'but that's probably too much to hope for. In the meantime, we just have to hope that the charges against Samantha Wells will stick. Did you go to see Florence?'

'Yes, she's back home. The hospital sent her off after a few hours. They'd probably had enough of her. She showed me the marks around her neck, which don't look very attractive. She's pissed off about that.'

'So she didn't thank you for saving her life?'

He laughed. 'Not a bit of it. Her mum suggested she should, but Florence described what I did as an assault. I tried to explain that the scruff of her neck was the only thing I was able to grab hold of, but she wasn't interested. She said the state of her neck was going to make it impossible for her to continue posting on her platform. I was waiting for her to say she was suing me for loss of earnings. So I told her she should show her injuries to her followers, get the sympathy vote, and she liked that idea.'

'Of course,' said Murphy. 'She'll be a victim of police brutality. Why not? The point is she hasn't yet had any earnings, nor has Derek, come to that. As far as I can gather, all the money went into a bank account in Samantha Wells' name and the other two had no access to it. They won't be getting their hands on it now, either. I imagine it will all go towards funding Samantha's defence. Derek really wasn't very clever, agreeing to all these arrangements. And it's lucky Alison Weaver didn't go ahead with selling the house, because it's not difficult to speculate where Florence's share of the money would have gone. We've talked a bit about grooming in respect of this case, and we thought Derek was maybe grooming Florence, but really Florence wouldn't be that easy to groom. She's too aggressive. The person being groomed was actually Derek himself. He was easy prey for a clever older woman. She was attractive and a lot more sophisticated than the girls he'd previously had relationships with – like poor Kelly – and he probably thought he was well cool, pulling in a woman like that, but he was really just a pawn in her game, as they say. It's a pity Florence didn't tell her mum about this sister of Cal's. According to our records, Derek was the only child of a single mother, so our attention would have been drawn to her earlier. But not early enough to save Amy.'

'So will co-operating with the police get Derek off the hook?'

Murphy shrugged. 'I don't think he deserves to get off the hook. He was a conspirator in all three murders, but he can spin all of them to some degree. He took Kelly to the club and he saw Samantha talking to her, but he thought that was all it was. He didn't know Samantha was going to poison her. He was supposed to push Richard under the train, but we know he didn't. And in the case of Amy Horsfall, Samantha fetched the drinks and he took Amy's phone in order to photograph her. How was he to know that her drink was spiked and that Samantha was going to push her off the edge while he was taking the picture? Poor innocent him. Like one of those dangerous drivers who've never had an accident, but they've left a trail of them in their wake.'

'But the CPS won't care about that. They're looking for a conviction so they will want to go for her and use his evidence.'

'That's right. We've pretty much got her bang to rights. We've got Derek's evidence regarding Kelly. Stan's identified Lindy/Samantha as being in the pub on the night Richard was spiked. She's a good-looking woman. Just as well, otherwise he might not have noticed her. The bar staff in the pub down on the Embankment recognised her. Amy's phone was found in her flat. And she can't really talk her way out of the attack on Florence.'

'So Flo and Cal will carry on in business? That was the impression I got from Florence.'

'They may well do. If Cal manages to wriggle out from under all this. And we know he's an accomplished wriggler. But the fingerprints on Amy's phone were his, the messages she sent were to him, he can't get away from that. He was the one who set her up to be killed. I'm hopeful that the CPS will take the view that all of these deaths arose from a conspiracy and go after both of the conspirators. But if he does escape justice again, I don't think he will have it all his own way. I think with Lindy/Samantha out of the way Florence will be the one calling the shots. Derek will just be manipulated by a different female.'

'I didn't get the impression that Florence feels herself in any way responsible for what happened to her dad.'

'No, she certainly won't give that impression,' said Murphy. 'To show remorse would be to show weakness, that's how she would see it. She's somebody who needs to be right, even if that involves making everybody else wrong. And from what I can gather, Alison is anxious that no blame should attach to Florence. I can understand that. But I think somewhere, in a hidden part of her soul, Florence knows what her responsibility for it was. Anyway, enough about her. I'm off to Enfield now.'

'Enfield?'

'Yes. I'm going to visit Amy's dog shelter. If there's a dog up there that looks like it would fit into my unorthodox household, I'll make it an offer.'

She climbed into her car, started the engine and swerved out of the car park. Looking in the mirror she saw Wilcox shake his head cover his eyes.

Next in the Detective Miranda Murphy Series

vinci-books.com/sudden-death

Some love stories end in death.

A young man frozen in his armchair.
Mysterious love letters that promise forever.
A body abandoned on cold streets.
And one woman who connects them all.

Turn the page for a free preview…

Sudden Death: Prologue

WHEN HE HAD MADE the decision, when he knew that he was going to do it, he went through the rest of the steps in something like a dream. He felt a bit sick and his knees were shaking, but he kept walking. It was as if this was an appointed task which had been given to him and he was trusted to carry it out – just like Frodo. And when it was over, when he had done this thing, he would never have to be afraid again.

He had bought the rope from the hardware store. They didn't know him there. Nobody had asked him his age, or what it was for, so that was good. And he knew how to tie the right knot. They had practised it in Cubs.

There was nobody around in the woods. The sun shone through the trees and he heard a dog bark in the distance, but it sounded far away. All the others would be in school, they'd be having playtime soon, and he hated playtime. When he came to his favourite tree, standing there, waiting for him, he stopped for a moment and thought of all the people he would miss. He hoped his mum would be OK. He hoped it would be quick.

Sudden Death: Chapter One

DETECTIVE INSPECTOR MIRANDA MURPHY was walking Barney on Hampstead Heath on a Saturday morning when the call came in on her mobile. Maybe actually walking was only a small part of it. The bigger part, certainly as far as Barney was concerned, was plunging into the boggy area created by the torrential rain of the last three days and bathing luxuriously in the mud. Trying to stop him was a failed mission. What was it with dogs and mud? Perhaps he thought it was good for his complexion.

Murphy hadn't been expecting any call from the station because, as far as she could remember, she wasn't on the rota for this weekend. When she queried this with the despatcher, she was told that Inspector Fulbridge had called in with flu and somebody had to attend a flat in Dalston where a body had been found. Great. She had to get this filthy dog home and then get to work. Right now, he looked like a dungheap with eyeballs. Checking that there were no swimmers nearby, she threw his ball into the Ladies Pond and he dashed in after it, causing a bunch of ducks to

Sudden Death: Chapter One

retreat in alarm. That would get the worst of the mud off. Of course, he picked up another layer of slime on the way out. Nobody had told her that there would be so much bloody housekeeping involved in having a dog. She didn't remember the children being this much trouble, but that was probably selective memory.

An hour later, having left the heaving mass of filthy fur with James and Clive, she was on her way to Queensbridge Road, Dalston. The car still smelled a bit whiffy, so she had all the windows open. 2C was a second-floor flat in a purpose-built block in a side street just off the main road and the entryphone was answered by PC Julie Fraser. Julie and her partner had responded to the original call and he was in the kitchen making the tea. Murphy pulled on her plastic overshoes and gloves and started by texting Wilcox. No reason not to ruin his Saturday as well.

The deceased was a young man of about twenty-seven, wearing jeans, T-shirt and trainers. His eyes were closed, there were no obvious marks of violence, and the way in which he was slumped in the armchair looked pretty natural to Murphy. For a moment she wondered if he wasn't just asleep, but the rise and fall of the chest was definitely absent and one of the paramedics she had encountered on the way in had shaken his head in a way that told her all she needed to know. What looked like a suicide note on the coffee table in front of him appeared to give further confirmation.

His flatmate who had made the 999 call was sitting in the kitchen. She introduced herself as Sophie Carter and told them that the deceased was called Liam Webster. She was a fragile-looking girl with red hair and exceptional bone structure. Her mascara had run catastrophically and wiping a tissue across her face wasn't improving the look. Murphy could see her hands shaking and encouraged her to drink the tea that Julie was placing in front of her.

Slowly Sophie told her story. Liam had been living here about a month. She had just arrived back from spending the night with a friend in Oxford and she had found him lifeless.

'I couldn't wake him.'

'Did you move him at all?'

'No, I wouldn't have been able to move him, he's too big for that, but I did shake him and then I looked for a pulse and there was nothing there. He was stiff.' She shuddered and bit back a sob.

Wilcox appeared in the doorway at that moment, looking as if he'd just been pulled off the pitch, which he probably had. The combination of football strip, tracksuit bottoms and overshoes and the streak of mud on his forehead seemed to shock Sophie out of her grief, and she almost smiled.

'Kevin, good to see you,' said Murphy. 'Hope you weren't about to score the winning goal.'

He shook his head. 'Nah, they were trouncing us.'

'Alright' said Murphy. 'Sophie, do you have contact details for Liam's next of kin?' Sophie shook her head. 'This is now a possible crime scene, so you will have to leave. When you're ready, we'd like you to go down to the station with Julie and make your statement, so we can get it all written up and signed.'

Sophie picked up her jacket and handbag and turned as she went out of the door. 'That note...' she said, 'I know how it looks. But he never seemed to me like that sort of person. What if he didn't kill himself? What if somebody else was involved?'

Sudden Death: Chapter One

The door closed behind her. Wilcox exchanged a look with Murphy. 'Shock,' he said. 'People say weird things.'

FRANK, THE PATHOLOGIST, arrived at that moment, banging the door open, sliding across the carpet on his plastic overshoes and almost smacking his case into the coffee table.

'So, no Linda today?' said Murphy.

Frank shook his head. 'The boss doesn't do Saturdays.'

'Smart woman,' said Murphy. 'I guess she has more clout than me.'

'Definitely dead,' said Frank, kneeling in front of the body, 'but you'll have had that from the paramedics. No immediate sign of what caused it. No injuries that I can see. No sign of poisoning. We'll know more when we've done the PM. Rigor well established, wearing off a bit. Time of death will be between the last time he was seen and when his body was found.'

'Thanks a heap, Frank,' said Murphy. 'Even Linda sometimes gives me more than that.'

'You're joking. Linda says we can only accurately tell time of death if the victim was wearing a watch which smashed when he fell over, and you can't even be sure about that. What she'd say if I stuck my neck out and gave you a time of death in advance of the PM, well, we won't go there.'

Murphy admitted defeat and turned her attention to the rest of the evidence. The flat had two bedrooms and it was not difficult to see which belonged to Liam. Both were relatively untidy, but one had male underwear strewn on the floor and the other had a bra draped over the mirror. Neither of them gave any kind of clue as to why Liam Webster was sitting dead in an armchair.

Sudden Death: Chapter One

'I've got his phone and laptop,' said Wilcox, when she returned to the sitting room. 'Can't get into them yet.'

'We'll need to get into them to find out how to contact his family,' said Murphy. 'And the other item to secure is that.' She pointed to the note on the coffee table, written in small neat caps.

I'M SORRY ABOUT THIS, I COULDN'T TAKE ANY MORE. AXIOM IS NEVER GOING TO WORK.

Sudden Death: Chapter Two

MURPHY AND WILCOX DROVE back to the station in her car. Wilcox sank as low as possible in his seat and braced his feet under the dashboard, which was his usual precaution. Then he found this made it impossible to get his head far enough out of the window to escape from the smell.

'I've had Barney in here,' Murphy explained. 'And he'd been rolling in God-knows-what, so that's the less than fragrant atmosphere. So, you'll have to choose between sudden death and asphyxiation.'

At that moment the taxi in front decided to change lanes without warning and sudden death immediately looked the more likely option. Wilcox hurriedly withdrew his head. 'Well anticipated,' said Murphy. 'If that hadn't gone our way, your head could have been severed at the neck.'

Something about the careless way she said this made Wilcox feel decidedly unnerved, but he saw that they were now approaching the station and a few minutes later he was able to make his escape.

Sudden Death: Chapter Two

After getting past the duty sergeant, who brightened up when he saw Wilcox and offered some impenetrable joke about the offside rule, he tracked down Fiona, the technician who had drawn the short straw and had to work this Saturday. The phone was unlocked in a matter of minutes.

'Just like that, access to all his secrets,' said Murphy, putting down the statement she was skimming. 'It always seems like the worst sort of prying. Anyway, enough of the scruples, we need to find his next of kin as Sophie didn't seem to know. I guess you don't ask for next of kin information when you take in a flat mate. Here we are, mother and father in Gravesend. Can you send the uniforms out to inform them? Poor people. And I think we'll have a few words with Sophie while she's here. This statement doesn't say much more than she told us in the flat. Let's see if we can get her to expand a bit.'

Sophie was sitting in the least ghastly of the interview rooms, Wilcox was pleased to note, and had been given tea (more tea!). If she had her wits about her, she wouldn't drink it, but it was the thought that counted.

Wilcox started the tape and intoned the preliminaries. Sophie looked a bit alarmed.

'Don't worry,' said Murphy. 'We're not charging you with anything, but we have to keep a record of all our interviews. Can you just explain the domestic set-up between you and Liam Webster. I gather he's not your boyfriend.'

Sophie shook her head. 'No, we're not in a relationship,' she said. 'It's my flat and he's my lodger – or he was my lodger. I originally bought it with my ex-husband and when we divorced, I bought him out – with a bit of help from my mum. There's quite a big mortgage so I need to have somebody else in to help with the bills. Liam's been living with

Sudden Death: Chapter Two

me for about a month. Before that I had a girl called Alex, but she got married and moved out.'

'And you decided to pick a man this time. Any reason?'

She shrugged. 'Not really. Well maybe. Perhaps I thought I would feel safer – as a woman – having a man around the place. No, that's wrong, I don't think I need a man for protection. I just liked Liam. I met him and he seemed like a nice guy, very easy going. I could see I would have no problem getting on with him.'

'And is that how it worked out?'

'Yes. Pretty much. We don't see a lot of each other, but we get on OK.' Her face fell. 'I mean we got on OK.'

'Alright. Now can you just tell us again what happened this weekend.'

Sophie sighed. 'I went up to Oxford after work on Friday to see my friend Cass, we were at university together. I've already given you her contact details.' She looked towards Wilcox, who nodded. 'We had dinner and drinks and I knew it would be late so I stayed over.'

'Did Liam know you wouldn't be back Friday night?'

She thought for a moment. 'I don't think he did. I don't remember seeing him Friday morning. He must have gone in to work early. I would probably have told him if I'd seen him.'

'So you came back Saturday morning,' said Wilcox.

'Yes. I got the train arriving into Paddington at 11.13. Then I got the Elizabeth Line to Liverpool Street and the 149 bus. I got home just after 12.'

'And you called emergency services straight away?'

'Yes, as soon as I realised he wasn't going to come round. It was a shock to see him like that.'

'What did you think when you saw the note?'

Sudden Death: Chapter Two

'I was really upset that he was so unhappy living with me that he would kill himself. I still don't believe it.'

'Did you recognise the handwriting?'

'No, but then I've never seen his handwriting. And it was all in caps.'

'Yes, that's right,' said Murphy. 'What's your job Sophie?'

'I'm an engineer,' she said. 'I work for Sevills – they're a big contractor.'

Something stirred in Wilcox's brain. 'So you worked on Crossrail?' he said.

She smiled briefly and nodded. 'Yes, that was a really great project. I felt so lucky to be part of it. Liam's a kind of engineer too – or he was. He was a data engineer. We had that in common.' Her smile died. 'We were both engineers, but very different jobs.'

'Did you meet any of his friends or family?'

Sophie shook her head. 'No, nobody. But then, we hadn't been sharing the flat for very long.'

'Alright Sophie. I think that's all we need to know for now.' Murphy gathered up her papers. 'Thank you for your time. We're still going over your flat so you can't go back there at the moment. Do you have somewhere else to stay?'

'I can stay with my mum in Bethnal Green.'

'That sounds like a good idea. Just write the address here for us in case we need to talk to you again.'

WHEN SOPHIE HAD GONE, they escaped from the interview room. Murphy stretched and put her feet on her desk. Everything felt stiff and the morning dog walk seemed days ago. Was it really just this morning?

'We've got her on CCTV at Paddington,' said Wilcox, coming out of the control room. 'She's definitely getting off the Oxford train, she couldn't have been that side of the barrier otherwise. And we've got her a bit later at Liverpool Street. So that seems to check out. Julie's shuffling through the CCTV from Queensbridge Road.'

'OK. Let's go see.' Murphy eased her feet down carefully and they left the CID room.

The image was grainy but three men could be seen getting out of a taxi on the corner of Queensbridge Road at 1.30 am on Saturday morning. The taxi remained in place and ten minutes later two of the men reappeared and got back into the taxi, which then drove off.

'Let's look at that again,' said Murphy. 'Looks like the one in the middle, being supported by the other two, is Liam, as he doesn't reappear. They drop him off and then ten minutes later the other two come out and they set off again. He's definitely drunk or incapable in some way.'

'So that's the last sighting of him alive,' said Wilcox. 'Wonder if he was alive when they got back in the taxi?'

'Well those are the two individuals we need to track down,' said Murphy. 'What have SOCO come up with so far?'

'They're still processing samples. Liam's parents and sister are coming to identify the body. Sophie's already identified him, but it's better to have next of kin. It was explained to them that there would have to be a post-mortem. They're very upset.'

'Of course they are. At least it wasn't a violent death, so there are no marks on the body. I don't know how much better that will make it for them. We'll have to go see them after the PM. I don't have anything I can tell them until then. I'm going home now, to apologise to my lodgers for dumping a dirty dog on them. Can I give you a lift?'

'No, I'll get the tube.' Wilcox shook his head emphatically.

Murphy set off on the drive home, negotiating the Saturday afternoon traffic and remembering she hadn't done any shopping. A bark greeted her as she put the key in the lock and she prepared herself for the onslaught of dirty claws and matted hair. What she saw instead was a glossy creature that looked like it had emerged from a grooming parlour.

'Blimey. He smells amazing.' She buried her nose in the back of his neck.

'Jo Malone bath scrub,' said Clive. 'Heavenly. And I put conditioner on his hair – coat I mean.'

'Thank you so much,' said Murphy. 'I was only expecting the hose in the back garden.'

'Yes, we started with that,' said James. 'And that got off the worst of it off. But he still wouldn't have been fit to sit on the sofa. He seemed to really enjoy his bath.'

'I'll bet he did,' said Murphy. 'Attention. It's what we all want. Or most of us.'

Grab your copy...
vinci-books.com/sudden-death

About the Author

Eva Maclean read her first Agatha Christie (*Death in the Clouds*) at age ten and has been obsessed with detective fiction and writing ever since. After a past life as an accountant, she is finally doing what she wanted to do in the first place.

Eva lives in London with her husband and two cats, her children having grown up and made good their escape.

Her favourite living authors are Kate Atkinson, Donna Leon and Mick Herron. The dead are too many to count.